Healing Hearts in Port Berry

ALSO BY K.T. DADY

PORT BERRY SERIES
Book 1: Welcome to Port Berry
Book 2: An Invitation to Port Berry
Book 3: Winter Magic in Port Berry
Book 4: A New Arrival in Port Berry
Book 5: Healing Hearts in Port Berry

Healing Hearts in Port Berry

K.T. DADY

Choc Lit, London
A Joffe Books company
www.choc-lit.com

First published in Great Britain in 2025

© K.T. Dady 2025

This book is a work of fiction. Names, characters, businesses, organizations, places and events are either the product of the author's imagination or are used fictitiously. Any resemblance to actual persons, living or dead, events or locales is entirely coincidental. The spelling used is British English except where fidelity to the author's rendering of accent or dialect supersedes this. The right of K.T. Dady to be identified as author of this work has been asserted in accordance with the Copyright, Designs and Patents Act 1988.

No part of this book may be used or reproduced in any manner for the purpose of training artificial intelligence technologies or systems. In accordance with Article 4(3) of the Digital Single Market Directive 2019/790, Joffe Books expressly reserves this work from the text and data mining exception.

Cover art by Dee Dee Book Covers

ISBN: 978-1781898888

Friendship changes the world.

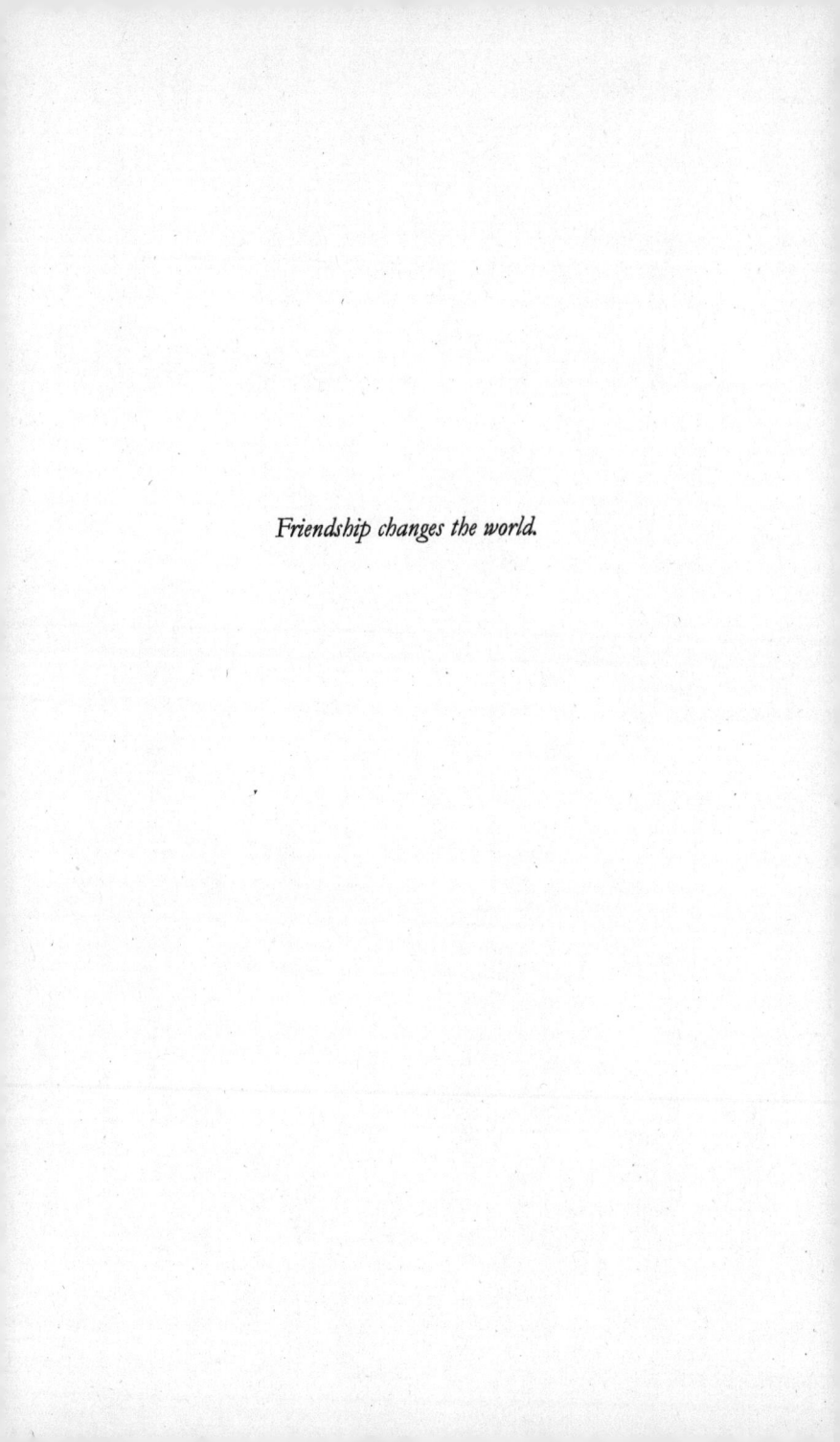

PROLOGUE

'Lovely spread, Demi. Can't beat a prawn cocktail vol-au-vent.'

Demi Lewis smiled politely at her elderly neighbour, Mrs Radcliffe, then thanked her for coming to the funeral. She perused the small gathering in the local pub, noticing they seemed to have settled in for the evening. She didn't need to stick around any longer.

A few more sympathetic smiles came her way as she tried to sneak towards the exit.

'Thirty-four is no age to be a widow.'

'How will she cope now?'

'Do you think she made the food, what with her being a chef?'

'It was a good funeral. I do love a good funeral.'

'Her daughter has no father now.'

'Poor love.'

She'd heard all the comments throughout the day. There was no room for any more.

Colin tugged her arm as she reached the car park. 'Getting some air, sis?'

She took in his pale face and deep dark eyes that matched her own. 'I'm tired. I'm heading home. You can see everyone off later, yeah?' She didn't move until her brother gave her a nod.

'Do you want me to take Jade home with us tonight?'

Demi glanced at the pub, knowing her fifteen-year-old daughter was in there somewhere. 'No, you can bring her back when she's ready. She's all right with her mates for now.'

Colin's head bobbed again. 'I can come back with you if you want. I'll just let Alana know. She'll—'

'No, it's fine. Go be with your wife. I'm going straight to bed.'

'Has Jade got her keys?'

'Yeah.'

Colin pulled her in for a hug. 'I'll speak to you tomorrow.'

Demi was glad when he released her. All day she'd been hugged and kissed by people offering their condolences.

Colin walked her to her car and waved goodbye.

Driving away, Demi had never felt so tired of life, her husband's funeral having drained her on more levels than she knew she possessed. It had been a surreal day, but at least he was finally laid to rest.

The trauma of his death washed over her as she found a spot to park along her street. She sat there for a while, engine running, going over the what-ifs once more.

A minute before. Perhaps one after, then he wouldn't have been standing there. He wouldn't have been in the way of the man attacking random members of the public with a knife.

Five injured. One dead. Had to be Terry, didn't it? Demi shook her head at how cruel life could be.

Taking a breath, she turned off the engine and locked up. She headed to their small terrace house at the end of the road, stopping for a moment by Mrs Radcliffe's rose bush, not knowing why. For years she had walked that route. She could remember moving in to Terry's house thirteen years ago, just one year after meeting him. What a catch he was.

After Jade's father died when she was barely a month old, Demi was sure she'd spend the rest of her life alone. Little did she know Terry was in her future. A man willing to raise her child as his own.

Demi could see them unloading his car with her things. The smiles, the laughter, so much happiness. That was a good day. Terry brought a lot of good days into her life, and Jade adored him.

The bitter chill of February had her scrunch her dark scarf into her chin as she hurried along.

She didn't want to put the key in the door, knowing Terry wasn't on the other side and never would be home again, but it was cold, and she needed her pyjamas and Terry's dressing gown. Parts of him were still there. She could hold on to him where possible.

'Excuse me. Are you Demelza Lewis?'

Demi turned towards the Geordie accent that had come from nowhere using her full name. The woman facing her was maybe a few years older, looking slightly lost and a touch tearful. 'Erm, yes.'

The woman's head dipped, then she took a noticeable deep breath and looked up.

'Are you okay?' asked Demi, seeing how pale the lady was.

'Oh no. I'm far from okay,' she said flatly, those watery blue eyes turning stern.

Demi's fingers holding the key at the lock were starting to numb. Winter by the Cornish coast had no mercy. 'It's been a long day. I'm—'

'It's been a long day for you, has it? My heart bleeds.' The coldness in her tone, words, and expression came as a complete shock.

A sudden snap of anger heated Demi's bones. 'Excuse me! Who the hell do you think you are? I've just come from my husband's funeral. Do you—'

'Well, aren't you the lucky one. I didn't get to bury my old man. Didn't even get to see his body. Didn't even bloody well know he'd died until I saw him on the news! So, excuse me if I have no sympathy for you, Mrs Lewis.' She huffed out a laugh. 'Lewis. What a joke!'

Demi had no idea what was going on or what the death of this woman's husband had to do with her. 'What you're saying isn't my fault.'

'Yes, it is.' The northerner took a step closer to Demi and her shiny red door.

Demi shrank away, wishing she had escaped into the house already. 'Who are you?'

'I'm Crystal Lewis. Terry's wife.'

Processing was a bit of a problem as Demi's mind had gone blank. 'Terry who?' was all she managed.

'Who do you bloody think?'

She couldn't think. That was the point. Clarification was needed, because it was coming across that this Crystal woman was married to the man she'd left at the crematorium, and that couldn't be right.

Crystal whipped out her phone from the dark handbag slung over her shoulder. 'Here. That's him. You tell me otherwise, because I need to know the truth myself.'

Demi peered at the screen to see a picture of Terry down by some boats. He was in his early-beard stages then, and she smiled inwardly at him changing his mind every five minutes about keeping it or shaving off the lot.

'Is that your husband, Terry Lewis?'

'Yes,' Demi replied, her voice barely a whisper.

'Well, pet, he's mine too.'

A cold wind blew Demi's dark hair across her face, numbing her lips and perhaps her heart, which she was sure had stopped beating. The phone was still aloft, held by a shaky hand, so she glanced once more at the screen. It was definitely Terry.

'I have more proof.' Crystal tapped her bag. 'Could we go inside? I can't feel my feet.'

Demi lowered her gaze to the black heels on her pathway, then opened the door and switched on the light and heating automatically. She hung up her coat, put her slippers on, then showed Crystal to the living room.

Crystal didn't bother to compliment the cosy décor or soft furnishings. As soon as she sat on the cream sofa, she whipped out a file.

Demi pondered over the idea of offering tea but sat instead. Her head ached, and her stomach swirled. Was this really happening?

'This is our wedding photo and certificate,' said Crystal, handing over the picture and document, which Demi took without thinking. 'And as you can see, we've been married eighteen years.' She looked up from her file. 'How long have you been wed?'

'Thirteen years. Together for fourteen.' Demi stared blankly at the date before her.

'Took me a while to track you down.' Crystal's tone had softened. 'Saw the victims of the stabbing in London on the news. And I couldn't get through to his phone. I never had a work number, as he was always travelling with his job, but I knew the HQ was in London, not far from the flagship hotel he worked for. Not that they helped much. They hadn't heard of me. Knew you though.' She quickly swiped a tear. 'So, his funeral was today. Trust me to be late.' She glanced at the ceiling rose. 'Bet that made him laugh.'

It was hard for the words to register. If what this woman was telling her was true, then she wasn't Demi Lewis at all. Her marriage was null and void — just how she felt.

Crystal stood abruptly, snatching back her proof of marriage. 'I guess our solicitors will have to deal with things from now on.'

'Solicitors?'

'Yes. I'm his wife. His things belong to me now. Me and our son.'

'Son?'

One side of Crystal's mouth curled as though she was enjoying herself. 'Oh yes, lady. We have a little lad. Three he

5

is. TJ. Terry Junior. Don't think you'll be keeping his inheritance.' Her eyes narrowed as she spotted a framed photo of Terry with Jade. 'Do you have kids?'

Demi followed her gaze. 'Not with Terry.'

Crystal seemed to perk up again at that snippet of information. 'Well, I guess that's one silver lining in this mess.' She waggled a finger around at the room. 'Did Terry own this?'

Demi nodded. 'Yes,' she replied quietly.

'Is your name on it too?'

'No.'

'That's pretty straight forward then.' Crystal headed for the door. 'I'll give you time to process. Lord knows I needed it. But you listen to me, lady, I'm as angry about this as a person can be. After what that scumbag did to me, he owes me big time — and I plan to get everything I can. Not just for me, but for my boy.'

Demi swallowed the dryness in her throat, hoping it would help her speak more clearly, but her head was so frazzled, not much happened. Terry had another wife, that much was clear, and now said wife was, quite possibly, about to take away her home.

'Oh, and I'll be wanting his ashes.' Crystal turned on the doorstep. 'I take it you cremated him. It was his wish.'

Demi nodded.

'Right, well, I'll be off.' The woman stopped at the end of the path. 'Look, I'm sorry he did this to you, and I'm sorry you had to find out this way, but I haven't got it in me to sit and hold your hand. I just needed to see your face. Tell you the truth. Now it's between the solicitors. You won't be seeing me again.' She glanced up at the dark sky. She looked as though she were turning her nose up at Newquay.

Demi slowly closed the street door and went upstairs. She still hadn't put her pyjamas on.

Terry's stripy dressing gown lay on the bed where she'd left it. It hadn't been washed so still held his scent. She lifted it for a sniff, wishing she could talk to him. Have him explain the woman who'd just sat in their living room, flashing documents that told her she was back to being Demi Carter again.

Not a lot made sense until the sound of the front door opening startled her back to life.

Oh no, Jade. What if that woman is still out there?

Demi dashed from the bedroom as her daughter called out from the hallway. She was still clutching Terry's dressing gown, and the belt somehow tangled around her foot, causing her to topple down the stairs and bang her head.

The first thing she heard when she woke was someone saying something about an operation, then everything went black.

CHAPTER 1

3 Years Later
Demi

Demi Carter smiled at the summer sky as she happily made her way to work. It was a beautiful late June morning that put a spring in her step. She loved the feeling of the sun on her face, warming her, and the way people seemed to look happier at this time of year.

The seagulls were low, scanning the tables outside the eateries along the high street, checking out what they could steal from customers having elevenses.

Tourist season had arrived, and Penzance was just as popular as the rest of Cornwall. Demi hoped business would pick up in the restaurant where she worked, as it had been slow for a good while. If any staff were to be given the boot, she'd be one of the first to go because she was one of the last to be hired.

Entering Seafarers, she immediately knew something was wrong. Marco had the staff sitting in the dining area, with all eyes on him.

'Ah, Demi, I was just waiting for you.'

She checked her watch to make sure she wasn't late for her shift.

'Now you're all here,' continued Marco, 'I have an announcement to make.'

Demi didn't like the way he wasn't keeping eye contact with anyone, not even Kevin, who was his head chef and best friend.

'As you know, things have been slow . . .' Marco cleared his throat.

She wished he would get on with it. She hated guessing games, and whatever her boss was trying to say, he was making a right pig's ear of it.

'Are we getting fired?' asked a waitress.

Demi offered her a friendly smile. Lois had been there longer than anyone, so it was likely her job would be safe. There were more cooks in the kitchen than was needed though — Demi knew it was her time at the restaurant that had come to an end and slumped a little in her seat.

As Marco waffled on, avoiding his point, Demi wondered who else would hire her. She'd have to disclose her criminal record, and she was sure that would push her to the back of the queue.

'I've gone bust,' blurted Marco, waking Demi from her trance with the salt pot.

A few words were muttered and others spat as the owner of the fish restaurant tried to settle his team.

'I have no choice. I'm closing down.'

'When?' asked Kevin, proving he was also in the dark.

'Today. Right now.'

Gasps and some expletives filled the air followed by Marco's endless apologies.

Demi sat back. She had nothing to say on the matter. As far as she was concerned, Marco was a good man. He'd been part of the back-to-work scheme set up by The Butterfly Company, known for helping ex-criminals get jobs. She'd been working as a chef in Seafarers for ten months thanks to them.

9

It took a while, but in the end everyone said their goodbyes and went their separate ways. Demi thanked Marco for his support and kindness, then went back out into the sunshine to take a breath. She needed to find work. That tiny bedsit she lived in wasn't about to pay for itself, and her savings were needed to help her move soon, as the owner of the bedsit wanted to sell, rather than renew the tenancy.

The Butterfly Company was only a bus ride away, so she figured she'd start there. If anyone could help, it was them.

It had been a while since she set foot in their offices. Not much had changed. The open-plan space was bright and practical, but Roddy wasn't at the front desk to greet her with his big smile and bright flowery shirt.

'Hi, is Roddy around?' she asked the young woman behind the white counter.

'I don't know any Roddy.'

That was disappointing. Roddy helped people no end. This woman had all the charm of a slapped rhino.

'I'm looking for one of the mentors to talk about finding a job.'

'Have you just been released?'

Demi shook her head. 'No. I came out just over a year ago.'

The woman peered down at Demi's feet. 'No tag?'

'No.'

'Are you on licence?'

'Not since last month.'

The woman frowned while pouting ruby red lips. 'You don't really need us then.'

Demi wasn't expecting that. 'Oh, I was told I could come here whenever I needed help.'

'Yes, but you're not really classed as an ex-offender anymore.'

Try telling that to my CV.

Demi sighed inwardly while keeping her polite smile firmly in place. She went to speak but someone called out her name, causing her to turn.

'I thought that was you, my dear.'

She smiled at the social worker, Henley, waving her over. 'Hello, mate. Good to see you.'

His amber eyes glistened as he gave her a high-five, before leading her to a colourful seating area in the far corner. 'Sit. Sit. Tell me everything. This is about Seafarers, right?'

Demi stopped smiling. 'I lost my job.'

Henley nodded. 'I just got off the phone to Marco. He called to let me know his business is out of the scheme. Shame. He was our only restaurant.'

Great!

Henley tapped her arm. 'Not to worry. I'm sure we can find you something.'

'I don't really need too much help. After all, I have the qualifications under my belt. I've been a chef for years, but you know what it's like when you have a police record.'

'Indeed.'

'I was hoping you had more restaurants signed up, but now I know.'

Henley shook his head, his light-brown face catching the sunlight pouring in from the large windows, accentuating his handsome features. 'It's hard to get any business to join the scheme, but . . . Ooh, look, there's Jan. Maybe she knows someone in the trade.' He stood and waved. 'Jan. Got a sec?'

Demi smiled at seeing another familiar face.

January Riley had been the first mentor to come into her life. Bringing understanding and hope while Demi, locked away in prison, suffered with withdrawal, anxiety, and confusion. Her dark brown skin held its usual healthy glow, and her dark eyes such warmth. Being in Jan's presence always made Demi relax. She was sure the therapist was an actual angel.

'Hi, Dem. What are you doing here?' Jan came in for a hug.

'Seafarers just closed down. I was seeing if there were any other restaurants on the scheme, but Henley's just told me there aren't. It's okay, though. I have some savings that'll cover my rent for a bit while I check out the job centre.'

Jan flicked back her mass of blonde curls as she sat. 'Aw, that's a shame. Marco helped a lot of people get back on their feet through that place.'

'Yeah, and I don't think he wanted to stop. He left it right till the last minute to tell us he's shut up shop.' Demi flopped back into the orange sofa and folded her arms. 'A heads-up would have been nice, though.'

'Hmm, I can see the dilemma.' Jan lifted her big bag onto her lap and rummaged around for a notebook. 'Not sure I know of any chef jobs yet, Dem. But I'll make a note.' She looked up and smiled. 'The job centre will see you good. Just got to keep your fingers crossed.'

Henley spotted someone entering the building. 'Ooh, be right back.'

Demi watched him skip off. 'The woman at the desk said I can't get help here anymore. Is that true?'

Jan glanced at the main desk as she scribbled in her notebook, then turned back to Demi. 'They don't shoo away anyone here. I'll get Henley to have a word with her later. Make sure her training is up to speed.' She put her book away and shuffled to face Demi full on. 'Now, I haven't seen you since you got your two-year recovery chip last month. You still going to meetings?'

Demi nodded and sat up straight. 'Yeah, but do you know of another one I could attend? I'm not keen on this one.'

'Oh, why not?'

'It's Jodie. She keeps picking fights, and she brought me into it last time.'

Jan frowned. 'What on earth is she doing?'

'Looking down her nose at some of the recovering addicts, that's what. Started spouting off about how we're different because we didn't choose to take the drugs we got hooked on.'

'She didn't.'

'She did.' Demi sighed. 'It was okay when I first joined that group, but a lot of the regulars have moved on, and I'm struggling to feel at peace there.'

'Okay, well, I'm glad you've brought it to my attention. I'll sort that pronto.'

'Do you know of any other meetings I could attend?'

'Let's see. You live on the border between Penzance and Port Berry, so if you don't want to go to the one in Penzance anymore, there's one held at the church hall in Port Berry. There's a meeting at lunch today. I'm just heading that way now.'

Demi perked up. 'All Saints?'

'That's the one. And I happen to know they have a grief support group starting up tonight. It runs for six weeks, and you have to commit to going each week. Check the noticeboard while you're at the church.'

Demi rolled her eyes. 'Really? That old chestnut.'

Jan leaned closer, narrowing her eyes. 'You need grief counselling, Dem.'

'It's been three years.'

'And I've been telling you for the last two years that you need this to help you heal.'

'The people at these sessions sit around talking about people they loved. What am I supposed to bring to the table? I still don't know how I feel about . . .' She sighed, slouching into her seat, not wanting to say his name. Not wanting to remember.

Jan linked her fingers on her bag as she sat back. 'You can't avoid talking about this forever.'

'Been doing all right so far.'

Jan raised her brow. 'You think?'

Demi shrugged, reminding herself of how her daughter, Jade, would act whenever she didn't want to talk. The thought of raking up the past did little to spark joy. She'd been on one hell of a journey these past three years. All she wanted was to keep pushing forward and pretend parts of her life never happened.

'Hey, Dem. It's good to talk. You do recovery meetings. You can do bereavement. I can stay with you if you want.'

'No, I'm fine, but I'll come over there with you now. See what the recovery group is like.'

'Come on then. Let's get a wriggle on. Got a bus to catch. We'll grab a sarnie en route. No one needs to hear my belly rumbling while they're trying to open up about their life. It really echoes in the church hall, you know.'

Demi laughed as they stood. She waved goodbye to Henley, and he told her he'd call if a job became available. It was comforting to know she had support. Even though she'd been clean for two years, and out of prison for one, her brother, Colin, and his wife still held little faith in her, so she was grateful for people like Henley and Jan.

She popped into a coffee shop with Jan to get their food to go.

'How's Jade doing?' asked Jan as they sat on the bus.

'She's good. Still hasn't heard if she's got into the uni she wants. Should hear something soon.'

'How do you feel about her going so far away if she does get into York?'

Demi shrugged, tearing open a cheese-and-ham sandwich. 'I guess I'm used to being away from her now.'

Jan nudged her arm. 'She might want to live with you again one day.'

'That's why I need to get another job soon. I've been saving for ages to get a two-bed so she can have those choices.'

'You'll get there. I believe in you.'

Demi smiled. 'Thanks, Jan. I just wish my brother would.' She stared out the window at the cottages dotted around a village green as she ate her lunch. 'I don't blame him, but he needs to move forward with me.'

'Is Jade happy living with him and Alana?'

'She says she is. They are good to her. I can't complain.'

Jan offered her crisp packet, which Demi declined. 'At least she's settled. That's a weight off, right?'

'Yeah. I'm glad they didn't put her in care.' Demi felt the guilt hit hard. What a lousy mother she had been.

'Don't go down that road.' Jan always could read her mind.

Demi finished her sandwich in peace as the single-decker bus bounced its way along the country road.

'Ooh, come on. This is us,' said Jan, wiping crumbs from her skirt as she stood.

Demi thanked the driver for delivering them safely, then stared up at the steeple. The church doors were open, and she did ponder over the idea of going inside to light a candle, but then she remembered some people weren't worth the thought, so she turned towards the hall at the side.

Jan pointed out a woman waving from the church door. 'You head into the hall, Demi. I'll be one sec. I'm just saying a quick hello. I'll see you inside.'

Demi entered the hall, surprised to see it empty. Whoever the host was, they hadn't arrived yet to put out the chairs. She wondered if she should. It wouldn't hurt to get involved.

Foldaway chairs were wedged behind a stack of tables, not making access easy, but she managed to pull a couple free, then set about creating a circle.

'Oh, that's kind of you,' said a male voice, making her jump.

Demi shot around to see an athletic man with the most gorgeous piercing blue eyes she'd ever seen. *Did I just blush?* 'Thought I'd make a start.'

'Are you signed up for the group?' he asked, moving to grab a couple more chairs.

Demi chastised herself for homing in on his forearms. They were as fit as him. She figured he was about her age, but whatever demon he had, he wore it well. She suddenly hoped her panda eyes were having a good day.

Bet he's been clean for a long time.

'I was hoping to start today,' she replied, standing back to check the circle for leg room. One time, she had a fella manspreading, and it reached a point where she could take his leg touching hers no more.

'Oh, that's okay. Everyone's welcome.' He unfolded two more chairs. 'That should be enough.'

Demi eyed a table. Noticing the lack of refreshments. 'No bickies?' she asked playfully.

'Someone will bring food. They always do when I set these things up.'

'You been doing this long?'

'A few times now, on and off. Always have the same people turn up, so you'll have all eyes on you for a bit, but don't worry, they're a good bunch, and it won't take long for someone to start talking about themselves.' His eyes seemed to smile, causing Demi to smile back. 'Please don't feel you have to speak on your first time.'

'It's okay. I know how these things work.'

'Not your first rodeo?'

Demi shook her head as she sat on a chair furthest away from him.

He sat opposite and leaned forward. 'I'm Robson McCoy, by the way.'

'Demi Carter.'

'Who did you lose?'

She glanced at the doorway, thinking he might be talking about Jan. She was taking a long time outside. 'Erm . . .'

'Sorry. I just said you don't have to talk, and here I am probing.' He raked a hand through his dark hair, looking uncomfortable for a moment.

Demi was confused. 'That's okay. I just didn't know what you meant, that's all.'

'Oh. I meant who passed away.'

'Passed away?'

Robson nodded, now looking as confused as she felt. 'The reason you're here at bereavement group.'

Jan came bustling in, surrounded by a small group of people. 'Looks like the gang's all here,' she chimed, making a beeline for Demi. 'My fault. I got the meetings mixed up.'

Demi tightened her lips as she side-eyed her mentor.

How convenient.

Jan flopped to the seat by her side. 'We're here now. We can just listen . . . or leave,' she whispered. 'Totally up to you.'

'Fine, I'll stay,' Demi whispered back. 'Just this once.'

Jan nodded, and Demi could see her smile being held back.

'Hey, everyone,' said Robson, gaining attention. 'We have a newcomer today. Please make Demi welcome.'

'Hello, love,' said an elderly woman, placing a ball of yellow wool and some knitting needles on Demi's lap. 'You can do some knitting with me. Helps settle the heart.'

Demi looked at the wool, hoping it did hold such magical powers, because the way she was feeling, she needed all the help she could get. Once more, she glared at Jan.

Jan smiled. 'You'll be fine,' she whispered.

It was the man with the piercing eyes who seemed to calm Demi's agitation — all he did was smile her way.

A woman named Lizzie pulled out a packet of pink wafers and handed them around, so Demi shoved one in her gob and got on with some knitting. There was no way she was sharing her backstory. She was sure she could sit and listen for a bit though. And as soon as the elderly man called Jed started talking about the price of fish, she gathered it might not be so bad after all.

CHAPTER 2

Robson

Robson smiled with warmth as Marisa spoke of her beloved deceased cat, Buttons.

'Twenty years is a long time to have a pet,' said Jed, handing the elderly woman a tissue that Jan had passed along.

Marisa's pale eyes dried. 'He was my baby.' She looked at Demi, who she'd shared knitting needles and wool with. 'I don't expect people to understand.'

Robson studied the newbie for her reaction, not that he normally sat there doing that to members of his bereavement group.

'Loss is loss,' said Lizzie. 'It all hurts.'

Demi gave a slight nod, then went back to staring at the knitting in her lap.

'And we have to talk about these things, Marisa,' said Jed. 'Gets it off your chest.' He gestured at Demi. 'Should we tell our stories?'

Robson knew the group had come together before, so they were way ahead of Demi, but he wasn't sure if she was interested. He got the feeling she didn't want to be there at all.

The young man sitting the other side of Jan leaned around her to look at Demi. 'Unless you want to go first.'

Demi glanced up and shook her head.

'She's new, Colby. Let her be,' said Jed, rubbing over his grey wiry beard. 'Tell her about your young fella.'

Colby's green eyes glistened as his slim shoulders dropped, and he waited until Demi gazed his way. 'It was two years ago now. My boyfriend, Ossie, got knocked off his motorbike. Died instantly. We were only twenty-three then. Sometimes it seems like a lifetime ago.'

'I'm so sorry,' said Demi.

'Thank you,' he replied quietly, dipping his head.

Jed sighed. 'I've lost a wife and son. Not at the same time. My missus went first. Storm took my lad. Out on his boat. One of those things. Life can be tough.'

Robson had known the old fisherman all his life. He remembered when the tragedy struck.

'I'll go next,' said Lizzie, raising a hand slightly. 'Lost my daughter, love. Cervical cancer. My Lisa was twenty-seven, so you make sure you have your smear tests when offered. My other daughter goes around schools doing talks on the subject. Could help save a life.'

Demi was chewing her bottom lip while nodding, and Robson wondered if she might open up after all. She certainly looked sympathetic, but who wouldn't?

He turned his attention to the yellow wool when her gaze fell on him, as just for a moment he forgot he hadn't told his story.

'It's a good thing your Alice does, Liz,' said Jed.

Everyone nodded and hummed out an agreement.

Robson looked at Jan. 'Do you want to talk about anyone today? I know you come here as a buddy, but feel free.'

Jan scrunched her nose as Marisa pulled out a KitKat. 'Not really. I haven't lost anyone close. My grandparents, that's about it, but I was young, and I didn't really know them well.'

'Ooh, I loved my old gramps,' said Jed, chuckling. 'Not met anyone as direct as him since.'

'Direct?' asked Colby, removing his emotional support bottle of water from his duffel bag, as he liked to have something to cool him whenever he became over anxious and heated.

Jed grinned. 'Told people straight, he did. Not one to mince his words.'

'I prefer people like that,' said Colby. 'You know where you stand, even if they do come across as rude sometimes.'

Jed laughed. 'Yep, he definitely was a blunt old sod.'

'Ossie was way too polite for his own good. Even if someone wound him up, he would rather silently seethe than say a word.'

'Depends on my mood how I react,' said Lizzie, her blue eyes smiling at Demi. 'My mum, on the other hand . . . Ooh, if you ever need to speak to the dead, she does all that. Psychic, you see. Her name's Luna. She's banned from these groups. Went to one once, the whole thing ended up like a seance. There were tears, tantrums, threats to call the police. It all kicked off. Best people just seek her out if need be, rather than Mum throwing herself in the ring. Do you want another wafer, love?'

Robson bit back his grin as Demi frowned.

'I should take Luna out on the trawler with me,' said Jed, grinning. 'Hopefully she can predict where the fish are.'

'Does she talk to your Lisa?' asked Colby.

Lizzie shook her head. 'Says Lisa won't come through for her. Too upsetting.'

'I talk to Ossie. Not that I'm psychic or anything. I just like to think maybe he watches over me from time to time.'

'I heard Buttons the other day,' said Marisa, biting down on her snack. 'Went to the back door. Nothing.'

'I had some woman come in the shop the other day just to tell me she didn't believe in life after death.' Lizzie turned to Demi. 'I own the newsagent's along Harbour End Road. Treasure Chest. Pop in anytime for a chat.' She looked around the circle. 'Not sure why the woman thought I needed to hear her opinion. Mum came out from the back and told the woman not to bother buying a scratch card if she didn't believe people from the other side could make contact.'

'What's that got to do with the price of fish?' asked Jed.

Lizzie grinned. 'Well, Mum told the woman, the next scratch card was a winner and someone up above was wanting her to buy it.'

'And did she?' asked Colby, widening his eyes.

'Oh yeah. Suddenly the non-believer believed.'

'Was it a winner?' asked Marisa.

'Twenty quid.'

'Amazing,' said Colby, folding his arms and legs. 'I'm coming in your shop for a scratch card next time your mum's there.'

Lizzie laughed. 'It was a lucky guess. Mum was on the wind up, that's all. She likes to mess with the sceptics sometimes.'

'It doesn't matter if people believe in life after death or not,' said Robson. 'All that matters is we remember our loved ones and try to take comfort from the memories we shared.'

'What if you don't have any happy memories?' asked Demi, surprising the group.

Robson studied her expression for a moment, but it stayed neutral, and she was back to knitting again.

'People are people, love,' said Lizzie. 'Just because they're dead, doesn't mean we should talk like they're now saints. It's okay if life was sometimes a bit wobbly with them. Blimming heck, my Lisa caused the most arguments in our house.'

Robson waited for Demi to respond, but she kept quiet, so he turned to the circle. 'Does anyone want to light any candles today?'

Colby's hand shot up. 'Me. Ossie loved a candle. Scented ones everywhere.' He slapped his hand to his chest. 'Oh, I miss him. Sometimes it hurts so much, I swear I can't breathe.'

Lizzie stood to hug him. 'Come on, love. Let's go sort one of those tea lights for your man.'

Sniffing, Colby followed her over to the side door that led into the church.

'You know what, I think I'll light one for my grandparents while I'm here,' said Jan, creaking to a stand while looking at Demi.

Demi handed Marisa the wool, helping her place it back in her large carpet bag. 'I'll wait here.'

'Anyone want to join me?' asked Jan.

Jed stood, offering his arm to Marisa. 'Come on then. We're with you.'

Robson remained seated, looking over at Demi. 'I'll make some tea.' He gestured at the side door. 'There's a small room just there, linking the hall to the church. We put some money in the pot, and it goes towards teabags and milk.'

'I can help with that if you like.'

'Sure. Follow me.' He led her to the side room and set about filling the small cream kettle at a stainless-steel sink wedged in the corner. 'So, how you finding the group so far?'

Demi was lining up some disposable cups. 'Everyone seems nice. Their stories are sad, but they seem to be handling their loss well.'

Robson breathed out a small sigh. 'I think we do most of the crying alone, right?'

Demi shrugged.

'You can talk about other things here,' he added quickly. 'Marisa grows a lot of herbs in her garden, and she loves talking about things like that. If you need any, let her know. She'll happily bring some along next time.' That seemed to perk her up.

'Ooh, lovely. I could do with some herb plants to liven up my kitchen. Well, it's more of a small unit.' She smiled, and he noticed how much her face came alive.

'Marisa will love you forever.'

Demi chuckled. 'You can't beat fresh produce. I've bought some from farm shops before. Shame there isn't one around here.'

'Sounds like a mission for you. See who you can seek out in Port Berry for home-grown stock. Perhaps get them together to open stalls or something for a weekly or monthly farm shop, something affordable. Ooh, my mate Ginny has a barn on her farm. Not far from here. We could talk to her. See about getting a Sunday market opened there or something. She's been wondering what to do with the outbuilding.'

Demi stopped shuffling cups to stare at him. 'Wow, you're just full of ideas.'

Robson flashed her his cheeky smile, one he didn't pull out very often, and he wasn't sure why he was going for cheeky charm now. 'I'm just used to brainstorming. I'm a volunteer for the Happy to Help Hub down by the harbour.'

'I've heard of it.'

'We're always coming up with ideas to raise funds for the place. I just run on autopilot now.'

'It's a good thing you do because it's a great idea, and I definitely think we should speak to Ginny. Port Berry Farm Foods, or something like that.'

'My friend Lottie grows her own, and she adds bits and pieces to our food bank. I know she'd have a stall. She'd sell some just to make money for the Hub.'

'Sounds like you know all the right people.'

Robson laughed. 'I own a pub. I know a lot of people.'

'Which pub?'

'The Jolly Pirate. Harbour End Road. Got a restaurant inside too, so if you ever fancy some pub grub, pop along.'

'Ooh, you don't need a chef, by any chance, do you? I lost my job this morning.'

'No way!' He looked at the ceiling and shook his head.

'What is it?'

'All that talk from Lizzie about Luna and messages from the other side. Maybe someone up there is helping you.' He noticed her mouth tighten and was worried he'd said the wrong thing. Everyone dealt with grief in their own way, and whatever was happening with her, she didn't seem best pleased about it. 'Erm, it's just my sous chef broke his leg a couple of days ago, so Joseph, my head chef, mentioned we should get someone to cover his sick leave.'

Demi glanced up, then at him. 'Could I apply?'

'Don't see why not. You'll have to do the interview with Joseph, as he deals with the hiring and firing in the kitchen. He'll know if your CV is up to scratch.'

'When could I see him?'

'Come back with me after this if you want.'

'Really?'

Robson smiled. 'Sure. Do you need to go home and get anything first?'

'No. My CV is in my emails. I can easily pull that up or send him a copy.'

'Here, you can send that over now. I'll text him a message. Let him know.' He showed her the email address, and she quickly got to work on her phone.

'This is incredibly kind of you.'

He smiled, putting his phone away. 'I think you'll find you'll be doing me a favour. It's only temporary though.'

Demi nodded. 'That's fine. If I get the job, I won't be out of pocket while I find something permanent.'

Robson looked over at the doorway to the church. 'I won't pour their tea till they come back, but we can have one now if you want.'

'Yes, please. My mouth's a little dry from those pink wafers.'

They shared a laugh, and Robson knew she was going to be a good fit for the group. At least, he hoped she'd return. He also hoped Joseph would give her the job, as he found he was enjoying her company already.

'After the interview, I'll take you to see Ginny. As well as owning the farm, she runs the tea shop along by me.'

Demi nodded. 'I really am having a day of two halves.'

'If I'm honest, you didn't look like you wanted to be here earlier.'

'I didn't, but it's okay. I just don't know what to say about my loss because...'

He watched her head dip as her voice trailed off.

'I don't always talk about my late wife,' he said softly, gaining her attention.

'Oh, I'm sorry,' she said sweetly.

'It's okay. Just know you're not alone. We do this in our own time, in our own way. There's no right or wrong. Just being in this group is sometimes all someone needs. I want you to know you have somewhere to go and people to talk to.'

'Thanks. I just think my story of loss doesn't fit anywhere.'

'It fits here.' He placed a hand over his heart, hoping she would understand. He knew all too well what grief felt like, and he certainly didn't want anyone around him to feel they had to cope with that alone.

Demi slowly reached out and lightly touched his hand on his chest, taking him by surprise. She paused for a moment, then dropped her arm to her side.

Robson took a silent breath. 'How about that tea?'

CHAPTER 3

Demi

Demi was no stranger to interviews so was relatively calm during her informal chat with the head chef at the Jolly Pirate pub.

Joseph had deep-set eyes that seemed to bore further and further into her soul with each question he asked.

What could she tell him that her CV hadn't already? There was some shop work after leaving school, then a pregnancy, followed by going to culinary school, thanks to Terry giving her the nudge. She'd been in kitchens ever since qualifying. All that was left to talk about was her gap year. Never her favourite subject, as she knew how easily people judged.

'I was in prison for theft,' she said confidentially. Should she elaborate? She didn't have to with Marco because he was part of the back-to-work scheme for ex-offenders, so he knew the backstories before he met the people. 'Shoplifting. Two-year sentence. The first year I spent in prison, the second outside on licence, but I was allowed to work.'

Joseph simply bobbed his head, and Demi fixed her gaze on his thick white curls. He gestured at the gas rings behind him. 'Go make me a mushroom omelette,' he said simply.

'An omelette?'

'I'm not a fan of repeating myself.'

Demi immediately got to work, eyeing up her work station quickly to see where everything was as she washed her hands, knowing hygiene was a must. She had to laugh as the memory of her first day in a restaurant sprung to mind. She happened to think the risotto she'd made that day was on point, but it was sent back, and that put her in the doghouse straight away.

With Joseph standing close by, looking as though he was taking mental notes, Demi tried hard not to overthink her chore. A mushroom omelette was child's play. She was sure he was messing with her but quietly made the order.

Robson was working the bar while she was in the kitchen, but Joseph called him in to sit at the small table in the corner.

Feeling like she was suddenly on a cooking show, Demi carefully placed the plate on the table, then stood back, hands behind her back.

Joseph sat opposite Robson, handing him a fork, and they both tucked in as Demi chewed the inside of her cheek.

She wondered if she should tell Robson about her criminal record or if Joseph would do that. Would this be her life now, always wondering if she should mention the part of her story she wished didn't exist?

'Best omelette I've ever had,' said Robson, bringing her out of her thoughts.

Demi smiled warmly. He was being kind, she could tell.

Joseph glanced over his shoulder. 'Do you know what's so special about omelettes?'

Not a clue.

'It's one of those things where you have to break something to make something,' Joseph added before she could reply.

Demi wondered where he was going with that.

He stood to face her. 'It's not about then. It's about now. So, you think you're up to the job?'

Demi nodded with enthusiasm. 'Hundred per cent.' She watched him glance at Robson, who simply smiled. 'Okay, you can start tomorrow. I'll email you the details later. Now, go, both of you. I have work to do.'

'Thank you so much.' Demi quickly linked her fingers to stop herself from clapping.

Robson waved her over to the doorway which led to the bar. 'Congratulations,' he said.

'That was way more intense than I expected.' She laughed, mocking a swipe of the brow.

Robson gestured at the long bar. 'Glass of wine to celebrate?'

'No, that's okay.'

'On the house.'

She stared at the Jolly Roger flag behind the bar. 'I don't drink.'

'Tell you what, how about some juice and a slice of cake at Ginny's instead?'

Demi smiled. 'Sure, but I'm paying. You're the one that just gave me a job.'

He gestured towards the kitchen. 'Joseph's decision.'

'You're the boss.'

Robson pointed at a covered outdoor grill area as they walked into the front beer garden on their way out. 'I let Joseph be the boss in the kitchen. I cook out here sometimes.'

'Will I be doing that too?'

He chuckled. 'Aren't you overqualified for flipping a few burgers?'

'Hey, I'm not a job snob.' She grinned as she perused the high ceiling, brick pillars, and small sink beneath the shelter.

'I don't normally get much help from the kitchen staff out here.'

Demi shrugged. 'I'll help — if Joseph lets me.'

'I'll bear that in mind.'

They walked along Harbour End Road, stopping outside Ginny's Tearoom, and Demi stared out at the calm sea across the road, then at the pretty bunting hanging in the windows either side of the tea shop's door. She'd rarely been down to Port Berry's harbour since moving to the area. Her job at Seafarers had been in Penzance and then there was focusing on getting her life back together and trying to rebuild a relationship with Jade.

'It's lovely here, isn't it?'

'My favourite place,' said Robson, motioning towards the red-and-white lighthouse in the near distance. 'Great view.'

Demi thought about the view from her bedsit. The small communal garden downstairs that led on to another red-brick block wasn't as quaint.

'Come on,' said Robson, opening the door to the tearoom. 'I'll introduce you to Ginny.'

Demi smiled at the boat-print tablecloths and framed harbour paintings, then at the petite pregnant woman by the glass counter.

'This is Ginny,' said Robson, pointing down at the baby bump. 'Plus one.'

Ginny's smile was filled with friendliness. 'Hello, chick.' She reached up to kiss Robson's cheek.

'Ginny, this is Demi. Newest recruit at the Jolly Pirate.'

'Hi,' said Demi. 'It's just temporary while the sous chef's leg heals.'

Ginny reached for the red scarf in her hair. 'Ooh, I heard about that. What a nuisance.'

Robson chuckled. 'Yeah, I'm sure that's what he thought.'

Ginny eyed Demi. 'Is our Robson showing you the sights?'

'No, just along here.' Demi smiled at him as he moved towards a table.

'Well, you've come to the best place.' Ginny laughed. 'Don't tell the others I said that.'

'We've come for some cake, and some juice would be good.' Robson glanced at the window. 'It's warm today.'

Ginny agreed. 'Let's hope it stays that way.'

Demi sat opposite Robson and picked up the small menu, thinking the blueberry muffin would hit the spot.

'Let me get you both a drink while you decide which of my sweet treats suits your needs.'

'All of them,' said Demi, chuckling.

Robson ordered an orange juice, and Demi decided to have the same. She watched Ginny plod over to the counter and couldn't help think she resembled a 1940s Land Army girl.

'You thinking about the war?' asked Robson, as though reading her mind. 'Ginny's style does that to people.'

Demi nodded. 'I was, yes. She wears it well though.'

'She does.'

'Have you known each other long?'

'Yeah, we both grew up around here. Ginny was a couple of years below me in school.' Robson lowered his menu. 'You from Penzance?'

'No. Newquay.'

'What made you move here?'

Demi had little choice when it came to accommodation once released from prison. It had been Jan, working with The Butterfly Company, who had helped find the bedsit, as Colin flat-out refused to house her ever again. Apparently it was too much for Alana last time, and Jade didn't need the disruption.

Demi didn't blame them. She knew what she had put them through, or rather, what trouble her addiction had caused.

'To be closer to my daughter,' she replied.

'She lives in Port Berry?'

'Penzance. My place comes under Port Berry but is on the border between here and there.'

It was the closest Jan could find that was affordable. There wasn't much to the poky property, but it was her home for now. She had to make the best of things.

'How old is your daughter?'

'Eighteen. She lives with my brother and his family.' Demi wanted to make things clear, as she'd had enough of secrets from the past. 'Joseph will no doubt tell you, but there was a gap year on my CV due to time I spent in prison for shoplifting. That's when my daughter went to live with my brother. As a family, we're in the process of rebuilding.' She met his eyes, wondering if he'd have more questions. 'Do you still want to hire me?'

Robson's smile was warm. 'Both Joseph and I are happy to give people a second chance.'

'Thank you. I've come a long way, and I'm a different person now, so you won't get any bother from me.'

'Life changes are hard, so good for you. I wish you well.'

A moment of silence sat between them, but Demi didn't feel uncomfortable, more relieved that he hadn't tried to delve further into her life. She was glad he knew about her record and was still willing to let her in the door.

'Have you got kids?' she asked, thinking it time to move on from her own story.

'No. It's just me.'

She noticed he didn't seem sad about that fact, so she simply bobbed her head, then thanked Ginny for the drinks she brought over.

'Do you know what you want yet?' asked Ginny.

'Blueberry muffin for me, please,' replied Demi.

'Strawberry cheesecake, ta, Gin.' Robson sipped his juice, then grinned. 'Cheesecake is my weakness.'

'I think all food is mine.'

'Ah, so that's why you became a chef.'

'I've always liked cooking.'

'I can take it or leave it. I don't spend much time at home since Leah died. I mostly eat downstairs in the pub.'

'I can see you miss her.' She wished she could say the same about Terry. At least she missed Jade's dad, Ray, even though she no longer thought about him often.

'It's been three years now.'

Ginny placed the cakes before them. 'I'll come and have a natter in a minute. Just need the loo.'

'Yes, please do,' said Robson. 'I want to talk about your barn.'

Ginny frowned, but her bladder was getting the better of her, so she dashed off.

Robson tucked into the cheesecake, giving off a small groan of delight. 'This is good.'

Demi sliced her muffin in half, not wanting to pick it up to take a large bite, which was what she would have done if at home alone.

'Do you like being on your own?' Demi asked, not sure why.

'It's okay. I'm busy all the time, so I'm always surrounded by people.'

They both knew it wasn't the same as intimacy.

Demi picked at a blueberry, wanting to say how lonely she felt, but she kept quiet.

'I know you're going to be working at the pub for a while, but when you're not and you just want to hang out, feel free to give me a call. I'm always up for a slice of cake and a chat.' Robson finished his food without looking up, but Demi could still see his warm smile.

'Right, I'm back,' said Ginny, stating the obvious as she plonked herself down next to Robson. 'What do you want to know about my barn?'

'Demi mentioned there wasn't a farm shop in Port Berry, so we were thinking, what if your barn was used as a weekly or monthly farm food market sort of thing? You've been thinking of ideas for the place. You could charge per stall, and the locals will have one place to buy all their farm goods.'

Ginny nodded her agreement. 'Worth some thought. With the baby on the way, everything else has been on the back burner, but I'll speak to Will.' She looked at Demi. 'He's my other half.'

'It would be nice to have a Sunday market or something that isn't linked to a car boot sale.' Robson shrugged. 'Also, would save me going from farm to farm to buy fresh produce. I'm sure the farmers would get on board.'

Ginny grinned. 'Yeah, and those making their own jams and honey.'

'We already know a lady who grows her own herbs,' said Demi, excited to be part of the planning committee.

Ginny affectionately rubbed over her stomach. 'It's definitely worth exploring. Leave it with me. I'll get back to you after I've spoken to Will.' She groaned as she stood. 'Ooh, my knees are giving me the hump today.'

'Why don't you sit down for an hour or something. I'll help your staff serve the customers,' said Robson, standing to put her back on a seat.

Demi listened to them debate her putting her feet up and letting him take over the shop. They seemed such good friends. Something she'd never had.

Both Ray and Terry had been her best mates when she was with them, pushing all her friends aside. It wasn't something she did intentionally, she just never cared much for a big circle. Perhaps if she'd invested in better friendships, she would've had more support when her life came tumbling down.

Colin had tried his best, but Alana gave barely an inch of her time. Jade was too young to be a rock, and even if she had stepped up, Demi wouldn't have allowed it, as she didn't believe children should carry their parent's weight, and what a weight she was back then.

For some reason, Crystal Lewis popped into her head. It wasn't often she came up. Not anymore. Demi hated thinking about the woman who had changed her life. One moment on her doorstep had taken more than she could ever have imagined.

Demi sighed silently, trying to control her breathing without gaining attention. Robson and Ginny were still discussing Ginny being stubborn, even though he'd already cleared the table and was holding the stacked plates and glasses like an experienced waiter.

'Sorry about this, Demi,' he said, moving towards the counter.

Demi smiled at Ginny resting her back against the exposed brickwork wall. 'Would it be okay if I help too? I've got nothing else on today.' She hadn't planned to call Jade till the evening, knowing she was out for the day with friends, celebrating the end of school life.

It was hard to believe her daughter was eighteen and would hopefully be off to university in a few months.

'Are you sure?' asked Ginny, her hazel eyes coming alive with amusement.

Demi gestured towards a small group of people heading for the seating area outside. 'Looks like you could do with another pair of hands.'

Ginny called out to the young woman behind the counter. 'What do you think, Lilac? Do you want the help?'

Lilac beamed at Robson, who didn't notice. 'Yes, please.'

'That's that settled,' said Ginny. 'But half hour, then I'm up.'

Robson laughed. 'Don't make me call Will.'

Ginny scoffed. 'Oh, what's he going to do?' She turned to Demi. 'Nag me, fuss me, faff about, and kiss me to death.' She winked as she chuckled. 'You got a partner, Demi?'

'No,' was all she cared to say, as adding anything else seemed complicated. There was a time during the first year after Terry died when she'd tell people she was a widow, even though she wasn't his legal wife.

Ginny glanced at Robson, then back at Demi. 'Looking for love, chick?'

Demi smiled politely. 'No, just the sink so I can wash my hands and get stuck in.'

Ginny laughed and pointed to the back of the shop.

'It's good of you to offer to help,' said Robson as she headed for the small stainless-steel sink.

It wasn't really for Ginny. Demi felt in control of her life when she was busy. Her addiction could come knocking any day, and the idea of going back down that rabbit hole scared the living daylights out of her. It was best to keep active, give her mind something to focus on, and pretend she was just another average everyday person going about life as though nothing bad had ever happened.

CHAPTER 4

Robson

Robson felt the need to apologise to Demi for how long they spent in Ginny's Tearoom.

'It's okay,' she told him as they stepped outside.

'I wasn't expecting her to fall asleep.' He chuckled, glancing over his shoulder at the window.

Demi smiled. 'I guess she needed it, but how on earth she managed to stay asleep through all the noise is beyond me.'

'Thanks for helping out.'

'Broke up the day.'

'What you got planned now?'

Demi stared out to sea as they came to a halt at the pub. 'Going home and getting some dinner.'

'You could join me for dinner in the pub, if you like. Just so you know, all staff get a discount on food, and it's a tradition of mine that they have their first meal on the house as a bit of a welcome.'

Demi checked her watch. 'Sure, I can do that. Thanks.'

Robson shrugged. 'No worries. I'll need to get back to work after. I like to put in my hours.' He pointed at the bend in the road. 'I just need to pop into the Hub first. Do you want to come check it out?'

'Yeah, okay.'

'We opened the place early last year. Thought it might be of use to people in need. A small group of us came up with the idea after a couple of homeless people were spotted sleeping in the harbour.'

'Oh, that's very kind of you all.'

Robson bobbed his head. 'We all need help from time to time.'

They stopped at the Happy to Help Hub, and Demi pointed at the smiley face sticker glued to the front door.

'So what exactly goes on here?' she asked.

'All sorts now. At first, we asked local businesses if they had anything to offer a homeless person who came in. We got a dentist on board, hairdresser, that sort of thing, then we joined forces with a homeless hostel, providing guidance to both us and our visitors. We also partnered with the Les Powell Trust so we could open a small food bank. Plus we have things like a noticeboard advertising local jobs, group sessions at the church, free furniture, stuff like that. Sometimes someone might just pop in for a chat.'

'Wow, it sounds like the Hub has come a long way.'

'Yep, we even have a baby bank now too. Food, clothing, the occasional pram.' He opened the door and stood back so she could enter first.

'Oh, I love the affirmations on the wall,' Demi said as she looked around the small cosy area.

Robson straightened one of the frames. 'We tried for positive vibes.' He gestured at some potted plants surrounding a mini water feature by the window.

Demi was reading the noticeboard, and Robson wondered if he should put the kettle on.

'Thought I heard you,' said a voice from the back room.

'Alice, come meet Demi.' Robson waved his friend forward.

'Give me one sec,' said Alice, placing a large box on a shelf before stepping through the doorway. She wiped her hands down her blue culottes, then swiped back her long dark hair. 'Don't mind me. I'm a bit flustered. Had a load of donations dropped off a minute ago. Been trying to fit everything in.'

Robson moved to her side to peer inside the storage room. 'Got much left to do?'

'Just a couple more boxes need unpacking.' Alice smiled over at Demi. 'Hiya, come and sit down for a bit. I think I might join you.'

'Yeah, you do that, Al,' said Robson, entering the back room. 'I'll sort these.'

Demi sat in a green high back chair as Alice opted for a large comfy blue one.

'There's not much room left on the shelves, Rob,' Alice called out.

'I'll pop them up to HQ,' he replied.

Alice grinned at Demi. 'That's what we call Sam's office above Harbour Light Café. Samuel Powell, that is. Owner of the Les Powell Trust.'

'Used to be Ginny's flat,' said Robson, managing to find some space for the boxes of cereal he'd just unpacked.

'You know Ginny?' asked Alice.

'I just met her today,' said Demi.

'We just did a shift for her while she fell asleep,' said Robson, poking his head out the door.

Alice laughed. 'All she does lately is sleep. Still, best she does. Mum reckons she won't get much kip once the baby is born.' She turned to Demi. 'You got kids?'

'One daughter. Jade. She's a grown-up. Eighteen.'

'Goes quick, doesn't it? My Benny's fifteen now. He's my nephew, but I adopted him when he was younger after his mum died.'

Robson gestured at Alice. 'This is Lizzie's daughter.'

Demi shuffled in her chair. 'Oh, I met your mum at lunchtime.'

'You were at the bereavement support group?'

Demi nodded. 'First time.'

Alice shook her head slightly. 'I don't go to those things myself. Suits Mum though.' She snorted a small laugh. 'My nan's been banned for turning one meeting into a seance.'

'I heard about that. Psychic or something, right?'

'Clairvoyant, medium, oracle, crystal ball gazer, you name it, she's it.' Alice gave a nod to Robson, making him laugh. 'Mum prefers the tarot, and I don't tend to dabble too much, but that's my family. Even our Benny charges his crystals every full moon. You a believer, Demi? Doesn't matter if you're not. Each to their own.'

Demi raised one shoulder to her cheek. 'Not sure. I'm not much of a spiritual person.'

Alice smiled. 'It's not for everyone.' She turned to Robson. 'Are you here to help Lottie and Sam when they arrive to sort the stock?'

'No, I came here to get a pram down from HQ. Someone's due in soon to collect. We made the arrangement yesterday.'

'Oh, she's already been. Came early. Samuel brought it down.' Alice looked at Demi. 'Lottie and Samuel are partners, just so you know who is who around here.'

'You'll meet the whole team soon, Demi, now you're working at the pub,' said Robson.

'Ooh, you got a job with our Rob here?'

Demi nodded. 'The sous chef broke his leg, so I'm filling in while he recovers.'

Alice's light-brown eyes widened. 'I heard about that. Poor sod. Well, good luck in your new job. Did you know Robson gives his staff their first meal for free?'

'Yes, he told me.'

'And we're going to have that meal right now.' Robson headed for the door. 'Unless you need me to stick around, Al.'

'No, I'm good. I'm just going to sit here and make up some food parcels. Don't get many people come in this time of day, and Sam and Lottie will be here any minute.'

Demi got up and followed Robson outside. 'Nice to meet you, Alice.'

'You too, Demi.'

Robson walked by Demi's side. 'Been a bit of a day, hasn't it?'

'Something like that.'

'Please don't feel obligated to join me for dinner. I'll understand if you're ready to go home.'

Demi checked her watch. 'No, I'm okay. I've got somewhere to be later, but I've got time to eat. An early dinner will suit me today.'

'Me too. I'm famished.'

They headed inside the pub and straight to the dining area to grab a table for two, and Demi laughed at the menu, making him frown.

'Sorry,' she said. 'I can't see any omelettes on here, and it made me giggle.'

'Oh, I see. Well, you can take that up with Joseph. He always has his cooks breaking eggs.'

They both chose barbeque chicken with fries and enjoyed some light conversation while they ate. Robson usually rushed through his meals as though they would be taken away at any moment, but he took his time, happy to engage and spend more time with Demi. He wanted to learn more about her and was curious about why she had been shoplifting, not that he would ask — but it wasn't long before she told him she had to go.

'I'll see you tomorrow.' Robson waved her off at the double doors of the pub, then made his way around the side to go up to his flat.

The large home was as empty as ever, showing hardly any lived-in signs.

He stood in the open-plan kitchen and stared over at the living room area. Once more he wondered if he should move. There was so much space, and he barely used any of it. The first room along the passageway was supposed to be an office, but it was mostly filled with clutter. Next to that was his bedroom, and opposite was a toilet and shower. He couldn't remember the last time he ventured to the next floor. Upstairs was as empty as he was feeling.

Robson went over to the kitchen table and sat still for a moment. He could feel the numbness creeping over him, and normally he'd work to make himself busy to take back control, but this time he wanted to sit in a trance, to have the respite that came with feeling comfortably numb. It was better than pain, and he'd had bucketloads of that since Leah died.

He glanced over at her picture in a frame on the windowsill as all energy left his soul.

CHAPTER 5

Demi

Demi was having a surreal day. She truly felt as though she'd been pulled from pillar to post. One minute she was heading to work, the next she'd been fired, sat in a grief support group, got a new job, worked a shift in a tea shop, made some friends, and had a free meal. Not what she was expecting when she woke that morning.

She sat on a bench outside All Saints church, knowing she had arrived too early for the recovery meeting. She was sure Jade would be home by now so thought it a good time to give her a call to see how her day went.

'Hi, Mum. I haven't got long. I've just got in, and I'm due back out any sec. Just looking for something to wear.'

'You out for dinner?'

'Yeah, with my mates.'

'The ones you've just spent the day with?'

'Yep.'

Demi paused, waiting to see if her daughter would ask after her day. She knew the odds were slim to none, as Jade never seemed to want any info. 'So, how was your day?'

'Great. We went sailing and had a picnic on the beach.'

'That sounds lovely.' She sat back and listened while Jade rattled on about her friends and their conversations about the future. It was nice to hear her daughter so happy and wanting to take on university.

'You just finished work?' asked Jade, finally taking time to bring Demi into the chat.

'No, I got fired today.'

The line went silent.

'Seafarers closed down,' Demi quickly added, worried Jade might think the worst.

'Oh, so it wasn't . . . you?'

'No, I'm good. About to go into a meeting.'

'That's great, Mum.' Her tone had changed to quiet, almost dismissive.

'I have a new job already. The Jolly Pirate. Do you know it? It's in Port Berry. Down Harbour End Road.' Demi hoped that would lift her daughter's mood.

'Yes, I know the pub. I'm glad you found work so quickly.' She sounded as though she meant every word, which was a relief.

Demi knew her daughter had little faith in her. She had ruined the girl's life, put her in danger at times, and left her to be raised by relatives.

All conversations with Jade were strained and quite the challenge since Demi had been locked up, but it wasn't prison that was the problem. Jade had witnessed her mother relapse a couple of months out of the rehab centre Colin had placed Demi in back before prison life. Why should Jade have any confidence in her mum? Demi knew rebuilding a relationship with her daughter was going to take time.

'Look, Mum, I have to go. I need to jump in the shower.'

'Yes, of course. Erm, maybe you can come over the weekend or something.'

'I'm busy. Besides, it's a bit cramped at yours.'

'I'm still saving for a two-bed. It'll be homelier for you then.' Demi knew it wouldn't be. Jade already had a lovely home life with Colin and Alana. Her own bedroom, en suite, pocket money on tap, and more importantly, stability.

'I'll speak to you later, Mum. Bye.'

Demi went to speak, but Jade was gone.

How you coping, Mum? Got any more good news, Mum? I love you, Mum.

Demi inhaled deeply as she put her phone back in her bag. She didn't deserve her daughter's time after what she'd put her through, so she told her chatty brain to shut up. Jade had stopped investing her emotions a long time ago, and who could blame her? It still hurt plenty.

A tall dark-haired man was entering the church hall, so Demi assumed he was part of the recovery meeting.

She went inside to see if she could help with setting out chairs or anything. 'Hiya,' she said as the man around her age turned to greet her.

'You here for the meeting?' he asked, pale-blue eyes twinkling.

Demi nodded. 'Am I early?'

'No, everyone should be here any minute.' He grabbed a foldaway chair. 'You wouldn't be Demi, by any chance?'

She frowned, amused. 'Yes.'

'Jan said you might pop along. I'm Matt.'

Now things made sense, Demi relaxed. 'Is she coming?'

'I don't think so. She doesn't always join. Depends on her schedule or if she's needed. She's always helping someone, so you never quite know where she'll be.'

Demi smiled. 'You been here long? I detect a strong London accent.' It instantly reminded her of the few times Terry had taken her to London for the occasional weekend to stay in one of the hotels he worked for.

'I moved to Port Berry last year. Don't live too far. Cockle Cottage. My missus owns the fishmongers along Harbour End Road: Sea Shanty Shack. Fresh fish on the counter every day. Pop along.' He beamed a smile. 'I need to work on my selling skills.'

Demi laughed. 'It was all right.'

Some people came in and sat in the circle Matt had created with the chairs, and Demi decided she would just listen to the others and see how she felt in their group. She knew she wouldn't be forced into talking so took the evening in her stride, which seemed to pass quickly.

'Who would like to end with some motivation?' asked Matt.

An elderly man leaned forward. His dark eyes held all the depth of a difficult history. 'Think of life as a computer game. You've got one energy bar left to reach the next level, and there's a monster in the way. All around you are distractions. Play the game strategically. Take that one piece of energy you have and use it to take down the beast, because if you use it on the distractions, you'll spend the rest of your life on that same level, never knowing what lies ahead. Choose wisely, my friends. Level up.'

Demi woke from her daze, as his words hit home. If she was playing a game, she would box clever, and he was right about one thing. She only had a small amount of energy that kept her from breaking down each day.

As soon as she got home, she set up her phone to record some more content for the social media account she'd been planning for months. Her quick and easy meals for one were sure to help someone. It sparked so much joy in her when she made the videos.

'Let's do this, Demi,' she said to herself, sitting opposite her phone.

All that was left to do was set up an account, post a video each day, and she had plenty ready, then see if anyone followed her little cooking show.

'First thing's first,' she muttered, getting comfortable.

The first content she wanted was an honest direct message about herself so her followers would know a little bit about why cooking saved her soul.

With no script and a deep breath, she pressed the record button.

'Hello, I'm Demi. Welcome to my account. I'm here to show you easy recipes for single meals that are healthy and affordable. I've always had a love for cooking, but little did I realise it would one day save my life . . .'

CHAPTER 6

Robson

Ginny was at home at Happy Farm, resting her knees, and Robson had arranged that he and Demi meet Will at his café, Harbour Light Café, after Demi's first shift at the pub finished, to go and see the barn.

All day, he'd kept busy at the pub, clearing his head first thing by going for an early-morning run. The weather was nice, the tourists out, and his staff upbeat. It all helped.

Demi was excited to go to the farm with him, wolfing down the chocolate fudge cake Will served them before they headed off.

Robson was feeding off her energy, eager to make plans and get involved in something new.

Demi was chatting happily to Will as he chauffeured them in his dark pickup truck. She asked all about his origins in Wales and wanted to know more about his past in the navy.

Robson sat quietly, letting his two friends get to know each other. He already knew Will's story. Not so much about Demi though. She gave him the impression she didn't like to talk much about herself, which was understandable, seeing how she had been in prison. She appeared more focused on her present and future. It just wasn't something he was used to, working in a pub, as all he heard was other people's life stories, usually filled with doom and gloom told into the dregs in their glass.

Happy Farm came into view. A new wooden sign staked to the ground welcomed them onto the drive.

Demi leaned closer to the windscreen, peering at the large farmhouse. 'Oh wow, I love your home.'

'Thanks,' said Will, clambering out the truck.

Robson got out and stood by Demi. 'It's definitely a happy farm since these two moved in. They've even got chickens.'

'Do you breed them?' she asked.

Will raked a hand through his mousey hair, his large biceps flexing as he stretched. 'Rescue them, more like. My Gin won't even eat chicken now. Oh, and we have a donkey, Ralph. He'll be pottering around somewhere. Got his own paddock, but when Ginny's home, he has free rein.'

Demi's dark eyes gazed up at Robson. 'I think I want to live here,' she whispered, adding a warm smile.

He knew how she felt. Everyone loved Happy Farm.

Ginny opened the front door, waving them inside. 'You want some cake?'

'No, ta,' replied Robson. 'We had some at the café.'

'Used to be mine,' Ginny told Demi. 'Will had the tea shop, then we swapped. Not that it makes a difference now we're a couple.' She rubbed her tummy. 'This little one will inherit the lot.'

'Let's not put us in our graves just yet, eh, love.' Will leaned over to kiss her cheek.

Robson and Demi shared a small smile.

'I hear you have chickens,' said Demi.

'Yes, come look.' Ginny led them through the rustic, cosy house to the back door.

'There's a certain peacefulness to your home, Ginny,' Demi said as they stepped outside. 'If that makes sense.'

'It makes sense,' said Robson. 'It's calming here.' Maybe he needed to move away from the hustle and bustle of pub life, or perhaps he just needed to make his flat feel homely once again.

Everyone leaned on the fence by the chicken coop, watching as the hens mooched over to see if Ginny had anything for them.

Robson stared out at the fields surrounding them. It was a great view, but there was no lighthouse, no rolling sea, no pier to sit on. He'd always loved the view from the pub. Leah loved it too. He quickly turned to Will. 'Let's have a look at this barn of yours then.'

Will nodded and led the way. 'It's in pretty good shape. Needs a tidy and a lick of paint, that's all.'

'And a clear out,' said Ginny. 'Some machinery bits left behind by the previous owner. Not sure why they thought we'd want them, but nothing a skip and some elbow grease won't sort.'

Will laughed. 'And by that, she means me doing the heavy lifting.'

Ginny latched on to Demi's arm. 'Well, you can't expect us to get our hands dirty. I'm pregnant, and Demi's new.'

Robson laughed, glancing over his shoulder at the women walking behind. 'Newbie privilege. That's a good one.'

'I really don't mind helping,' said Demi.

'I know that, chick. Proved it when you took care of my tearoom.'

'It was actually a lot of fun. I can see why you enjoy it there.'

Robson called back to them, 'Better than being a chef?'

Demi shook her head. 'Never.'

Will opened the large barn doors, revealing just how spacious the place was. 'I can just see this with stalls dotted around. Corn on the cob in baskets. A scarecrow in the corner.'

Ginny laughed. 'It's not autumn.'

'I know, but you get the gist.' Will grinned at Demi. 'What do you see?'

'Erm, pretty much the same thing. I think we could dress up the scarecrow each season to blend in with any other décor we come up with. Makes it look farm-ish.'

Robson chuckled. 'Farm-ish?'

Demi shrugged, then pointed at the back wall. 'We could use some of the wood here to make a stall or two, and look, those old wagon wheels would look perfect screwed to the front of one of the stalls.'

Ginny cooed. 'Ooh, I love those kinds of stalls.'

'Apart from the tidying and creating, how are we going to go about starting this up?' asked Will, looking to Robson.

Robson turned to Demi. 'Ask around. Put the word out, see who fancies a farmers' market first. If there's little interest, then no point looking into things any further.'

'Well, we've been meaning to do something with the place, so it's still worth cleaning up,' said Will.

'And if you make any stalls you don't end up needing, you can always sell them,' said Demi.

'How are you with a saw and a screwdriver?' Will asked her.

'I'm willing to give it a go.'

'Do you have time, chick?' asked Ginny.

'I can grab an hour here and there after my shifts at the pub.'

'And I can come too,' said Robson, glad to squeeze more into his day to keep him busy. With the amount of staff he had, he didn't really need to work at the pub if he didn't want to. He always wanted to. Not only did the Jolly Pirate lift his spirits, it gave him something to do with his time.

Demi screamed, making everyone jump. They quickly turned her way. She was by the door and Ralph had nudged her elbow. 'Ooh, sorry,' she said, placing a hand over her heart.

Robson moved to her side. 'You okay?'

'Yeah. Just gave me a fright.'

Ginny tutted at the donkey. 'Not the best way to make friends, Ralph.'

Ralph rested his head on Demi's arm, and by the look on her face the gesture melted her heart a touch.

Robson stroked Ralph's back. 'Aww, you're a good boy.'

Demi giggled. 'Yes, pleased to meet you.'

'You'll get used to him poking his nose in,' said Will. 'So, I was thinking, if we do this, we can set a small charge for stall hire like they do at the car boot sales, but what do you two want out of the deal?'

Robson looked at Demi, who shook her head.

'I don't want anything. Just local fresh food, reasonably priced of course.' she replied, and Robson agreed.

'You were looking for ideas for the barn,' Robson told Ginny. 'So I found one for you.' He shot his palm out to Demi. 'Top chef on board too.'

Demi dipped her head a touch, and he was sure she blushed. 'Can't beat a Sunday morning mooch around a farmers' market.'

Robson thought about his own Sunday mornings. A run first thing, as usual, followed by the Sunday dinner rush. Not exactly a day of rest for his business. Demi knew about restaurant life, so he had little doubt Sunday at the pub wouldn't faze her. Perhaps they could both fit in an early-morning stroll around Happy Farm.

'Okay,' said Will. 'I'll look into the legal side of things, see if any licences are needed. Spread the word in the meantime, and see if there's interest.'

'Let's just hope people like the idea,' said Ginny.

Demi gave a sharp nod. 'I know I do.'

'Right, well, now we know what we're doing, I'm going to head off.' Robson thumbed over his shoulder. 'I've got a shift on at the Hub.'

'I can give you both a lift home,' said Will.

Robson shook his head. 'No need. The bus stop is just up the road. Won't take five minutes to get back. You can take Demi.' He turned her way. 'We're not in the same direction, are we?'

'No. I live further inland, but I can get the bus too. I need to pop to the supermarket on my way home anyway.'

'I don't mind,' said Will.

'You put your feet up for a bit.' Robson grinned. 'I'm sure you'll be back up and out later.'

Will nodded. 'I will.'

Robson and Demi walked to the driveway and said goodbye to Will and Ginny, both looking pleased with themselves, before heading up towards the road.

'I really love the farmers' market idea,' Demi told him.

'I should think so, seeing how it was your idea.'

'Yours really. I just said it would be nice to have one around here, but ideas and it actually happening are two different things.' Demi pressed into his arm as they met the front gate. 'Aww, farm life.'

Robson blew out a laugh as he lightly nudged her back, feeling a slight flutter hit his stomach. 'Countryside or seaside, which would you prefer?'

'Anything's better than my built-up area. It's all new-build blocks that aren't so new anymore. The builders couldn't possibly squeeze another thing into the small area.'

'You got a flat?'

'Bedsit.' He saw the glow in her cheeks fade. 'I'm grateful for the roof over my head. It's cheap as chips to rent, but it's just so tiny, and I haven't had room for my daughter to sleep over.'

'Have you tried for a home swap?'

Demi scoffed. 'No one wants to downsize to a bedsit, and I need a two-bed, which I've been saving for. My tenancy isn't being renewed, so I'm currently looking for somewhere to rent, and I'm hoping for a bigger flat, but they cost a bit.'

Robson pointed out the bus stops on either side of the road. 'I'll keep my eye out for any full-time chef jobs.'

'I won't look just yet. I wouldn't want to leave you in the lurch.'

'It's not a problem.'

She gave a small nod as she went to cross the road. 'Erm, thanks for . . . well, everything.' Stepping forward, she gave him a quick hug.

Robson closed his eyes for a second, absorbing her warm embrace. *She's simply saying thank you*, he reminded himself. 'No worries,' he said, moving back. He watched her cross the road, then walked over to his own bus stop to sit and wait.

Demi waved over, making him smile, and he raised his hand her way.

He figured he was lucky to have so much room at his home. He had a nice place and a great business. Perhaps it was time he started to live properly again. He was doing so much for others, even hosting bereavement groups. Surely it was time for change within himself. Being at Happy Farm had inspired him to want more for his life, and meeting Demi, who was showing strength and positivity when it came to life changes, was motivational.

CHAPTER 7

Demi

Seeing how Demi didn't get to speak much to Jade yesterday, she thought she'd go to Colin's house before her shift started at eleven. Knowing her daughter, she should be crawling out of bed soon, especially if she had a late one with her friends.

The bus ride took longer than expected, then the fifteen-minute walk to the house slowed her with every step going uphill. Light rain started to fall, forcing her to get a wriggle on in case the heavens opened up and she got drenched.

At the time of Jade's eighteenth birthday, Demi wasn't impressed with Colin and Alana buying her daughter a car, but each time she took the journey to their large home on the back roads, she felt pleased Jade didn't have to travel by foot.

A delivery man was just exiting the side gate when Demi arrived, so she slipped inside and jogged up the drive to the oak double doors and knocked on the solid wood.

Colin was wearing a smile when he answered, but it dropped immediately on seeing who was on his doorstep. 'Demi, I thought we talked about this.'

She frowned, swiping her damp hair off her forehead. 'Talked about what?'

'You showing up unannounced.'

'I'm your sister, Colin, and my daughter lives here. I shouldn't have to call in advance.'

'Is that the taxi already?' called Alana.

Colin stepped back, allowing Demi to enter the large white hallway. 'No, it's Demelza.'

'Oh,' said Alana, from the bottom step of the wide winding stairway. She placed a designer carry case down on the shiny floor without taking her eyes off her sister-in-law. 'Were we expecting you?'

Demi ignored the disgruntled edge to her tone. 'No. I just popped by to see my daughter before I go to work.'

Alana glanced up the stairs as her son came trotting down to place a small suitcase by his mum's bag.

'Hiya, Aunt Dem,' said Damien. His dark eyes glared at her dripping locks. 'Oh no, it's not raining, is it?'

'Just a little.' Demi offered her fifteen-year-old nephew a small smile. She never liked him much because he could be quite the brat, but she always made sure she was polite. After all, it wasn't his fault he was spoiled rotten.

Damien sprinted back up the stairs. 'I hope we don't have any tropical storms where we're going,' he muttered.

'Are you going away?' asked Demi, eyeing her brother. He turned to his wife as though she should be the one to reply.

'Yes,' said Alana, twiddling with the bottom of her long blonde hair. She cleared her throat as she straightened her shoulders. 'Barbados for a couple of weeks.'

Demi already knew the answer but asked anyway. 'Is Jade going with you?'

Alana scoffed. 'Of course. Since when have we left her home alone?' One of her perfectly shaped eyebrows quirked. 'Not our style.'

That was a direct hit. Demi had left Jade home alone in the small hours while she went out to buy drugs. Jade had been scared and called her uncle, and Demi still felt the guilt, but she was also tired of the past being shoved in her face every time she stepped foot in their house. She understood they, too, had been affected by her life and that they still worried she might relapse, but Alana could be quite cold towards her at times.

'She never said,' was all Demi was willing to say.

Alana's wide smile lit up her whole face. 'We sprung the surprise on her last night.' She started checking out her manicured fingernail on her index finger. 'Well, she studied so hard and sat all those exams. Least we could do. We thought we'd enter July with a bang. She deserves a nice holiday now the exams are over, don't you think?'

'Yes, it'll be nice for her — but it would also be nice if you let me know.'

Alana's button nose wrinkled. 'We've been her legal guardians since she was fifteen. We don't need your permission, Demelza. Besides, she's eighteen now. She makes her own choices.'

'And I'm sure she was going to tell you later,' said Colin.

Demi clenched her jaw, trying to fight off the feeling of abandonment. It wasn't as though she had a right to feel that way after everything she'd put her daughter through.

'Probably when she had more time,' added Colin. 'Maybe at the airport.'

'I'm part of this family too,' said Demi.

'We know that,' said Colin. 'We're not trying to pretend you don't exist. It was all a bit last minute, that's all. I'm sorry, I should have told you.'

Alana turned to go back upstairs. 'We did our time, keeping our lives on hold for you. In case you haven't noticed, we don't do that anymore.'

'And in case you haven't noticed, I'm not that person anymore.' Demi's heart raced, but she remained perfectly still.

Alana huffed and went upstairs.

'Look, Demi, Alana still worries you might . . . slip again. She just wants to keep Jade stable and give her a good life.'

Demi held a palm to her chest. 'I know, and I appreciate all you've done, but she's still my daughter, and you two never tell me anything.'

'It's just a holiday.'

'That's not the point.'

Colin stepped closer, lowering his voice. 'Just give everyone more time to believe in you.'

There was no way Demi was going to cry, even though his comment struck her straight in the heart. 'I've been clean for two years.'

'Yes, but you were locked up for the first year.' He gave a small shrug. 'I mean, does it really count?'

'It counts.'

'You know, it doesn't help when you get angry.'

Demi almost choked on her laugh. 'I'm not angry. I just want to be included. You hardly roll out the welcome mat.'

'Well, what do you expect? We gave you a home. I paid for the best rehab I could afford, and what did you go and do? Came out and went back on the gear. You didn't give a crap how it was affecting your kid, let alone the rest of us. All you thought about was where you could get your next fix. And now, just like that, you expect us not to be wary of you. Oh, and I heard you lost your job.' His hands were on his hips as he frowned down at her.

Demi's hands started to shake, so she clasped them together, rubbing her fingers. 'Seafarers closed down, and I got work again the same day. Shame you didn't hear that part.'

'I'm glad you're sorting your life, I truly am, but we've all got a life too, and Alana's right, it doesn't revolve around you.'

'I'm not asking for anything other than to be notified about things that involve my kid, that's all. I never asked to come back into your home. I never asked for money from you. And I never asked to have Jade living back with me. I know she's happy here, and I can see how well you love and care for her, and I'm grateful to you, Colin. I always have been, but bloody hell, just let me in.'

Colin sighed. 'We are, Dem. Just slowly, okay. Things will improve over time. As long as you stay on track.'

'I've been out of prison for over a year now, and I haven't come off track, but it's not good enough for you. It never will be, will it? Come on, be honest.'

Colin reached out for her, but she moved back. 'You're my little sister, and I want you to be well.' He gritted his teeth as he leaned closer. 'You put me through hell and back watching you spiral out of control. You have no idea what that feels like. I've never felt so bloody helpless.'

'Yeah? You should have tried being in my shoes.' Demi caught her breath as she lifted her chin. 'But that's in my past, so stop knocking on doors where I no longer live.'

'That's not what I'm doing.'

'That's exactly what you do every time I see you.'

'Mum,' called Jade from over the banisters upstairs.

Demi took a calming breath and put on her best smile as Jade came jogging down to greet her. 'Hello, love.'

'I was just packing. We're going to Barbados to celebrate the end of my exams. Did you hear?'

'Yes, I heard. That's great.' Demi rummaged around in her handbag. 'Here, let me give you some spending money for your—'

'No need,' said Jade. 'I've got plenty.'

Demi looked up from her bag and smiled. 'Right.'

Jade smiled back, looking so much like her father, Ray. The same thin lips, pale eyes, and fair hair. There wasn't any of Demi in her. She even had a lot of Terry's mannerisms.

'Our taxi will be here soon,' muttered Colin, eyes on the door.

'We'll catch up when I get back,' said Jade.

Demi nodded. 'Sure.'

'You should come away with us one day,' said Jade, and Demi could see she didn't mean her words.

'Your mum has to work,' said Colin. 'Especially now she has this new job.'

Jade stepped forward, giving her mother a half-hearted hug. 'Yeah, course. Good luck with that, Mum.'

'Thanks,' said Demi, missing her daughter already. She used to be such a tactile child. Always loved to snuggle and cuddle on the sofa while watching the telly. Demi turned to the door. 'Best get off then. You have a safe trip and send me some pictures.'

Jade walked back upstairs. 'Will do.'

'Love you,' called Demi, but there came no response.

Colin saw her to the door. 'I'll call you when we get back. Sort some dinner out or something. Like I said, slow and steady, Dem.'

Demi looked out to see the light drizzle had stopped. She said goodbye and slowly made her way to the bus stop, not feeling like going anywhere, let alone to work.

Round and round in circles she'd been going with Colin the last year, and not much had changed. It was a hard battle to fight, as she wasn't sure who was right half the time. She could see his point of view, but she needed him to see who she was now.

It was a bitter pill to swallow not having her family believe in her. Jan once told her she had to believe in herself. That was all that mattered.

Demi sat at the bus stop and without warning burst out crying. Something she rarely did. Suddenly a hand was on her shoulder and a soft voice in her ear.

'You all right, love?'

Demi glanced to her side to see an elderly woman with white hair tied in a bun. Demi sniffed as she straightened on the wooden seat inside the bus shelter. 'I'm okay,' she lied.

The woman handed over a tissue, her midnight-blue eyes searching Demi's blotchy face. 'It's good to have a cry every so often. Releases stale energy.'

Demi was starting to feel a little calmer. 'Just one of those days.'

'There are never days that bring you down. Just moments. And we can deal with them one at a time.' She lightly tapped Demi's arm. 'The rest of your day will be good, I promise.'

Demi wiped her eyes and blew her nose as the bus pulled up. She let the old lady board first, then sat by her side when offered the seat.

'I'm going all the way to the harbour in Port Berry,' said the lady, opening a packet of mints, waggling them at Demi.

Demi took one and smiled. 'Thanks. I'm going that way too.'

'Doing a bit of shopping?'

'No. Work.'

'Ooh, I work down that way too. Well, I help out from time to time. Family business. Treasure Chest, the newsagent's. Pop in anytime.'

Demi stopped staring out the window. 'I met Lizzie who owns that place.'

'My daughter.' The woman breathed out a small laugh. 'Small world. So, where do you work?'

'The Jolly Pirate. I'm a chef.'

'I know Robson. Good lad.'

Demi continued to suck her mint, pondering over whether to mention the psychic abilities she'd heard about.

'I'm Luna,' said the woman.

'Demi.'

'Is that short for anything?'

'Demelza.'

'Ooh, I've been there. Nice place.'

'It's where I was born.'

'Makes sense your parents named you that then.'

Demi smiled at the memory of her mum and dad. If only they were still alive. Her mother would believe in her, she was certain. She was glad her parents weren't around to see the state she had got into after her knee operation. It would have broken their hearts. It sure as hell broke hers.

Luna peered at the sky. 'Sun's trying to poke its nose out.' She nudged Demi's elbow. 'See, told you the rest of the day would be good. And look, there's a penny by your foot. You know what that means?'

'That it fell out of someone's pocket?'

Luna grinned. 'It's a penny from heaven, love. Whenever you spot one, pick it up, as it's a gift from someone watching over you.'

Demi twisted her mouth to one side. 'You believe that?'

'You have to believe in things. Helps make the journey here easier.'

Demi bent to pick up the penny and plopped it in her bag.

I believe in me.

CHAPTER 8

Robson

The empty rooms on the top level of Robson's flat gave him the idea of advertising for a lodger. Perhaps if he added someone else into his home it might not feel so lonely, and no doubt there was someone looking for a large space with a sea view and cheap board.

After hearing Demi talk about her bedsit the day before at the farm, he figured his premises would be snapped up. But could he really share his home with a stranger? The idea had whirled all throughout his early-morning jog.

Robson stared at the kitchen. It would be the only area he would have to share, as the lodger would have the top floor for all their needs.

He went over to his cereal bowl on the draining board and put it back in the cupboard. It was only breakfast time he used the area. Perhaps if he found someone quiet. No night owls. He would have to conduct interviews.

Shaking his head at his unexpected bizarre idea, he went downstairs, set the alarm, locked the door, then headed around the side to the pub to open for the day.

Joseph was already waiting. 'You running late this morning?'

Was he? He hadn't realised.

The cleaners appeared too, so Robson left everyone to their jobs and went out the back to the small office to check on some orders. He glanced up at the large wall calendar to see when his next shift at the Hub was.

After lunch? He was sure he wasn't rostered on until tomorrow.

There was a funeral gathering due in at three. At least he'd be back by then to help serve drinks.

The noise of vacuum cleaners filled the air, distracting him from his morning chores. He couldn't concentrate, so he went out to the front beer garden to stare over at the choppy sea. The end of the short pier looked misty, but at least the rain had stopped now, unlike when he'd been jogging earlier, and the sun was trying to peek through some clouds.

Robson smiled on the inside. The first time he'd kissed Leah was on that pier. God, he was nervous. Would he have kissed her had he known their time together would be short and he'd be left with so much pain? Yes, he decided. The pain was worth the memories.

'Morning, Robson,' said a voice, waking him.

He saw the owner of Seaview B&B strolling towards her premises. His elderly neighbour looked a touch frail today. 'How you doing, Mabel?'

'Mustn't grumble,' she replied.

'Need a hand with anything?'

She giggled and flapped a hand. 'Leave off, son. I'm fitter than you. At least we can pretend.'

Robson smiled at her wit. 'Always here.'

'I know you are, lovey, but I've got Alice coming in to help out. Got a lovely surprise for her today.' She tapped the side of her nose, then carried on her way to the large chalky white building two doors down.

'Morning,' said a voice behind him, causing him to turn.

'Hey, Demi. You all set for your second shift with us?'

She gave a slight shrug, and he could see a touch of sadness in her eyes. 'Ready as I'll ever be.'

Robson moved closer to her. 'Are you okay?'

The big smile she gave did not meet her eyes. 'Yeah, fine. Bit tired.'

'Not much sleep?'

'Probably.'

He tried to make eye contact with her, but she was looking at her feet, so he opted for a subject change. 'Hey, you gave me an idea yesterday.'

Finally, she looked up. 'Oh?'

'When you were talking about your bedsit. It made me think about all the space I have at mine. I'm contemplating advertising for a lodger. What do you think?'

'Bold move.'

'Yeah, I'm a bit dubious. It's not as though they would have entrance to the pub or anything, as there's no entrance from the flat, but it's that thing about sharing your space. Although, technically, it would only be the kitchen, as they'd have upstairs while I stay down.'

Demi shrugged. 'I guess if you need the money. You'd have to put up with—'

'Oh no, I don't need the money. It's more about giving someone else some space.' He dropped his shoulders, not wanting to mention his loneliness. 'Oh, I don't know. It's just an idea at the moment. I've not done anything like this before. If I do go ahead, I guess it'll be trial and error.'

'You just need someone who is tidy, respectful, and no night owls.'

Robson laughed. 'I thought about the night owls too.'

'Well, whoever gets to move in will be lucky to have so much space.' She pointed up at the roof. 'I take it the flat has the same floor space as the pub.'

'Yeah. And it's just me rattling around up there.'

'It is big.'

'Leah and I planned on having a load of kids. It would have been suitable for all of us, but breast cancer had other plans, so we only got to spend six years together, not the lifetime we had expected.'

Demi reached out for his arm. 'I'm sorry, Robson.'

He breathed out a small huff. 'Life can be unpredictable, eh?'

'Yep. And unfair.'

He followed her eyeline up to the top windows. 'Oh, crap. Sorry. There's me going on about all that space when you're trying to save to move to something bigger.'

'That's okay. I don't hate you because your home is bigger than mine.' She laughed, but it gave him another idea.

'Move in with me,' he blurted.

'What?'

'Oh, sorry, that came out wrong. I meant to say, how would you feel about being my first lodger? Think about it for a sec. You need to move out of your bedsit soon, and I'm looking for a lodger. You could help me test the water. And you'd have room for your daughter here. It's a bit of a win-win.'

Demi's eyes widened. 'Are you serious?'

Robson shrugged one shoulder. 'It could be good for both of us, and if nothing else, it'll give you some breathing room if you want to look for somewhere else to live. I can only imagine it's been a bit stressful trying to find somewhere to live when you're on the clock. You can have this place while you figure things out, and we'll work out affordable rent.'

'I ... erm ...'

'You don't have to give an answer right now. Think it over and let me know. Why don't you come and have a look?'

Demi gestured at the pub. 'I'll be late for work.'

He lifted an index finger. 'One sec.' Sprinting inside, Robson headed straight for the kitchen, where Joseph raised his eyebrows at him.

'You look flustered.'

'No, I'm good,' said Robson. 'I'm just here to let you know Demi has arrived, but I need her for a moment. Ten minutes, tops.'

Joseph gave him a stern glare followed by a curt nod.

Robson jogged back to Demi. 'All sorted.'

'What's sorted?'

'Your shift. It starts in ten minutes.' He waggled a hand towards the side of the pub. 'We should be five.'

Demi followed him, and he watched her check out the large bins along the wall by his front door.

Robson opened the door and switched off the alarm. 'Come up.' He walked up the stairs that led straight into the open-plan area.

'Oh wow, this is big.'

He gestured at the living room side. 'So, this is mine, and you'd have a living room upstairs.'

'You have two living rooms?'

'No. I have three empty large rooms upstairs, plus a bathroom. You could use two rooms as bedrooms, and the other as your lounge. We'd only share the kitchen and the balcony down here.' He splayed one hand that way. 'As you can see, there's plenty of cupboard space, so we could have a side each, perhaps.' He moved to the wide two-door fridge. 'Same in here, maybe?'

Demi gave a slight nod as she glanced down the passageway.

'My bedroom is down there, an office, and shower room. That's all I use.'

'Why do you have your bedroom downstairs?'

Robson controlled his sigh. 'Not long after Leah passed away, I kind of lost it and stripped our bedroom in a rage, then tossed everything out. I wasn't left with much, so I relocated down here and pretended our old room no longer existed.' He pursed his lips and shuffled his feet. 'I know, it sounds—'

'It doesn't sound like anything. Grief has its own mind.'

He smiled at her kindness. 'Let me show you upstairs, that way you've seen everything and can have a think.'

'Okay.'

They went upstairs and viewed the empty rooms that all needed a duster and lick of paint.

'Would make a nice home for a lodger, wouldn't it?' he said, watching her mull over the idea.

'It certainly would.'

'And look—' He gestured at the window in what used to be his bedroom — 'a sea view.'

Demi's face lit up. 'Oh, that is amazing.' She placed her hands over her mouth as she giggled.

'What you laughing at?'

'I'm not sure I have enough stuff to fill one room, let alone three.'

'Bed in here, sofa in the other room. You'd make it work, I'm sure.'

'My sofa is my bed.'

He widened his eyes. 'You sleep on your sofa?'

'It's a sofa bed.'

'Oh, right.'

Demi followed him out to the landing. 'I'll think about it. When do you need an answer?'

'Whenever is fine. It's not as though I've had the idea long.'

They shared a friendly smile, then headed back to the pub, where they both received a glare from Joseph.

Robson went to his office, this time with a small skip in his step.

CHAPTER 9

Demi

It had been three days since Robson's housing proposal and Demi still hadn't given him an answer. It was such a good deal he had offered. The space was just what she had been dreaming of, and she was sure the gorgeous sea view would encourage Jade to have sleepovers.

She glanced at her phone as it buzzed, hoping it would be Jade. She still hadn't heard from her, not even a message to say they had arrived safely.

The text was from Robson, saying the skip had arrived at Happy Farm and would she be able to go there with him today to help out.

As it was her day off, and she'd already finished filming some cooking content for her social media account, she agreed. She let him know she would meet him there. It would be a good opportunity to talk to him about his flat.

It was a hot July day, the start of a mini heatwave according to the weather reports, so Demi put on some dark dungarees with a pale-blue tee shirt, layered on sun cream, popped a floppy hat on her head, gave herself the once over in the narrow mirror attached to the en suite door, ignored the fact she resembled a scarecrow, put on her sunglasses, picked up her bag, and made her way to the bus stop.

Demi was having a good day, and it wasn't even lunchtime yet. She was determined that nothing was going to get her down. Work was good. She had a couple of thousand followers on her account, giving thanks for the recipes, and then there was Robson and the opportunity to have two bedrooms.

She thought about him during the bus ride to the farm. He seemed happy enough, but she could see the sadness behind his smile, and whenever he spoke of his wife, his voice would catch. She knew what he was feeling, as she had once felt that way too.

The next grief group meeting was coming up, and Demi had already decided she was going to attend. She wasn't ready to share her story, but she was going to commit to the course. Besides, even if she didn't need the support, she felt Robson did, and she was sure he just wanted company around his home, rather than a lodger.

Perhaps she could be the friend he needed. He sure was a good friend to her.

Ginny was standing at the end of her drive, waving at Demi as she approached. 'Hey, chick. Will's working today, but Robson's already in the barn, and he's brought Spencer with him to help. You met Spence yet?'

Demi shook her head.

'Come on. I'll introduce you. He's one of the Hub volunteers, and he's part owner of Berry Blooms.'

'The flower shop along Harbour End Road?'

Ginny nodded. 'That's the one. Owns it with his sister, Lottie.'

'I've heard her name mentioned.'

'Ooh, we need to do something about a meet and greet with you and the gang.' Ginny scratched at her dark bob and rubbed her baby bump at the same time. 'Hmm, let me see. How about a barbeque here? That way, Robson can put his feet up, as we mostly have get-togethers at the pub. We could have a painting party for the barn once it's cleared. Have a bit of a bonfire. Ralph will have to stay in his stable for the evening.'

Demi chuckled. 'You sound like Robson. I don't think he stops brainstorming.'

'We've been this way since we opened the Hub.'

'He said that too.'

Ginny nodded. 'We're always trying to come up with fundraising ideas, that's why. We have pirate days, pub quizzes, we've had a pram race, and our Matt did a sponsored swim out to the lighthouse once. Ooh, and Lottie did a wheelchair fun race. It all helps.'

'She's in a wheelchair?'

'Yeah. Got knocked off her bicycle a couple of years back. Spinal cord injury. Just like that her life was changed. We raised enough money last year to buy her two wheelchairs, one for everyday and one for racing, but she's with Sam now, and he's a millionaire, so she can have any wheelchair she likes. I swear he'd buy her the world if she asked.'

Demi smiled.

'You never know what's around the corner, eh, chick?' added Ginny, motioning towards the barn.

Demi followed her eyes to see Robson topless, tossing something metal into the skip.

'Ooh, it's a hot one,' said Ginny. 'You go get stuck in, and I'll fetch some cold drinks out. Won't be a sec.'

Demi's gaze was fixed on Robson catching the sun on his toned abs. She swallowed the dryness suddenly stuck in her throat, then quickly dipped her head when he glanced over. Mimicking his actions, she raised a palm, then made her way to the barn.

Robson reached for his tee shirt as she approached, first using it to wipe the sweat from his brow, then pulling it over his head. 'Jeez, it's hot today. You okay, Dem?'

It was the first time he'd shortened her name, and it sounded nice the way he said it.

'Yeah, erm, I have some sun cream in my bag if you need it.'

'I'm okay. I'm in the barn mostly. Got my top back on now anyway.'

'Oh, please don't feel you have to cover up around me.'

And I said that why?

'I mean, it's hot. Feel free to strip,' she added.

Stop talking.

Demi bit her lip as Robson smiled.

'I'm about to get rid of some wood that's no good, and I don't want any splinters in my chest, but, hey, good to know you're into naturism. You learn something new about someone every day.'

Demi opened her mouth to correct him, but his laughter as he walked into the barn had her laughing too.

'Dem, come and meet Spencer,' he called.

She removed her sunglasses as she stepped inside. She was surprised the barn was cool. She had expected it to be muggy enough to make her hair frizz.

A man with copper hair, sat on the floor, screwing pieces of wood together. 'Hello, Demi. I've heard all about you.'

Demi's heart flipped. 'You have?'

Spencer chuckled. 'New chef. Small town.'

Of course.

She smiled, relieved that was what he meant, as for a moment there she thought he was about to bring up her past.

He patted the dustsheet on the floor. 'Come and join in. Just seeing what I can build with what's here. I was thinking we could get some hay bales for décor or something.'

Demi sat by his side, glancing back at Robson collecting wood. She tugged off her hat and placed it on a stool with her bag. 'Sure, and even if we can't make any large stalls, we can always use trestle tables and foldaway chairs.'

Spencer nodded. 'We might have to raise some cash to buy those though, and we're still not sure yet if this will happen. Will is checking all the guidelines, and we're asking locals what they think. Either way, we can't expect Ginny and Will to fork out, not with the nipper on the way. I heard you've got a kid.'

'Not so much a kid anymore. Eighteen now.'

'I've got a son, Archie. He'll be one this November.'

'Aww, that's lovely.'

'Tiring.'

Demi grinned, remembering. It felt far worse for her because Ray had died just before Jade turned one month old. 'Yes, but the first year flies by, so try to enjoy it the best you can.'

Spencer's face lit up. 'Oh, I do. He's the best thing that's ever happened to me. Well, and his mum, my missus, Beth. Oh, and my little sister, Lottie.' He looked up. 'Then there's my aunt who raised me, plus George . . . Okay, let's just say there's a lot of love all around.' He chuckled to himself, then went back to his task.

Demi wished she had love around her like she used to have. A husband, child, brother, parents. How could half her life have been a lie? It still baffled her how Terry lived that way. How awful to leave a legacy of deceit.

Robson crouched down, a glass of cold lemonade in his hand. 'Here. Let me know if you want any more,' he told her, smiling.

Demi watched Spencer widen his blue eyes in amazement as Robson walked away.

'Erm, what about me?' Spencer chuckled.

'Oh, yeah, sorry. One sec.' Robson came back with another glass from the tray Ginny had left in the doorway, and Spencer grinned at Demi.

An hour later, Ginny called them into the farmhouse for a bite to eat, and Demi was grateful for the fan in the kitchen.

They all washed their hands before joining Ginny at the table for sandwiches and soft rolls.

Demi ate in silence as the others chatted about the Hub, the Port Berry Craft Fayre coming up, and how baby Archie was getting on.

A knock at the front door got Ginny back on her feet, and she quickly called out to Spencer to help her with the animal feed delivery that had arrived.

Demi took the opportunity to speak to Robson while they were alone. 'Hey, I wanted to let you know I'd like to move in to your flat, if the offer is still there?'

Robson's whole face came alive. 'That's great! Anytime is okay with me. I'll put the mop round tonight.'

'I'll start getting things sorted my end.'

'I can get you a contract to sign. I've got a mate who is an estate agent. He'll be able to sort us something we can both sign. I'm not bothered, seeing how it's you, but I want you to have the security of knowing I can't just throw you out, which I wouldn't do anyway.'

'Okay, that would be great. Stability is really important to me.'

'Yeah, of course. I'll get on to that first thing tomorrow.'

Demi leaned closer, breathing out a quiet laugh. 'Are we really doing this?'

'Don't see why not. It suits us both.'

'Yes, it does. I'll look at it as temporary though, as I want my own place with Jade one day. At least now I don't have to rush, although it would be nice to have one by Christmas.' She liked the idea of that being a gift for Jade. With a bit of luck, and hard work proving she was stable, perhaps Jade would spend the festive holiday with her, no matter where she lived.

'I'm really looking forward to this,' said Robson.

'There's just one thing you need to know...'

Actually, there are a few things, but one at a time.

'I'll use the kitchen a lot,' she finished.

'Oh, right, course, you're a chef.'

'It's not really because of that, well, it is, oh, let me explain. I have a cooking page on my social media account, and I show videos of how to cook small meals for one person. Basically, when I have time, I'm pottering around the kitchen creating content, and it can take time and get messy, but I do clean up after myself, and I don't make the videos every day because I already have loads ready to post.'

Robson smiled. 'Sounds like fun, for you I guess.'

'Yes, I love it. It keeps my mind occupied in the evenings. When I'm cooking, it's like I'm in another world and nothing negative gets in.'

'I get it. It's why I like to keep busy too.'

'I thought it best to let you know, in case you might not want the odd bit of chaos in your kitchen.' She raised a finger. 'Controlled chaos.'

'I might actually learn something. Or I'll keep out the way when you're filming.'

'It's your kitchen. I won't expect you to leave.'

Robson shook his head slightly. 'It'll be *our* kitchen, and you can do what you want. I mean it, Dem. I want you to feel comfortable.'

'In all honesty, I've never created any online content with someone watching me. Not sure if I'll be embarrassed.' She took a sip of lemonade and smiled.

'We'll figure it out as we go, yeah?'

She nodded, feeling better already about her decision to share a home with him, even if it was just the kitchen.

CHAPTER 10

Robson

Robson's morning run normally stopped at his street door, but Lizzie's daughter, Alice, was standing outside Seaview B&B, beaming up at the building while lightly clapping her hands, so he stopped jogging there to see what she was up to.

Alice flung herself onto his sweaty arm. 'I can't believe it,' she blurted.

Robson chuckled. 'What's got you so excited?'

She leaned closer to his cheek. 'Mabel's only gone and sold the place to me.'

'What? No way!'

Alice's eyes were wide with delight. 'Way.'

Robson laughed. 'This is Mabel we're talking about. Her family has owned that place since it was built.'

'I know, right, but she has other plans, and she wants me to take over.'

'I guess it makes sense. You're like a granddaughter to her, and you're always there helping.'

'She's been my mentor. She knows I've always wanted my own B&B around here. I've been saving forever.'

'I know. So, you're good to go now?'

Alice released his arm and stood back. 'I'll still have to get a bank loan, but with the discount Mabel offered me, I should be able to afford the place.'

'Discount?'

She nodded. 'Yeah. Reckons it was what she had planned for me in her will, so she's giving me that money now by knocking it off the price.'

'Wow, she really does think highly of you.'

Alice stopped smiling. 'I'm all she's got really, except for Betty.'

'I've never been sure if Betty is her best mate or girlfriend.'

'They've been friends for years, but this year they got closer and gave in to their true feelings for each other, so they're girlfriends now. But they don't get to see each other much, what with Betty living in Devon, and they both had this dream of relocating to Jersey, so now they're doing it, and you should see Mabel. She's alive with joy.'

Robson smiled over at the wide arched front door with the stained-glass top window of a boat. 'Aww, that's lovely. For all of you.'

'We've got to finalise a few things, then it's mine.'

'So she's off soon then?'

Alice shook her head. 'No, she's going to remain living here until Betty has sold her house, then they're leaving. They plan to rent over there while they look for their forever home.' She squealed quietly. 'It's so romantic. Living out your dreams when you're elderly.'

Robson laughed. 'I don't think there's an age limit on dreams.'

'I know, but you don't expect such adventure at their age.'

'Look at it as inspiration.'

'I am, because between you and me, this whole new business adventure I'm about to go on is a little intimidating to say the least.'

75

'You'll smash it, Al. You're been helping out here for years. You know how to run the place. Mabel taught you.' He nudged her arm. 'Perhaps she's been preparing you all along.'

Alice's eye narrowed as she glanced up at the sea-facing balconies. 'Hmm, now you've said that, it wouldn't surprise me.'

'She probably wanted someone she could trust with her family's history. Not as though she could leave that in the hands of her grandchildren. Shannon would sell it off straight away to property developers to turn into flats knowing her, and as for Jamie, well . . .'

Alice dipped back to one heel and folded her arms. 'He's doing his time peacefully. Hasn't got into any trouble in prison and should be out early next year, all being well.'

'Mabel tell you that? I thought she didn't speak to him.'

Alice shrugged, then beamed widely as Mabel came out to say hello to Robson.

'Judging by Alice's face, I take it she's told you the news,' said Mabel, her pink blusher looking extra pink today.

Robson nodded. 'She did, and I'm pleased for you all. And I'll want postcards when you get to Jersey.'

Mabel giggled. 'Will do, lovey.' She gestured at his running clothes. 'You look a bit sweaty there. Alice holding you back from your shower?'

He grinned at Alice. 'Yeah.'

'Oi,' Alice scoffed, nudging Robson's ribs. 'You stopped to be nosey.'

He nodded at Mabel. 'I did, but now I need that shower. You two have a good day, and when everything is finalised, we'll have a little party in the pub to celebrate.'

'Ooh, lovely,' said Mabel, and Alice agreed.

Robson walked the rest of the way home, looking forward to a good wash down. The sun was out in force already and it was only eight a.m.

'Morning,' sang out Demi, standing on his doorstep.

'Ooh, you made me jump. I wasn't expecting to see anyone standing there.'

'Sorry.'

He pushed back his damp hair as he opened the door. 'You're out early.'

'Yes, I wanted to speak to you before work. It's been on my mind all night.'

He glanced over his shoulder before turning off the alarm. 'You'd better come up then.'

As much as he was pleased to see her, and now intrigued, he was dying for a cool shower, as the sweat was making him feel itchy, and he was paranoid he might whiff a bit.

As though reading his mind, Demi gestured down the passageway. 'If you want to take a shower first, I don't mind waiting.'

Robson sniffed his armpit. 'That bad, eh?'

Demi breathed out a small laugh. 'No. You just look a bit hot and bothered, and what I want to say might take a little time.'

He frowned, amused. 'Okay.'

She waved him towards his downstairs bathroom. 'Go on. I'll rustle us up some brekkie if you like. I don't know about you, but I haven't eaten yet.'

Now he was concerned. Up early, wanting to talk, looking serious, hadn't eaten. Perhaps the shower could wait.

Demi shook her head. 'Everything's fine, honest. It's only about moving in here.' She waggled a hand towards the passage. 'Have your shower.'

He gave a brief nod, then headed for the bathroom. Never before had he showered so fast, eager to hear what had her showing up at his home so early. Everything seemed fine when they spoke of the arrangement the day before at Happy Farm.

'Oh, crap!' He realised his clothes were in his bedroom, which meant crossing the passage in his towel. Would that be inappropriate? He was going to have to adapt when he started having lodgers.

Wrapping a stripy blue-and-white towel around his waist, he decided to make a quick dash for his room, but

Demi was laying the kitchen table and looked up as he exited the bathroom.

Robson raised a finger. 'One sec.' He was sure he blushed. Quickly, he threw on cream tracksuit bottoms and a green tee shirt, mentally shook his head, took a calming breath, then met her in the kitchen to see a display of chopped fruit and bowls of cereal on the table.

'I wasn't sure you'd want a fry-up after your run,' she said softly, eyes on the food.

He sat at the table and smiled at her thoughtfulness. 'No, this is good, ta.'

Demi sat opposite him, twiddling a spoon.

'What's wrong, Dem?' he asked gently, trying to gain eye contact.

Her slim shoulders lifted and fell steadily. 'Full disclosure.'

He tapped his chest. 'Me?'

'No, me.'

'What do you want to tell me?'

She put her spoon down and straightened. 'I don't feel it's right to move in here without you knowing some facts about me first.'

'Okay. Like?'

'My criminal record.'

Robson shook his head. 'What about it?'

'There's just a bit more to the story, that's all.'

He gave a small nod, waiting for her to make her point. It was obvious she didn't want to talk about whatever it was.

Demi rested her arms on the table as she took a deep breath. 'I'm a recovering drug addict. That's why I was stealing. I needed the money for my next fix. I'd already had a warning before, but the police weren't about to keep warning me. I ended up with a two-year sentence. I spent the first year in prison and the second out on licence. That came to an end in May, so I'm free now, and I'm two-years clean, but it played on my mind that I hadn't told you.'

Robson bobbed his head as he watched her stare into her cereal bowl. 'I see.' He figured there had been more to her story, and he felt quite touched she was trusting him, but at the same time so sad for her.

'Three years ago, I fell down the stairs and had to have a knee operation. I got addicted to the pain meds,' she said, glancing up through her dark lashes. 'Life changed.'

His heart went out to her. 'Jeez, I'm so sorry, Dem.'

'When you're in recovery, you just want to move forward with your life, but I thought it was fair you knew about my past. I might always be an addict. You know, never fully cured, only in control. So it's right you know who you're living with.'

He shifted closer to the table. To her. 'Would I need to do anything if you got a craving or something?'

She shook her head. 'No. I have a sponsor I can call. Plus, I go to meetings, but it's easier for me if my life is stress free.' She blew out a laugh. 'I know that's not always possible, I just mean — I try for peace.'

'You won't get any trouble here. I like a peaceful life too.'

Demi smiled softly. 'It's okay if you change your mind about the whole lodger idea now. Honestly, I understand.'

'I haven't changed my mind. I'm pleased you told me, and I'm happy for you that you're in a better place now. I can only imagine how terrible it must have been for you back then.'

Demi's head dipped. 'Worst time of my life.' She met his eyes, hers filled with determination. 'I will never live that way again. I hated every moment.' She sniffed, and he saw her blink away tears. 'It took everything from me. My home, job, family, my character. All wiped out.'

Robson reached for her hand on the table. 'You got them all back,' he said, trying to offer encouragement, as it was quite clear she had drifted to the past for a moment.

'Getting there.'

'I think you're amazing.'

Demi smiled. 'You're kind.'

He shook his head. 'No, don't put that on me. Think about it for a sec. Look what you came back from. That takes guts. Strength.'

'Everything,' she added.

Robson gave her hand a light squeeze. 'It wasn't your fault what happened to you. You were a victim of circumstance, but you didn't roll over and accept the cards you'd been given. You fought hard for all you have today.'

Demi scoffed. 'I don't have much.'

'You have your life back, Dem. How's that for a happy ending?'

She slid her hand from his and picked up her spoon. 'It's a start.'

'Well, I'm in awe of you, and when you move in here, I'm going to make sure to let you know just how amazing you are every day.'

Demi laughed, swiping away an escaped tear. 'I might get bored if you're going to keep repeating yourself.'

Robson matched her smile. 'Once a week then.'

'Is everything really all right now you know about me?'

'Yeah, it's all good.' He gestured at the ceiling. 'You can start decorating if that's something you want to do. Move in before your tenancy agreement is up if you like. I won't charge you rent until you've stopped paying for the bedsit. That way, you can move in sooner. I'm going to sort your contract later.'

'I see what you're doing. Thinking it'll be less stressful for me if I move over here in stages, but I haven't got a lot to bring over. I only need a van.'

He thumbed towards the door. 'Spencer will lend us his work van. Just let me know when, and I'll give him a shout.'

Demi glanced down the passage. 'It might be nice to paint some walls, especially the room Jade would use.'

'Okay, well, you make a start on getting everything shipshape, then we'll bring your things over when you're ready.'

It was heart-warming to see her face come back to life. He pondered over telling her some things about himself. After all, she'd opened up. But no doubt part of the reason she'd told him her history was the possibility of it re-emerging and having an impact on his life. His own story didn't come with that complication, so perhaps it was best he didn't bring her down with his darkness.

'Up for a trip to the DIY shop after work?' he asked.

Demi was still smiling. A good sign in his books. 'Lovely,' she replied, then started to eat breakfast, which settled him even more.

CHAPTER 11

Demi

Two weeks had passed, and Demi was so excited that Jade had returned from Barbados that morning. She couldn't wait to show her daughter the bedroom she had prepared for her at Robson's.

All she'd been doing was working, helping fix up the barn at Happy Farm, going to meetings — recovery and bereavement — and spending time decorating her soon-to-be temporary home.

Painting walls, putting up pictures, buying two single beds, had all helped put Demi in the right frame of mind for when she got her own home.

If she spoke to Colin about her move before announcing it to Jade, he might just give her back some of her savings that he had pretty much forced her to hand over when he'd first found out she had lost her job and was buying illegal drugs.

It seemed like the best plan at the time, as she was sure she would be able to knock the habit on the head so didn't mind him taking charge of her finances to reduce temptation. Best to be safe than sorry, was the motto Alana had tossed into the mix, and once all was back to normal, the money would be returned. She had figured that would be within a few weeks, not realising how out of control she was.

Colin had assured her the inheritance from their parents she had squirrelled away would be safe in his savings account. Little did she know at the time she would have drained the lot if he hadn't shifted it from her bank to his. She hadn't the grip she thought, as denial was strong, and so were the cravings.

The memory of begging him for money hit hard. On her knees, pleading, crying, shaking. It wouldn't be that way now. Things had changed. She wasn't about to ask him to sort her next fix, she just wanted more furniture, and her savings were running low.

Perhaps if he gave her back everything, she could find her own home immediately, but Colin showed his stubbornness on that subject when she got out of prison and needed somewhere to live.

'It's my money,' she had told him.

'You're not having it until you've proven you'll stay clean,' he'd replied, then gave the estate agent dealing with the bedsit tenancy the deposit. Not even that was allowed to sit in her palm.

Demi was grateful for everything her brother had done, but she didn't feel her money had to be under lock and key anymore, and she knew she'd have to convince him it would be put to good use.

Surely Colin would understand. He'd often said the bedsit wasn't good enough, without saying the actual words, so Demi believed her step up to all the space she had at Robson's would please him a touch.

Once the living room was fully furnished and Jade's bedroom had a chest of drawers, Demi could move in the weekend.

Robson was downstairs in the pub and had said he would bring fish and chips up with him soon, so Demi took a breath and called her brother.

'A pub?' he yelled, making her pull the phone back from her ear.

Demi was quite taken aback by his furious response. She didn't know how to reply, not that she got a chance to.

'Jolly Pirate, you say? I'm on my way.' Colin hung up.

Previous to her day from hell, also known as Terry's funeral, Demi hadn't been treated like a child, but somewhere along the way, Colin had morphed into her dad.

She quickly got out the vacuum cleaner, then mop, then duster. The cleaning frenzy had her in a tizz. Not much needed going over, but she didn't want Colin to pick points. Very soon, the flat would be her new home, so it was good he was coming to check it out. He would see for himself how she had levelled up. It was all okay.

Demi flopped to a chair, breathing in through her nose and out through her mouth while counting breaths, determined to calm her racing heart.

Damn Colin, and damn how this was making her a bag of nerves. She stood facing the door, hands on hips, jaw clenched. She'd show him.

The doorbell rang, and Demi crumbled.

Colin was slightly purple in the face, and he didn't wait for an invite, just flapped a hand at the stairs. 'I can't believe you.'

Demi frowned as she followed him up.

'What are you playing at?' he snapped as soon as she walked into the kitchen.

'The owner of the bedsit is selling, so I had to find somewhere else, and this is less rent, more room, and living here for now will move me faster towards my own place for me and Jade.'

Colin scoffed, snarling at the living room. 'Why didn't you tell me before now?'

'Will you stop snapping?'

'Will you stop making bad decisions?'

Demi crossed her arms in a huff. 'This is a good decision, thank you very much.'

Colin raised his hands. 'It's a pub.'

'Above a pub restaurant, and it's short term, and Jade will be able to spend time with me here, as she now has somewhere to sleep. The whole of the top floor is mine. Would you at least come upstairs with me and take a look?'

Colin gave a curt nod as his nostrils stopped flaring.

Demi led the way, pointing out facts like the sea view and the nice tea shop a few doors down as though it would make a difference. The harbour was a lovely area, and she was sure her brother would find it suitable for Jade.

Colin checked out all the rooms, giving the place the once over as if he were looking to buy the property. He even kicked at the skirting in her bedroom, which she decided to stay quiet about, seeing how his cheeks still resembled beetroot.

'Colin, I want some of my money so I can kit this place out properly. It will all go to good use again once I get my own home.'

'I'm not giving you the money.'

Demi frowned. 'You know, you don't actually get a say in it.'

Colin looked calmer. 'Yes, I do.'

'It's my money,' she snapped, not meaning to. 'You can't hold on to it forever.'

He tapped his chest. 'I'm doing you a favour.'

'You were, but you're not now. In case you haven't noticed, things have changed. I've changed. And if you gave me back my money, I would already be in my own home with Jade.'

He rolled his eyes, which always annoyed her. 'That's Mum and Dad's money, in case you haven't noticed, and how do you think they would feel if I gave it back to you and you went out and got high again?'

'Why do you insist that's what would happen? You've got eyes. Take a look at me. At my life. Don't you see any of the changes?'

He threw his hand out towards her. 'I don't trust you yet, all right.'

'That much is obvious, but when will you?'

Colin shrugged and went to gaze out the window at the sea.

'This can't go on forever, Colin.'

'It's too soon, and Alana agrees.'

Demi scrunched her nose while his back was turned. As far as she was concerned it was none of Alana's business. She took a calming breath and tried once more. 'I want to rebuild my relationship with Jade, and if she can sleep over at mine, I think it will help move us along. Let's face it, things have been slow.'

He turned from the view. 'She's happy with how things are, Dem. She's settled.' He showed his palm. 'And before you start ranting about how you've changed, yes, we can see you're trying, but you can't just expect her to fall into your arms as soon as you come out of prison.'

'It's been over a year.'

'You know what I mean.' He blew out a huff. 'You traumatised the girl, Dem. You scared her. Bloody hell, you scared me.' He gestured at the room. 'This kind of thing proves you're still not stable.'

'Don't be ridiculous.'

He stepped closer. 'You showed stability in that bedsit. You were in a steady job, working towards getting a bigger property, and I was starting to believe in you, and now look.'

She followed his finger spinning around. 'I'm still working, I've found a temporary bigger property that accommodates me and Jade while I look for my own home, and if you did believe in me, you'd give me back my money.'

'It's a pub. Not exactly ideal.'

She shook her head. 'Above a pub. You're acting like I've just moved into a crack den.'

'Wouldn't be the first time.'

'I spent one night there, then you found me.'

'Yeah, and I'm still saving your arse.'

Demi slammed her hands on her hips. 'In the past you did, and I appreciate all you did to help me. You know I do, but now you're actually holding me back.'

'Oh really?'

'Yeah, really. Bloody hell, Colin, I just want to put the past to bed and move on with my life. I want my own home, and I want my daughter back.'

'It's too soon.'

Demi had never felt her blood boil before. She was sure her face was the same shade of purple as his. What right did he have to think he could continue to rule her life this way?

Footsteps came thumping up the stairs, and suddenly Robson was in the doorway.

'Demi, you all right?' he asked, sounding out of breath for someone so fit.

'Erm, yes,' she replied, unclenching her fists. She didn't know it was possible for those piercing eyes of Robson's to look so stern.

'Who are you?' asked Robson.

Colin frowned. 'Who are you?'

Demi stepped between them. 'This is my brother, Colin.' She swivelled her head the other way. 'This is Robson, my boss, new landlord, and friend.' She hoped the last part of her sentence might cool the air.

'You put her up to this?' asked Colin, waggling a finger at Robson.

'No, he didn't,' she replied, before Robson had time to open his mouth.

'My sister is in recovery,' said Colin.

Robson nodded. 'Yeah, and it doesn't sound like you're helping.'

'What would you know about anything?' Colin retorted.

Robson moved further into the room, and Colin took a step back. 'I heard raised voices from the street door, and I know Demi wants a stress-free life. She's told me about her past, and I'm just helping her out.'

Colin made his way to the exit. 'I don't know anything about you, so what's in it for you?'

Demi saw Robson's eyes narrow.

'She's my lodger, that's all. What you see up here will be rented out again once she's moved on.' His tone was flat, steady. 'As for me, feel free to ask around about my character. I own the Jolly Pirate, and I'm a volunteer for the Happy to Help Hub. I also help out at the Sunshine Centre in Penzance when needed. It's a respite centre. But like I said, ask around for references if you want.'

Colin stared at him for a moment, then headed to the stairs. 'My niece still won't be staying here.'

Demi ran after him. 'She's eighteen. She can make up her own mind.'

Colin turned in the kitchen, glancing down at the bag of fish and chips Robson had put on the table before he had sprinted up the stairs. The salt and vinegar was wafting up everyone's nose. 'Don't you get it, Dem. She doesn't want to sleep over at yours, no matter where you live.'

'You don't know that.' She hoped. 'She can see this place for herself and decide.'

'Fine. Let her do that then.'

His words failed to lift her, as she knew he would be discouraging the visit as soon as he saw Jade.

Demi pulled out her phone. Her hand shook, and a lump was wedged in her throat. 'I'll call her now and find out.'

Colin scowled. 'Don't do that. What's the matter with you? She's just had all the stress of her exams, had a lovely holiday to relax, and now you want to land all your crap on her. Could you be any more selfish?'

Demi went to speak, but closed her mouth. The last thing she wanted was to ruin Jade's happy mood. Maybe Colin was right. It wasn't the best time to bring Jade into the mix. Perhaps in a few days when Colin had calmed down and seen sense. Maybe she had gone about things the wrong way. She really couldn't be sure anymore, and her head ached too much to think clearly.

'Shall I take you home?' asked Colin, his voice softer.

Demi shook her head. 'No, my dinner's here,' was all she could think to say.

Colin shook his head and left, but his voice trailed up the stairs. 'I'll talk to Jade.'

She turned to Robson, standing behind her. 'Have I done the right thing?' she asked, her eyes filling with water.

'It's your life, Dem. Only you can say what feels right,' he replied softly.

'It did feel right till he showed up.'

'Look, I don't mean to step out of line or anything, but does he always talk to you like that?'

She shrugged one shoulder. 'Only since I became an addict. He took control of me until the law took over. He thinks he's doing what's best for me, but it doesn't feel too good in my shoes anymore.'

'Have you explained that to him?'

'I try, but it's not easy talking to Colin, plus his wife often gets her two pennies in, and he always sides with her.' Demi flopped to a chair. 'He won't give me my money back, and it's enough to buy my own home. I never used it after my parents died and left me the cash, as I didn't really need it at the time.'

'And he has full control over your finances?'

'Only the inheritance. I don't give him my wages.' Demi started to unwrap the chip paper, not that she had much of an appetite. 'It's not his fault. He just worries I'll buy drugs if I have too much money. Thinks me living a simple life will help keep me grounded.'

'But you're saving up for what he could give you, so what difference does it make? You'll have your own place one day.'

Demi shrugged. 'I just know he doesn't trust me and thinks the money is safer with him, and that way I'll only be able to rent. He seems to be okay with that. I guess he thinks I won't be able to sell my home to a dealer if the need should arise, which is why he's against me having ownership of a property.' She stuffed a warm chip into her mouth just for something to do. 'These aren't from the restaurant.'

'No, chippy.' Robson sat by her side and took her hand. 'Life won't always be this complicated. He'll see soon enough you're doing well, and that I'm no monster.'

'Sorry about that.'

'It's okay. But look, it's fine if you do change your mind about moving in.'

Demi met his eyes. They were filled with compassion, unlike Colin's, who always held either cynicism or rage. 'I've been looking forward to moving in. I want to carry on with our plan, and I will bring Jade over as soon as I'm settled, and she can see for herself how lovely things are here.'

Robson motioned towards the small framed photo of Demi and Jade, the little ornament of a jolly pirate, and the flowery plant pots on the kitchen windowsill filled with herbs that Demi had placed next to the picture of his wife. 'Looks homely already.'

She glanced at the living room, then back at his kind smile. 'Colin will be fine once he's had time to think. He just worries. Perhaps he always will. I put my family through a lot, so I don't blame their wariness. This isn't a bad decision. It's a step forward.'

'It's a good step.' Robson snaffled a chip and smiled.

'What do you really think, Robson?' she asked warily, feeling the need for some back up.

'I think you've been doing just fine for a long time now. You carry on working towards your goal and ignore the distractions.'

Demi smiled. He was right. She had been doing great. A meeting tonight wouldn't hurt though. She needed a bit of respite. Speaking of which. 'Tell me about this Sunshine Centre place.'

CHAPTER 12

Robson

Two days had passed since Robson met Demi's brother. It was hard not to think about her financial situation, but it was none of his business so he didn't bring it up again. Demi seemed fine, going about her life as normal. Colin hadn't been back, not even to visit the pub, which Robson felt was a good thing, as he saw how drained Demi looked around her brother.

She'd just left work, along with Joseph and the rest of the kitchen staff. Everything always seemed quieter once the kitchen was closed.

The last of the punters were ushered out the door by the bar staff wanting to go home, and Robson joked with them all as he followed them outside into the mild night.

The faint scent of sea salt filled the air, and he inhaled deeply as he said goodnight and watched everyone depart in different directions.

Harbour End Road was quiet once more. The moments Robson loved the most. He stared at the carpet of stars in the sky for a while, then headed back inside, his smile fading along the way.

A glass of brandy might help fight the sadness creeping in, so Robson bolted the door and headed straight to the bar to pour his nightcap.

He sat at one of the tables close to the fireplace and gazed blankly at the dark liquid waiting to warm his soul. It held no such magical power. Nothing did. He knew that.

Most of the lights were switched off, leaving the bar as the only beacon, but he didn't look that way. He wasn't seeing much no matter which way he turned, as emptiness settled in for a while, taking his concentration.

The darkness was an old friend. Not one he'd seen much of lately. He wasn't sure why it was making itself known this year, as last year it had disappeared altogether, and he was sure that was the end of that.

It was gone eleven p.m., so way too late to call Jan for a chat, not that he favoured talking when the numbness kicked in.

Robson pondered over what it would feel like to slip away to the other side.

There had been many times over the years when he had considered that question, but not once had he attempted to play out his thoughts. It never failed to amaze him just how logical his brain could be in the moments he felt he had no emotions. How could it plot and plan while the rest of him had no control?

Robson wasn't in the eye of the storm anymore, so it was a lot easier for him to pull himself back into reality. Still, it wasn't that simple waking when it was so comfortable sleeping.

He slid the untouched drink away from where he rested his hands on the table. A late-night run was needed. Exercise was his saviour not booze.

Even though he knew what he had to do, he stayed seated and simply stared at nothing in particular. Memories swirled, eating at him once more. If only he didn't hold such secrets, perhaps he would have been able to handle life. But he understood why his uncle had told him the truth. He just wished the truth wasn't so haunting.

He touched his phone in his back pocket, mulling over calling his uncle. What time was it in Australia? He shook his head. No, he wasn't going to bother his aunt and uncle with his troubles. They'd moved away a few years ago to start a new life with friends already living out there, and they were happy. They couldn't know about his pain. It would only hurt them, and that was the last thing he wanted.

Get up. Run.

With a slight bob of the head, Robson stood. If he didn't run, the darkness would win, and he couldn't allow it to return and take over his life ever again. In the here and now he had the strength to fight back. To take control. But it didn't stop him wanting to wallow. His truth was a hard thing to live with. How had his mother coped?

He took the drink back to the bar and emptied the contents of the glass into the sink all the while thinking of the mother he never knew. Had she been in his life he wouldn't have grown up in the Jolly Pirate. Would she have given him a better life than the one his aunt and uncle had? He would never know.

Robson placed both hands on the bar, leaning forward as though about to chat to a customer. He perused the area, appreciating the happy childhood he had thanks to his mum's brother. Shame his aunt and uncle couldn't have kids of their own. He figured they'd done each other a favour, as they could have easily placed him in care when his mother abandoned him.

Demi's daughter sprung to mind. Perhaps that Colin fella wasn't so bad. After all, he did the same thing as Robson's uncle. Stepped up, took someone else's kid on, made their life stable. It wasn't exactly the same. Demi didn't leave Jade. She was just sent to prison. Whereas his mum had to go because . . .

A thud on the door made him jump out of his thoughts. Who the heck was that knocking so late? He made his way towards the door, one hand on the large bolt.

'Hello?' he asked warily.

'Robson, it's me, Demi.'

He frowned as he quickly opened up. 'Demi? Everything all right?'

'Sorry to knock so late, but I think my phone might be here.' She gestured inside. 'I was halfway home when I noticed my phone wasn't in my bag, so I got off the bus and retraced my steps. I'm hoping it fell out into my locker. I was going to knock at the flat, but then I spotted the light.'

He glanced over at the bar. 'Yeah, I was just about to head out.' He moved to one side to allow her access. 'Come in.'

She entered and he locked the door while she sprinted off towards the kitchen.

'Found it,' she called, moments later.

Robson unlocked the door again as she approached. 'That's good.'

'Yeah. I was praying it was here. I'm so glad you were still up. I would have been fretting all night.'

He nodded towards the road. 'You've missed the last bus. Let me see if I can borrow Spencer's van to drive you home. He added me to his insurance a little while back to help me out when my car died a thousand deaths.'

'Oh, okay, thanks.'

Robson pulled out his phone. 'I'll send Spencer a text. If he's still up, he can toss the keys out the window. Not the first time he's helped me out that way.' He tapped away on his screen. 'I really need to go car shopping at some point. I keep meaning to get around to it.'

'I used to love my car.'

He looked up and smiled. 'Let me just set the alarm and lock up. One sec.' He quickly got on with his task, then met Demi on the pavement.

'All done?' she asked.

'Yep.' He followed her eyes up to the dark sky.

'They're all out tonight.'

'It's a better view at the end of the pier. No streetlights.'

Demi grinned. 'Bit creepy though.'

'Nah, not for me. I grew up here, so I'm used to it.' He nudged her arm. 'Want to see?'

She glanced at the phone in his hand. 'Have we got time?'

Robson checked to see if Spencer had replied to his text. He hadn't, so he nodded.

They made their way over to the pier, where the world looked darker, the stars brighter, and the only sound was the gentle whooshing of the waves against the pilings.

'Ooh, I wonder what it's like to be on a boat out there now,' said Demi quietly.

'You can find out one day if you like. I can arrange for Jed to take you out on his boat.'

Demi turned, smiling at him. 'Only if you come too.'

'Okay.' Robson's phone pinged. 'That's Spencer. Come on, he'll be at the window in a minute.'

'Does he live far?'

'Just up Berry Hill. He and his family are staying with Lottie and Samuel at the moment. They're about to move. He used to have the flat above the flower shop, but they bought a cottage recently. It needed work, so he moved in with his sister for a bit.' He gestured to the coastal houses on the top of the hill at the end of the road.

'Ooh, they have a nice view up there.'

'Yeah, that's where Spencer and Lottie grew up. Now Lottie and Samuel own three of the houses along there having knocked them into one.'

'Sounds lovely.'

'Ginny mentioned having a barbeque at hers so you can meet our circle of friends. You up for that?'

Demi nodded. 'Sure, whenever she's ready. We're nearly finished sorting the barn. All it needs is a lick of paint, and we've got ourselves a farmers' market. All being well.'

'It'll be handy having it all in one spot. A lot of the pub grub comes from local businesses.'

Demi stopped walking and laughed. 'Hang on, I'm a bit out of puff.'

Robson chuckled with her. 'It's a steep hill. When you move in around here, you can walk up and down here each morning, and that'll sort your fitness levels.'

'I'm sure it will.' She touched his arm as she started walking again. 'Hey, Robson, I was wondering if I can move in now.'

'Tonight?'

'No, I meant as soon as possible. The flat is almost finished, and I've decided not to talk to Jade about it, but to show her instead. I think she'll get a real feel for our future once she sees the two-bed all laid out.'

He nodded his agreement. 'Makes sense, and I don't see the problem with you moving in tonight.'

'It's late.'

Robson shrugged. 'We'll have Spencer's van. We can be quiet moving your things... Wait, how much is there to move?'

'Not a lot. The big things are the sofa bed, TV, and a couple of boxes of kitchen equipment. The bedsit was partially furnished, so the fridge isn't mine nor the oven or microwave. It's such a tiny space, there's not much you can put in there anyway.'

'We should be able to fit that all in Spencer's van.'

Demi stopped at the top of the hill. 'Aren't you tired?'

'Nope. Wide awake.'

Spencer opened the door and plodded down the pathway, yawning. 'Don't mind me,' he said through another yawn. 'Archie has a cough, so not much sleep happening in there.' He thumbed behind him.

Robson took the keys. 'Cheers for this. I'll pop them through the letterbox in a bit.'

'No worries,' said Spencer, stretching his arms. 'I'll see you both tomorrow.'

'Night, Spencer,' said Demi as Robson thanked him once more.

'Van's back at the flower shop,' said Robson, heading back that way.

Demi grinned. 'Yes, I noticed the big white vehicle with the painted Berry Blooms sign.'

'I was going to go for a run tonight, but carrying your sofa bed can count as my exercise.'

'Do you do a lot of exercise?'

'Mostly running. You?'

'No, but I'm willing to give it a go.'

Robson opened the van's passenger door for her. 'Great, you can come out for a morning run with me one day.'

They got in the van and drove off to Demi's.

The country lanes were deserted, and the cottages they passed showed little signs of life. All they encountered were a few wild rabbits and a fluffy white cat until they neared where Demi lived.

Someone in a nearby flat was playing their music loudly, and a group of teenagers were hanging around by a swing park. A few cars zoomed up and down the main street close to her bedsit, and the side street where her building sat was fully lit from streetlamps.

'Don't think we'll wake anyone around here,' remarked Robson, pulling up.

Demi got out and looked up to the next block where the pop song was blaring from. 'They have a lot of parties up there.'

'Bet they're popular with the neighbours.'

'To be fair, they invite everyone. We can pop there right now and we'd be welcomed with a Budweiser, a glow stick, and some Pringles.'

Robson laughed. 'Got my own back home, minus the glow stick.' He noticed her smile soften.

'It's so much nicer where you live.'

'Quieter,' he said, grinning. 'Let's get you sorted, then you can enjoy spending your nights staring out to sea.' Her face came alive again, warming his heart.

'First floor,' she told him, opening the main door.

She wasn't kidding about the bedsit being tiny. He was amazed there was room for her sofa bed, which wasn't as big as he was expecting. 'Is this a kid's one?' he asked, placing a hand on the back of the wine-coloured sofa.

'I had to buy a small one because the standard size didn't fit once opened.'

'At least this will be okay for your living room.'

'For now. I want to get a proper sofa.'

Robson gave it the once over. 'Well, it'll definitely fit in the van.' He scanned the area, seeing her things already half-packed. 'We won't need to do another trip.'

Demi shook her head. 'No, we won't.' She sighed, gaining his full attention. 'There's not much to me, is there?'

'Hey, you're not your things. This is just stuff. It doesn't define you.'

'I just meant I don't have much to show for my life.'

'You hit a rough patch, that's all. Can happen to anyone, and often does. You are at a stage in your life where you're rebuilding, and buying furniture isn't what I mean. Don't be hard on yourself. You've got loads to be proud of. Against all the odds, you bounced back.'

Demi's frown disappeared. 'I did, didn't I?'

'Yep.'

'Okay, let's get this show on the road, then when we get home, I'll make us some hot chocolate to celebrate.' She placed a hand to her mouth. 'Sorry, I meant your home.'

'It's your home too now, so no need to be sorry.'

Demi breathed out a small laugh through her fingertips. 'I'm really doing this, aren't I?'

'If that's what you want.'

She nodded. 'More than anything. I can just feel this is the right move for me.'

'In that case, you wedge the door open, and we'll shift the sofa bed first. The rest should fit around it in the van easily enough.'

Demi opened the door, jamming it with some recipe books. 'I feel like we're doing a moonlight flit.'

Robson chuckled. 'Let's hope no one calls the police thinking we're robbing the place.'

'You'll be all right, but I'll go straight back to prison.'

Robson was about to lift his end of the sofa. 'Ah, crap, that was a really naff joke. Sorry, Dem.'

She smiled. 'It's okay. I'm not that sensitive.'

'Still, bad form.'

'If we're going to live together, know one thing . . . You can't tiptoe around me, okay?'

'Okay, but I can be a bit more thoughtful.'

She reached to pick up her end of the sofa. 'Anything I need to know about you?'

Robson smiled warmly. 'Only that I like my hot chocolate extra hot.'

'Ooh, me too.'

'Looks like we're going to get along just fine then.' He decided to leave it at that, because he didn't want to burden her with his problems. Nothing about his life would have an impact on her, so there really wasn't any reason for him to share his secrets, especially the one about his mum. He'd never told anyone but January Riley during a therapy session. It was hard to deal with, let alone share.

He studied Demi as she concentrated on getting the sofa down the stairs. She had so much on her plate, and yet there she was, moving towards her goals.

As soon as they placed the sofa bed in the van, Robson sprinted up the stairs, using them as exercise. He was awake, energised, and focused once more on something that wasn't himself. All was good and back to normal. Not only did he have himself to thank for that, he also had Demi. Her positivity had definitely added an extra spring to his step.

CHAPTER 13

Demi

Demi had spent her first two days living at Robson's arranging and rearranging what little furniture she had, and now Jade was due any moment, and Demi couldn't be more excited. She was so sure her daughter would love the new flat. There were still a few items missing, but nothing that would make much of a difference, she hoped.

A wax melt had been filling the air with the combination of bergamot, coconut, and tonka all morning, and Demi had all the windows open to let in the fresh summer day. She'd baked some muffins and filled a small glass jug with freshly squeezed orange juice.

Robson was such a gem. He'd bought some flowers from Spencer's shop and placed them in a yellow vase on the kitchen table before heading downstairs to the pub to give her all the space she needed.

Demi scanned the area. The kitchen was clean, and looking rather homely, in her opinion. Robson's living room couldn't help go unnoticed, seeing how it was open plan, but he was quite the minimalist, so nothing was out of place, as there wasn't much to make a mess of. With his permission, she had placed a couple of her cushions on his long corner sofa just to liven it up a bit.

Upstairs was neat and tidy, showcasing a comfy, happy home that Demi was sure anyone would like.

Demi's phone buzzed, showing a message from Jade to say she'd just got off the bus and was walking to the pub. At least she had confirmation her daughter was definitely coming, as most of the morning she had felt sick with worry that Jade would change her mind.

She sprinted to the door, ready with a huge smile.

Jade walked around the corner and smiled back. 'Hi, Mum.'

Demi immediately gave her a hug, not wanting to let go, but also not wanting to act weird by over-hugging. 'Why didn't you drive down?'

'I wasn't sure what the parking would be like. Besides, I don't mind the bus. Alana said she'd drop me, but I wanted to come alone.' She gave a slight shrug as she swiped away her ponytail.

Demi couldn't see any signs of happiness in Jade's pale-blue eyes. It was disheartening to think her daughter had only agreed to check out the new flat through obligation. 'Come up. I made your favourite muffins.'

'Colin told me this place is quite big.'

Demi deflated a little on the inside. 'What else did he say?'

'Not much,' Jade replied, following her up the stairs.

Demi knew that to be a fib. Colin would have told Alana, and Alana would have taken great pleasure in trying to turn Jade off the idea of living above a pub. Or perhaps Demi was being a touch paranoid. She gave herself a mental shake as she watched her daughter enter the kitchen. 'Ta-dah!'

Jade frowned at Robson's living room.

'Oh, that's the landlord's space. We only share the kitchen. My flat is upstairs. This way.' Demi thumbed down the passage, believing the colours and furnishing upstairs would spark joy for her daughter.

Jade walked around quietly, and Demi hoped she was taking it all in, making plans about where she could put her things.

'This is your room,' announced Demi, splaying her arms. It's the biggest, and it has a sea view. Look.'

Jade peered out the window. 'I like the lighthouse.'

Demi smiled. 'It's a great view.' She waited for Jade to turn around. 'I wasn't sure what colour you'd want in here, so I went for pink. You used to love that colour, but we can change it, that's not a problem.' She followed Jade's eyes to the brown teddy bear placed on the pillow, which she thought held a nice friendly vibe until she noticed Jade didn't smile at the toy.

The silence was unnerving.

'What do you think? Better than the bedsit, right?'

Jade nodded. 'So much more room.'

'Do you like it?'

'Yes, it's nice.' Jade sat on the corner of the bed, which Demi would have taken as a good sign if it weren't for the stale atmosphere.

'Bed's new.'

Jade smiled softly. 'I gathered.'

'I got you a firm mattress. Good for the back. I would have bought the double size but—'

'Look, Mum, I might as well spit it out. I won't be living here with you.'

Demi sat on the white wooden chair by a matching dressing table she had bought especially for Jade's room. 'Oh, I wasn't expecting you to move in, love. I just thought it would be nice for you to have your own space when you stay over. It's not like Alana wants me at her house, so we haven't had a chance to do sleepovers since my release, but we can now.' She swallowed hard, trying to keep her composure.

'I'm not sure I want to do that either, Mum.'

'We have to start somewhere, Jade.'

'We meet up for coffee. Lunch.'

'I know, and I understand your reluctance to do more with me, but it's time for us to move up a gear. I want us to get back to how we were, or at least become a little closer.' Demi sighed deeply. 'I guess I just wish things could be as they were.'

Jade looked at the light-wood flooring. 'Things are different now.'

Demi's heart cracked, but she held it together, holding on to hope, to her dreams. 'I know, but we're moving forward, not staying put, so we have to work with what we have now.'

Jade's pale eyes were weighted with water as she glanced up. 'I don't feel I really know you anymore.'

Demi felt her heart break some more. 'I know, love. That's why we need to be around each other. That way, we can get to know each other again. The people we are now.'

'But we can't be sure you'll stay this way.' Jade's smile was small. 'I'm not trying to be rude, Mum.'

'It's okay. I understand.' What else could Demi add to reassure Jade? Could she offer a guarantee? She was a recovering addict now, and even if she wasn't, she knew life was unpredictable. She knew that more than anyone.

'I'm sorry, Mum.'

'No, baby girl, I'm the one who is sorry. I never should have put you through that terrible life.'

'Colin always told me it wasn't your fault, and now I'm older I know more about the subject.'

'It doesn't make the trauma go away though, does it?'

Jade gave a small shrug as she twisted her mouth to one side. 'It helps a little.'

'Well, if it helps some more, just know I'm on a mission to stay clean for the rest of my life. I'll die before I go back to that.'

'Don't say that, Mum.'

'I just want you to know how hard I'm fighting each day. I go to so many meetings, have therapy, knuckle down with my job. I'm staying on track, love. There's nothing to be afraid of.'

Jade started picking at her fingernail. 'I had therapy too, Mum. Alana took me to a private clinic.'

That was the first time Demi had heard that. 'I didn't know.'

'It's all good. I'm okay now. It was back when you went inside. I wasn't coping very well.'

Demi moved to Jade's side and took her hand. 'Oh, love, I'm so sorry.'

'Terry died, then you went downhill fast after your operation. It all seemed to be such a whirlwind. We lost our home, you were hooked on drugs, I felt so lost and alone, and if it weren't for Colin and Alana, I'm not sure I would have survived.'

Demi tried to hug her, but Jade pulled back. 'I'm sorry, love. I was too ill to think about what was happening to you.'

'I know.'

'And I can see how badly this whole ordeal has affected you, and I'm so grateful to your uncle, I really am. He's given you such a good life, and I'm proud of you. You've done so well for yourself. Off to uni soon, because we both know you'll get the grades. What a superstar you are, young lady.'

Jade smiled softly. 'Thanks. But you can see now why I don't want my life turned upside down.'

'It's not in my plans to hurt you, Jade.'

'I know.' Jade dipped her head. 'I just don't trust you,' she added quietly.

Demi had no words. There was nothing she could say that could change the past, and there was little she could do to show her daughter a future filled with moonbeams and roses.

Jade stood, sniffing, not making eye contact. 'I should go.'

'You don't have to.'

'I want to. This is too hard.'

Demi reached for her hand. 'Please, Jade. I just want us to rebuild.' She gestured to the room. 'I did this for you. For us.'

Jade tugged back her hand. 'Don't put this on me. I'm not carrying guilt because of you.'

'No, that's not what I'm trying to do. I just—'

'I'm not ready for these kinds of moves. I don't want to be pushed.'

Demi took a step back. 'I won't push you, love,' she said softly. 'Just know you have a room here with me whenever you need one.' She watched Jade scan the bedroom once more before leaving.

Jade went downstairs and stopped in the kitchen. 'I like my life, Mum,' she said quietly.

Demi gave a slight nod. 'I'm happy that you're happy. That's what I want for you.'

'I want you to be happy too, Mum.'

'I am. I'm doing really well.'

Jade smiled, but it looked weak, awkward. 'Good.'

Demi followed her to the top of the stairs, wondering if her daughter would turn to hug her.

'No need to walk me to the door,' said Jade, walking down the stairs without showing any signs of affection.

'Come back anytime,' was all Demi could think to say.

Jade waved at the bottom, then left, and just for a moment all that was left was the silence.

Demi slid down the wall to sit in a slump on the kitchen floor. Tears streamed, and her breathing was hard to control. She quickly whipped out her phone to call her sponsor, Nancy.

'Whoa, whoa,' said Nancy, her face appearing on the screen. 'Okay, just breathe, Demi. First step, remember? Just focus on the breaths. In through the nose, out through the mouth. Nice and slow. Easy now. You've got this.'

Trying to steady her breathing while a thousand tears fell wasn't an easy task. All Demi wanted was to curl up in a corner and numb the pain. There was so much pain, and she could make it go away with one pill. Maybe more.

'Come on, Dems. Breathe through the son of a bitch,' said Nancy, her deep tones hitting home.

Demi started to calm enough to speak. 'I can't take this anymore, Nance.'

'Yes, you can. It's just a setback. Part of the process. You know that.'

Demi nodded as she started to rock back and forward a little. 'I hate this. I hate this.'

'I know you do. We all do. But this is just a moment, and we're going to make sure it stays just that. Now, take a deep breath and tell me what's going on.'

The inhale Demi took was shaky but manageable. She stopped moving and pressed her head back against the wall.

'Did you slip?' asked Nancy, her dark eyes homing in on the screen.

Demi shook her head. 'But I want to. I just want to make life go away.'

'No, you don't. It's just a shit moment. Tell me, what brought this on?'

'Jade.' Demi took another deep breath, trying hard to stay focused. 'It doesn't look as though she'll ever live with me again. She doesn't even want to have a sleepover.'

'Did you show her your new digs?'

'Yes. Didn't make a difference.'

Nancy sighed. 'Give her time, Dems.'

'I don't think that will make a difference either. No one in my family has any faith in me.'

'What's important is you having faith in you, and I know you do. We have to.' Nancy tapped her collarbone. 'Remember when we met? What we learned at that meeting? Everything we do, we have to do it for ourselves. This whole journey is about us. We won't survive if we're only living for others. We have to want better and do better so we feel better.'

Demi remembered. It was how she lived her life. Focusing on her goals. Moving forward. Rebuilding with each and every step.

'Don't change it now, Dems. No matter how much I love my husband, I can't stay sober for him. This is my life, my pain. I have to want the freedom. You remember that part, because this is your freedom we're talking about. I know you love your life.'

'I do, but today was tough.'

Nancy stabbed a finger forward. 'And another day in the future will be tough, and so on. But you keep reminding yourself how much you hated life when off your face and lying in a gutter.'

Her sponsor's words were what she needed. The reminder of just how terrible things once were. There was no way she could go back.

'Take another deep breath, Dems. You've got this.'

Demi inhaled, then breathed out a small laugh filled with exhaustion. 'It's so unfair, Nance.'

'Don't start that, mate. No feeling sorry for yourself. You know that's a negative. Come on, chin up. It happened, we're past that. It's about the here and now, and right now you need to remember your goals and give yourself a break.'

'The worst part is, I don't even blame my family for their lack of trust in me. I put them through hell, so I don't exactly have an argument. I just thought our relationship would have improved by now.'

'It took a few years for my old man to accept my changes. It's not easy for them either. We know that.'

Demi bobbed her head. 'I just feel so tired right now, Nancy.'

'I know, mate. But those are the days we fight harder. And how do we do that?'

Demi smiled softly. 'We rest.'

'And what don't we do?'

'Beat ourselves up.'

'So you do listen at meetings.' Nancy smiled. 'How about you peel yourself off that floor and think of something positive to do.'

Demi perused the area. 'I've got the day off work, and there's nothing here for me to do.'

'What about a walk? Always clears your head.'

'There's a local craft fayre going on today. Perhaps I'll check that out.'

'Yes, that sounds like a great idea. I bet you find some home-made jams or foody bits you'd appreciate.'

The idea of getting some more feedback from stall owners about having a farmers' market up at Happy Farm came to mind.

'Thanks, Nancy. You know, for everything.'

Nancy waggled a hand. 'That's what sponsors are for.'

'Yeah, but you're the best.'

'You don't do too bad yourself.'

Demi grinned. 'Oh, we've come a long way, haven't we?'

Nancy chuckled. 'Who knew!'

Demi took another deep breath. 'Right, I'm going to sort my face and go to the craft fayre because that's my life now.'

Nancy showed her serious side again. 'You sure you're good now, mate?'

'Yeah, I just needed to get that out of my system.'

'We can talk some more.'

'Thanks, Nance, but I'm okay. I can't think about my family and see what they see. I have to carry on being me, doing me, and walk my own path. Just needed reminding.'

'That's good. You just remember, a bad moment doesn't have to ruin the whole day. But you call me back if you need to. The fact you called me proves you don't want that old life. You're one of the success stories, Demi. And you always will be. Believe in yourself. I believe in you.'

'I believe in you too, Nance.' Demi blew her friend a kiss, then said goodbye.

The silence was back for a moment, but it didn't seem as chilly as before the phone call. Demi felt so blessed to have a sponsor who she could call whenever she struggled. Just five minutes with Nancy always sorted her out.

Demi spotted her reflection in the mirror as she passed Robson's bathroom. 'Bloody hell, look at the state of me.' Not really thinking about personal space, she entered just to zoom in on her panda eyes and blotchy cheeks.

'Demi, you up here?' called Robson.

It was in that moment she realised she had entered a room that wasn't hers. Quickly, she stepped into the passage, coming face to face with him.

'I'm sorry,' she said. 'I just caught myself in your mirror and went for a closer look. I wasn't snooping or—'

'Hey, are you okay?' He stepped closer, reaching out a hand, concern in his eyes.

Demi couldn't help herself. She moved to his chest, wanting to rest there for a while. Wanting to be held.

Robson curled his arms around her, without saying a word.

It was so nice just standing there wrapped in his warmth, but she knew she couldn't stay there forever, so she slowly pulled back.

'You want to talk?' he asked quietly.

'No. I'm good, thanks,' she replied just as softly. 'I just spoke to my sponsor.' She briefed him on the conversation.

'I'm glad you have someone to talk to. I don't know how to be a sponsor, but just know you can always talk to me. I'll help wherever I can.'

'Thank you. All support is welcome.'

'I came up because I saw your daughter in the pub with some blonde woman.'

Demi silently sighed. 'That'll be my sister-in-law. I should have known she would be close by.'

'They were checking out the menu.'

'More like checking out where I work.'

Robson gave a slight smile. 'That's a good thing. They can see we're a family-friendly pub.'

He was right. It would be helpful for them to see the Jolly Pirate wasn't some drug den, which no doubt they had imagined. She didn't want to think about it anymore. The only control she had was over her own thoughts and actions.

'I wasn't sure if you were joining them,' added Robson. 'Then I got worried when you didn't show.'

'I'm okay. I'm just going to tidy myself up and head off to the craft fayre.' She looked towards the kitchen. 'Things with my daughter didn't exactly go to plan, so I need to clear my head.'

'Anything I can do to help?'

'Thanks, but there isn't anything anyone can do. I'm just going to carry on living my best life, and it's up to my family whether they want to spend time believing in me or not. Not much I can do about them. My actions speak louder than words, so, one day, they'll see everything's okay.'

Robson bobbed his head, looking as though he didn't know how to respond. 'Erm, would you like some company at the fayre?'

Demi smiled warmly. He really was so nice. 'You want to join me?'

'Sure. I'll just get changed into some shorts, as it's getting hotter out there, then I'll nip downstairs to let the staff know I'm off out, not that it matters. They've got it covered as usual. I want to be back by dinner though to open up the grill.'

'Hmm, sounds like that's my evening meal sorted.'

Robson laughed. 'You can help me cook.'

'Deal.' Demi gestured down the passage. 'I'll just sort my face and grab my sunglasses, and I'll meet you in the kitchen.'

'Okay. Don't forget to slap on some sun cream.' He motioned at his bathroom. 'There's some in the cabinet. And, by the way, I knew you weren't snooping.'

Demi dipped back to one heal. 'Oh.'

Robson lifted her chin. 'Let's get this show on the road.'

She smiled as she watched him walk away to his bedroom. Nancy was right. A bad moment didn't have to ruin the whole day.

CHAPTER 14

Robson

The Port Berry Craft Fayre saw Anchorage Park full of large cream tents. Arts and crafts were on display, and lots of visitors were out enjoying the hot summer day.

All Saints church was open, with its own bric-a-brac stall outside the stone-built hall, and food and drink was being sold over on the Old Market Square cobbles.

The winding road leading to a row of quaint cottage-style shops was just as busy, and the small slightly lopsided pub called the Crooked Hole had loud music pumping from inside the bar.

Robson was pleased he'd decided to go with Demi. She sure as heck looked as though she needed a friend when he saw her in the flat. He smiled her way as they walked along by the pond. She looked peaceful as she stared over at the large weeping willow and ducks mooching nearby.

Whatever had happened between her and her daughter was none of his business. It was obvious damage had been done because of the addiction, so the last thing Demi needed was painful questions, but he could still show up to let her know she had someone to talk to if need be. He knew how important that was.

'Hey, there's Will,' said Demi, nudging Robson's elbow. 'I think he wants us to go over.'

Robson peered at his friend waving away by the Sunshine Centre's tent, so he went with Demi to see what he wanted.

Demi immediately perused the art on display. 'Oh, wow, these are lovely. We should get a picture of the harbour for the flat.'

Robson nodded, then greeted Will. 'What's up?'

'Bad news about the farmers' market, I'm afraid.'

'Oh?' questioned Robson.

'Councillor Seabridge said the residents he has spoken to aren't keen about having a market on their doorstep, so to speak. They're worried it'll clog the roads with traffic.'

'Did they all say no?' asked Demi, stepping away from the artwork.

'Not the ones I've spoken to,' replied Will. 'Ginny's going to go through all the red tape with the councillor, then we'll take it from there. I think it might be too much for us to take on at the moment, what with the baby due, but Ginny stills wants to try, as she's got her heart set on the idea now.'

'You won't be alone in this,' said Robson. 'We'll all chip in like we normally do.'

Will smiled. 'Thanks, I know, but I didn't realise there would be so much hassle involved in people selling their wares.'

Demi indicated the fayre around them. 'I was thinking we could spread the word while we're here. Get some feedback from people.'

'Yeah, it'll be good to see how many are onside,' said Robson. 'Hear it for ourselves.'

Will nodded.

Robson spotted Samuel and Lottie in the art tent. 'I'll get them to ask around as well.' He held up a hand to Samuel. 'Sam.' He made his way over to where Sam stood and where Lottie was selling her paintings.

'Hi, Robson,' Lottie said — her smile aimed at Demi. 'You must be Demi. We haven't met yet, but my brother told me all about you. I'm Lottie, and this is my other half, Sam.'

Demi smiled back. 'Oh, you're Spencer's sister. Pleased to meet you both.'

'We're supposed to be having a gathering at ours so Demi can meet everyone,' said Will, who had joined them, 'but we still haven't managed to arrange that yet.'

Samuel swiped a hand through his dark hair. 'Everyone's been so busy lately.'

'Right, that's it,' said Will. 'Friday night at ours. It's supposed to be dry all week, so we'll have that barbeque. I'll double-check with Ginny, but I'm thinking all should be good.'

Lottie lightly clapped. 'Lovely.' She manoeuvred her electric wheelchair around some artwork so she was closer to Demi. 'And what's even lovelier is I hear you've moved to the harbour.'

Demi nodded as Robson rolled his eyes.

'Don't interrogate her, Lott.' He shook his head. 'We only popped over to see if you could help ask customers if they'd be interested in a local farmers' market.'

'We need the locals onside,' said Will. 'Speaking of which, I'm going off to continue to do that right now.'

Samuel nodded. 'Sure, we can help with that. Not a problem.'

'It'll be a shame if it falls through,' said Demi as Will walked away. 'The outbuilding is almost ready.'

'We'll check it out on Friday.' Lottie looked to Samuel for confirmation.

'Yeah,' he said. 'We've not been over there in a while.'

Lottie flicked her strawberry-blonde hair over her shoulder as she beamed at Samuel. 'I can't wait for our get-together now.'

Robson watched the love between them shine brighter than the sun. It always warmed him to see his friends happy and settled.

'I have an idea for the barbeque,' said Lottie. 'A surprise baby shower for Ginny?'

Samuel smiled her way. 'Great idea.'

She gazed up at him. 'I need to speak to Sophie and Alice to make arrangements.'

Robson nodded. 'We can all bring some food. And just in case Ginny and Will aren't into baby showers, well, all we've done is add to the party food and bought a gift for the baby.'

Lottie agreed. 'Yes. Although it would be nice to have a few balloons.'

Samuel laughed. 'How about you sort some flowers instead. If we're going to spring a baby shower on them, let's not go overboard.'

Lottie frowned. 'Can I at least get a cake?'

'Don't see why not,' said Robson. 'Just don't buy it from Ginny's.'

They all shared a laugh.

'I can make one,' said Demi, gaining everyone's approval.

'Are you sure?' asked Robson.

'Yes, I used to make all of Jade's birthday cakes. It's been a while since I did anything like that, but I think I know my way around a kitchen, so it shouldn't be too hard to remember.'

Robson beamed her way, then realised he was over-beaming so stopped.

'As soon as we've got the confirmation from Will about the barbeque, we can get organised,' said Lottie. She looked at Demi. 'Thanks for the cake offer. Ginny deserves all the fuss in the world. And Will, of course.'

Samuel turned to help a customer who had come to browse Lottie's pictures.

'We'd better let you get on,' said Robson, gesturing at her artwork. 'Put that one to one side for us, Lott.' He double checked with Demi, then pulled out his wallet, had a short debate with Lottie over what to pay for the painting of Port Berry Harbour, as she wanted to give him a discount, finally settled on the original price, then headed off to enjoy the rest of the craft fayre with Demi.

'Your friends are all so lovely, Robson.'

'We have a nice community.'

'I'm glad to be part of it. It's made a real difference to my life. What do you think about me offering to do a shift at the Hub?'

Robson stopped walking to face her. 'That's up to you. There's always room for more volunteers. We'll pop in on our way home and check out the roster.'

'I was thinking about the Sunshine Centre as well,' she said, pointing to their tent. 'Now I know about the place, I could ask the person in charge if they'd like some cooking classes to help with mental health or something. I find cooking so calming. It might be useful to someone else in that way.'

Robson smiled as he nodded. 'You really do want to get involved.'

'I have some spare time, and I'd rather keep occupied. Plus, it's nice to give something back. People helped me, so I'd like to pay it forward where I can.'

'Okay, well, I'll introduce you to Debra, if I see her.' He peered over at the tent. 'Not sure where she is right now, but she's the one in charge, and I'm sure she'll bite your arm off, as that's just the type of thing they do over there.'

'That's good. Meanwhile, shall we get some lunch? All this talk of cooking is making my stomach rumble.'

Robson laughed. 'Yeah. What do you fancy?'

'We're working the grill at dinnertime, so perhaps something light.'

He motioned towards the square. 'How about some seafood? Sophie's got her mobile stall out today.'

'Sounds perfect.'

'Sea Shanty Shack it is.'

They strolled to the white trailer to be greeted by Matt, who was just handing over a tub of peeled prawns to a customer.

'Hello, you here for a snack?' he asked Demi, before grinning at Robson.

Robson noticed a lot of his friends kept grinning at him lately. He knew they were thinking something more was going on with him and Demi. He could see it in their eyes.

'We thought we'd have a seafood lunch,' said Demi, browsing the goods on the cold counter.

'What about a dressed crab?' suggested Matt, pointing one out.

Robson nodded as Demi turned to him. 'Sounds good.'

'And I've just bought some buttered baguettes from the bakery,' said Sophie, entering the trailer. She smiled at Demi. 'You can have one each if you like. I've got plenty.'

Robson introduced the two women, then thanked Sophie as she handed over the bread.

'I'll pay for lunch,' said Demi, dipping into her purse.

Robson went to protest, but she quickly reminded him he had just paid for the picture for the flat, and he wouldn't have done that if she didn't want it. 'Thanks,' he replied, earning him a grin from Sophie.

Demi took the dressed crabs and a couple of small wooden forks from the counter. 'I heard you two are getting married this year.'

Sophie gestured towards the church. 'In December, and we can't wait.' She leaned into Matt, who kissed her cheek.

'Aww,' said Demi. 'Hope it all goes well for you.'

'You can see for yourself,' said Sophie. 'You're very welcome to come. I'll put you down as Robson's plus-one.'

Robson coughed on the baguette he'd just bitten into. 'Sure,' he croaked, giving Demi the thumbs-up sign.

They decided to sit by the pond to eat their lunch, and Robson felt a tad awkward after his clear show of shock horror at taking Demi to a wedding. It wasn't meant that way at all. He was just taken aback by Sophie's attempts at matchmaking.

Demi threw some crumbs to the ducks, then sat and ate her lunch in silence.

Robson felt the need to explain. 'About the wedding.'

'Oh, that's okay. I'm sure you'd like to ask your own plus-one.'

'I don't have a plus-one.'

Demi looked devastated. 'Bloody hell, I'm so sorry. Your wife, of course.'

'No, it's not that. I mean . . .' He didn't really know what he meant so stopped talking.

'You don't have to take me,' Demi said softly. 'It's okay.'

He glanced her way and smiled. 'I don't have a problem with that, Dem. Honestly. Sophie took me by surprise, that's all, but I'm happy for us to go together. We're flatmates, sort of, right? We work in the same pub. I'm sure we can manage hanging out at a wedding.'

'If you're sure.'

'Yeah. It's all good.' He felt a lot better now that was sorted.

Demi nudged his arm. 'Eat your crab before that seagull swoops in.'

He looked up to see the food thief circling. 'Those birds have no shame.'

They sat in silence again, this time more comfortably, and Robson stuffed their rubbish in the bin by his side when they had finished. It was so nice sitting in the sun, he closed his eyes for a moment and simply enjoyed the tranquillity of the park, even though there was a craft fayre taking place right behind him.

'I'm thinking of speaking at the next bereavement meeting,' said Demi, waking him, as he was about to drift off.

Robson straightened. 'You feel ready?'

'I haven't said anything at any of them. No one's mentioned it, but they must think it's pointless me attending when I don't talk about my loved ones.'

'Not at all. No one has to speak. Sometimes people find peace just by being in the company of others who know what they're going through.'

Demi shrugged. 'I want to say something.'

'Okay, but don't feel obligated. Grief is strange. You have to deal with it in your own time. No pressure.'

'I know, but . . . Oh, is that Marisa?'

Robson followed her eyes. 'Yeah.' He frowned. 'She looks a bit distressed.'

'What do you think is in that box she's carrying?'

'I don't know, but let's get over there.'

They jogged towards the elderly lady, whose head was down, showing her concentration was on the cardboard box in her arms.

'Marisa?' questioned Robson. 'You okay?'

Her eyes held water as she peered up to see who was talking to her. 'Robson.' The seriousness on her face lightened a touch. 'Demi.'

Robson peered into the box as he heard a faint meow. 'Are these your kittens, Marisa?' He knew how much she loved cats so it wasn't too much of a surprise to see her with some.

'No. I found them on my way here, dumped behind some bins, and I don't know what to do.'

'Here, let me.' Robson took the box, giving her arms a rest.

'Thank you, Robson. I was heading to the church to see if I could get help.'

Demi reached into the box to stroke a black kitten. 'Ooh, they're so sweet. How could anyone dump them?'

'There were six altogether,' said Marisa. 'But two were dead.'

'Let's get over to the vets,' said Robson. 'See what they have to say. They probably know a cat shelter.'

Marisa didn't look too keen, but agreed anyway, following him across the square and along the winding road.

'Is it far?' asked Demi, walking close behind with Marisa.

'Michael Lane's just opened a practice up here,' replied Robson, checking on the four skinny kittens.

'Ooh, Artie Lane's son?' asked Marisa. 'I didn't know he was a vet.' She turned to Demi, clutching on to her arm. 'I never took my Buttons to see him.'

'He moved away, but he's back now,' said Robson.

'We'll soon get these kittens seen to,' said Demi softly. 'They'll get good homes, I'm sure.'

Robson came to a stop at an old cottage-style shop, and Demi opened the door.

'Hello, Robson,' said the tall man behind a small wooden counter. 'What you got there?'

'Hi, Michael. My friend just found these. Been dumped.' Robson placed the box down for the vet to take a look.

'Aww, bless them. They look undernourished.'

'I can feed them,' said Marisa, placing one hand over the box in a protective manner.

Michael smiled at her, revealing perfect teeth. 'I'm sure you can, but I think my nurses are going to have to do some round-the-clock feeds first.'

Marisa frowned. 'I can do that.'

Robson could see the vet thought it might be too much for the elderly woman. 'Perhaps it's best to let the nurses make a start, then you can come in and help.' He glanced at Michael to see if that was an option.

Michael gave a brief nod. 'I'm sure we can arrange something. But you need to know, they're very weak and might not make it through the night.'

Marisa slapped a hand to her mouth as she gasped, and Demi quickly hugged her.

Robson turned his attention to the vet. 'And what happens if they do make it?'

'We can arrange for them to go to a local cat shelter. I know a woman who takes in strays and tries to get them adopted. She's very nice.' He pointed to a leaflet advertising the shelter on the noticeboard, trying to reassure Marisa, who still looked mortified.

'If they get stronger, can I keep them?' Marisa asked meekly.

'Of course,' replied Michael. 'If you think you could cope with four cats.'

Marisa scoffed as though he had offended her cat ownership skills. 'I've had cats all my life. I just didn't plan to have any more after my Buttons passed away.' She gazed at Robson. 'It's been so hard.'

'I know, Marisa.' He reached forward to pat her arm.

'But looking at these poor little souls, what am I to do?'

'You don't have to take them, Marisa,' said Demi. 'Someone will adopt them. People do.'

Marisa tapped her chest. 'I'm someone. I can do it. I don't want to leave them now.'

Robson looked at Michael. 'How should we move forward?'

'We'll take the kittens out back for a few nights, get them settled and fed, then if they pull through, they can be wormed and chipped and handed over to Marisa when they're strong enough.'

'And how much will that cost?' Robson thought it best to ask before everyone got carried away with ideas.

'Pfft,' scoffed Marisa. 'I've got money. I'll pay whatever it takes.'

'Are you sure?' asked Demi quietly.

Marisa nodded. 'I'm more and more sure with each minute that passes.'

Michael gestured to a doorway that led out back. 'I actually have a charity attached to my clinic that helps to fund situations like these when they occur, so the cost for care can be reduced. Would you like to come through, Marisa, and help settle them with the nurse?'

Her eyes lit up at the offer. 'Ooh, yes please, doctor.'

Robson shared a smile with the vet, then left them to it. He took a deep breath and sighed as Demi met his side. 'Well, that was unexpected.'

'Oh, I don't know. I had an idea she'd want to keep them.'

'No, I meant Marisa finding them.'

'I don't reckon I'll be talking much about me at our next meeting now, as we will all want an update on the kittens.'

Robson dropped his sunglasses to his nose as he smiled. 'What should we do now?'

'Grab the painting from Lottie and head back?'

'Yeah, that suits me. We'll stop off at each stall on our way and mention the farmers' market.'

'And buy an ice cream.'

He smiled in agreement. 'Good plan.'

Demi leaned into his arm as they crossed the narrow road. 'It's been a funny sort of day.'

'And it's only lunchtime.'

She chuckled. 'Let's focus on where we're going to hang our new picture.'

'You do know you get the same view if you just look out the window.'

Demi poked him in the ribs, causing him to wriggle away while laughing. 'We've bought it now.'

'It could go in the pub by the pirate stories.'

'Another good idea.'

'And when you move, you can take it with you to remind you of your time at the harbour.' As soon as the words left his mouth, he felt sadness hit.

'Hopefully, I might be able to stay close by.'

He watched her wave over to Matt as they entered Old Market Square. With a bit of luck, she wouldn't move too far away, because he was already used to her always being around.

While Demi stopped for a quick chat with Matt, Robson told himself to mind his own business when it came to her life. Just because she was his lodger, it didn't mean he could involve himself on a personal level.

Sophie wrapping her arm around his shoulders made him jump out of his thoughts. 'You look a million miles away there, Rob.'

'Just enjoying the sunshine.'

Sophie gestured to Demi over by the trailer. 'Is that all you're enjoying?'

Robson tutted. 'Stop that. She's just my friend, employee, and now lodger. Everything is professional.'

'What's professional about being someone's landlord?'

Now she'd put it to him, he found himself quite stumped. 'I don't know. It's just the way things are, so don't meddle.'

'I have never meddled in your love life.'

'Only because I don't have one.'

Sophie turned him to face her. 'In all seriousness, do you think you're ready now?'

He didn't want to ever be ready for that kind of commitment. Leah dying almost killed him. Could he really open his heart after that?

Sophie gave his hand a light squeeze. 'You're my friend, and I love you, and I just want whatever is best for you.'

He smiled as he pulled her in for a hug. 'I know you do, and all I can tell you is that right now, I'm happy with my life.' It didn't seem like a fib, as he was mostly happy.

CHAPTER 15

Demi

On their way back to the pub, Demi and Robson popped into the Hub to see that Alice and Beth were on duty.

'Demi wants to add her name to the roster,' said Robson, opening the door.

'Ooh, lovely,' squealed Alice, looking slightly flustered. 'The more hands the better. We've just had a van pull up and unload boxes of tinned food. We had to take most of it upstairs. But just like the last lot, it won't be there long. We're about to make more food parcels.'

Beth tied back her long mousey hair, removing damp strands from her forehead. 'It was a bit of a nightmare in this heat.'

Robson introduced Beth to Demi. 'This is Spencer's better half,' he joked, making Beth laugh.

Beth turned to Demi. 'Spencer's at the craft fayre with the kids he mentors at the Sunshine Centre. He's got our son with him too.'

'We just came from there,' said Demi. 'We didn't spot him.'

'It was busy this year,' said Robson. 'But then we were distracted by a friend of ours who'd just found some dumped kittens.'

Alice flopped into the big blue comfy chair. 'Aww, that's a shame. Don't know why people don't just drop them off at the vets.'

'They're with Michael Lane now,' said Robson.

Alice smiled. 'Best place. He'll look after them.' She motioned towards the painting Robson was carrying. 'Is that one of Lottie's?'

'Yep. Demi can't get enough of the view.'

Demi looked out the window at the sea, her heart warming. 'It's a lovely view.'

Robson agreed. 'We're still deciding where to hang this. Pub probably.'

Beth went out to the back room to fetch the weekly roster. 'Let me sort this, then, Alice, I'll make you a cuppa before we carry on.'

'I can do that,' said Demi, wanting to get stuck in already.

Robson moved towards the door. 'I'm going to head back to the pub. I'll see you in a bit.'

Demi nodded. 'Okay.'

'How you settling in over there?' asked Alice.

Beth sat at the table and glanced up. 'Ooh, I heard you moved into the pub.'

Demi grinned to herself as she made the tea. 'Word really travels fast around here.'

'Yep,' said Alice, chuckling.

'Well, I'm settling in nicely, thank you for asking.'

'What's Robson like as a boss?' asked Alice. 'I help him out when I'm in there and it gets super busy, but it's not as a job. Just a mate.'

'He's nice, but he's not really my boss, as such. Joseph is in charge of the kitchen staff.'

Alice shuffled up. 'Speaking of kitchen staff, I've an idea I want to run by you. Have you got time, or do you need to get back soon?'

Demi glanced over her shoulder. 'I've got time. I told Robson I'd help with the grill later, but that's all I've got on today.'

'Great,' said Alice. 'Pull up a pew.'

Demi made three cups of tea and placed them on the table, then sat down, expecting Alice to talk recipes, as most people did when they found out she was a chef. She also wondered if Alice had seen her online cooking shows and might want to talk about that.

'It's about the B&B I've just bought,' said Alice. 'Once Mabel moves out, I was thinking of hiring a proper chef and adding a lunch menu. As it stands, Mabel makes the brekkie, then it's up to guests to sort their grub somewhere else for the rest of the day. I want to change that and offer a hotel kind of lunch. What do you think?'

Demi liked the idea. 'Don't see why not. Your breakfast comes in with the price of the room, but your lunch can be a set menu.'

'And would anyone be able to eat there or will it be just for paying guests?' asked Beth.

'Anyone,' replied Alice. 'I want people to talk about my B&B. Recommend the lunch menu to their mates and so on.'

'Do you want my help creating a menu?' asked Demi, thinking that was where the conversation was heading.

Alice leaned forward for her tea. 'I was actually hoping that when your time comes to an end at the pub, you might consider being my chef at the B&B.'

Demi was quite taken aback. 'Oh.'

'I know it's probably not what you're used to, what with you being a restaurant chef and that, but would you think it over?'

Demi gave a brief nod. It wasn't the worst idea, and if they pulled in the punters, it would secure her a long-term job, and she would only have to make breakfast and lunch. She assumed. 'Would you want me to cook breakfast too?'

'That would be up to you. It's mostly a full English or continental that's served, so I can manage that by myself, and my Benny would help wash-up and stuff before school.'

Beth smiled. 'Since Alice told everyone her news, we've all been thinking of ways we can help out if needed. I'm a teacher, so I can only help during the school holidays, and Spencer has said he can do any heavy lifting, if beds need moving or anything.'

Alice shook her head. 'They do make a fuss, but I'm perfectly capable. I've been helping Mabel at the B&B since I was in my teens.'

Beth lightly tapped Alice's arm. 'Yes, but you didn't have fibromyalgia then.'

Alice turned to Demi. 'That's true, but over the years I've learned how to work with my body, and I have no shame in asking for help if needed.'

Without giving it too much thought, Demi said, 'If you can afford to pay me more hours, then I'd be happy to take on the breakfast shift as well.'

Alice quietly squealed. 'Does that mean you're up for the challenge? You'd be the only chef in the kitchen, as I can't afford a whole team, but I'd be there to help. Would that work?'

'How many covers?' asked Demi.

Alice frowned. 'How many what?'

'How many people fit into your dining room?'

'Oh, erm, there are . . .' Alice started to count on her fingers. 'About fourteen.'

Demi was doing her own maths. If there was a full house, and she offered a choice of three set meals that were quick and easy to get to the pass, she was sure with Alice's help it was doable. With all those meals-for-one she'd been showcasing on her social media account, she felt well and truly prepared for the task. All she had to do was come up with a menu that had customers wanting to return.

Excitement oozed through her at the thought of designing an actual menu of her own for a kitchen. Sure, it was for a B&B, but what a fantastic opportunity, especially as something small and homely suited her just fine.

'Have you ever wanted your own restaurant?' asked Beth.

'Not really,' said Demi. 'Perhaps when I'd just started, but then I saw how much was involved when you're an owner, so I prefer to do my job, then go home. No stress. No overheads.'

Alice nodded. 'I think that's why Robson takes on a lot of staff. I know it's a big pub, so he needs that many, but with everyone on duty, he doesn't have to do much work himself. He just chooses to join in when he wants.'

Demi thought it best to mention the pub grub on offer. 'You do know you'd be in direct competition with him at lunchtime, right?'

'I was thinking we could serve food that he doesn't have on his menu. I know fish and chips is the biggest seller around here, no matter where you choose to eat,' said Alice, nodding at Beth.

Demi laughed. 'We serve a lot of fish and chips at the pub. Not the same as buying from the chippy though.'

Beth rubbed her stomach. 'Ooh, you can't beat all that salt and vinegar over your greasy fingers.'

The women laughed, then finished their tea.

Demi had her thinking cap on. 'You know, for the B&B, you could lean more towards meals your granny would make. Hearty, homely, ones that warm the cockles.'

'I'm ready to eat there now,' said Beth, grinning.

'Me too,' said Alice.

Demi smiled at them both. 'At least that way, people will come to yours for a different reason. You could even give your B&B kitchen a name.'

Alice tilted her head. 'What like, Granny's Kitchen?'

Demi breathed out a small laugh. 'Yeah, something like that.'

'Well, it's worth thinking about. I'll have a chat with my family tonight. See what they think.' Alice leaned back in the chair and smiled a smile that seemed to be just for her. 'You know, my nan used to do all the cooking at home till her hands started playing up. One of the meals I loved was a chunky chicken-leek-and-potato soup. And I'm talking major chunks. It was so filling and definitely warmed you from head to toe.'

'We could serve food like that. Something that would keep the customers full till dinner.' So many recipes started to appear all at once in Demi's mind.

'I prefer the home-cooked style,' said Beth. 'Beats all that fancy-schmancy stuff that just looks pretty.'

Alice lightly clapped. 'Are we really doing this, Demi?'

It was the last thing Demi had expected to pop up in her life, but now it had been presented to her, why not?

Demi nodded. 'Let's give it a try.'

'And I won't offer dessert,' said Alice. 'I'll send the customers in the direction of Ginny's Tearoom for that.'

'They'll expect dessert. Perhaps get Ginny on board with that instead, that way you can help each other. She could supply the cakes, and I'll make any puddings needed. And you must push the coffee at the end of the meal,' said Demi. 'There's a huge profit in tea and coffee, so don't miss out on that.'

Alice nodded. 'Will do. I'll start making proper plans, but I won't change anything until Mabel has moved out, as I don't feel comfortable doing stuff like that while she's there. That place has been her home all her life. She has told me to do what I like now it's mine, but I think it's for the best if I wait. Won't be long now.'

'Besides, I'm still working at the pub for now. So I can't do much until the other chef is back on his feet.' Demi glanced at the door as it opened.

'Excuse me,' said an elderly man, leaning inside. 'I was wondering if you have any cat food?'

Alice stood to greet him. 'No, sorry, lovely. We don't have any pet food here.'

'But I know a place that might be able to help,' said Demi, reaching for a pen and notepad that was on the table. 'I was at a vet's earlier, and a cat shelter was mentioned. I noticed their advert on the noticeboard. Here, I'll write down the name and street. They might have a pet food bank.' She stopped writing and looked up. 'Actually, let me call them and find out for you. Save you a trip.'

Alice invited him inside and put the kettle on while Demi got on with the task of doing an online search for the phone number.

'Oh, hello, I'm calling to ask if you have a pet food bank.' Demi smiled at the man who was staring her way with hope in his eyes. 'Right, okay. Thank you.'

'Any luck?' asked the old man.

'They said they have a small amount of food to give, but you have to prove you're on a pension. They can't afford much so had to limit themselves,' Demi said.

The elderly man coughed out a chuckle. 'I'm well into my eighties, love. I think I can prove I'm on a pension, just doesn't cover everything anymore. I'm all right, it's just needing the bit extra for the cat now.'

Demi handed him the address. 'Do you know this street?'

'Ooh, yes, that's not too far from me. I didn't know they gave out food though. I thought the woman who runs things just takes in strays.'

'I guess they help wherever they can,' said Demi.

Alice handed the man some tea. 'Here, you drink that before you head off again. And how about a choccy bickie to go with it?'

He grinned. 'Go on then. Just the one.'

Demi smiled as she sat between him and Beth.

Beth nudged her arm while Alice chatted away to the old man. Sliding the timetable over, she asked, 'If I roster you on with Alice, you'll both have more time to talk about the menu and stuff.' She motioned to the following week. 'Show me when you're free.'

Beth pointed out two shifts she could do that week, but only one was with Alice, the other with Robson, which made Demi smile on the inside, as she loved hanging out with him.

Wait till she told him her news. She was sure he'd be happy for her, as he always showed support to others.

Demi turned to Beth. 'Perhaps we could put up a sign to ask for pet food, and if anyone comes along in the future, we might have something to offer.'

The elderly man smiled. 'That's a good idea.'

Alice wrinkled her nose. 'That's if we have room. We had no idea it would get so busy at times around here. Good thing it's not every day or we wouldn't cope. We're only small fry.'

'We can store some upstairs,' said Beth. 'We have to do that with the baby bank bits. Or we could take some over to the animal shelters. They might be interested.'

Demi gazed outside to the harbour. Whether it was prison, The Butterfly Company, or the Hub, there was always someone in need of help, and with a clear head and healthy body, she could put herself to good use and be one of those who helped others.

CHAPTER 16

Robson

One of the things Robson loved doing at his pub was working the grill outside in the front beer garden. Ever since he was a kid, his uncle used to fire up a barbeque for the customers, and the smell always reminded Robson of those days, even if his modern electric contraption wasn't as authentic.

He smiled at Demi serving by his side. She was so cheerful and got on well with everyone. It was a pleasure being in her company.

'Ooh, the customers have fizzled out a bit,' she said, lowering her tongs. 'Let's grab something to eat now.'

Robson moved to the chair over by the sink. 'You do yours first, then I can serve while you eat if anyone else comes up, then we'll swap.'

Demi slapped a steak on the grill. 'I've had steak in a bun on my mind all evening.' She laughed as she cooked.

'I didn't think you were coming back from the Hub, you were there so long.'

'I know. I got involved.'

He smiled, loosening his apron strings. 'Gets you like that.'

'I had a lot to talk about with Alice.' She grinned over her shoulder, making him laugh at the excitement in her eyes.

'Spit it out. You know you want to.'

Demi chuckled. 'Alice offered me a job at the B&B.'

Robson frowned, confused. 'Oh, doing what?'

'Chef.'

'Brekkie duties?'

She shook her head, flipped her steak, then turned. 'Lunch menu. It won't be until Mabel has left, and also not until I'm finished here, of course.'

Robson quirked an eyebrow. 'And what might she be serving at Seaview?'

Demi gave a teasing shrug.

Robson laughed as he joined her side, nudging her hip with his own. 'I feel like you're a spy now.'

'Joseph has his special sauce recipe under lock and key, so you're safe.'

He playfully nudged her again. 'You know what I mean.'

'It won't be anything you serve.' She flashed him a wide smile. 'Don't worry. I've got it covered.'

'Hmm.'

'Hey, trust me.'

He warmed at the smile in her eyes. 'I do.'

They held each other's gaze for a moment longer until a voice broke them apart.

'Excuse me,' said a young woman. 'Are you that Demelza's Dish of the Day lady?'

Robson watched Demi pull in her lips and slowly nod. Her cheeks had turned a slight shade of beetroot, and she'd dipped back to one heel.

'I thought it was you,' added the woman. 'I follow you online. I love your quick and easy meals, especially the ones you can put in the freezer.'

'Oh, thank you,' said Demi coyly.

Robson still hadn't had the pleasure of watching Demi create online content nor had he checked out her account.

He wanted to help snap her out of the shy bubble he just witnessed her disappear into. 'She's a great cook. Are you here to eat?'

The woman flashed a wide smile his way. 'I wouldn't mind a photo.'

Robson frowned. 'With me?'

The woman giggled. 'Well, there's an offer I can't refuse, but I meant with Demelza.'

Robson was sure he blushed, but he shrugged it off and stepped around the grill to take the woman's phone. 'I can take that for you.' He waved Demi over, who checked on her food before moving.

'Thank you so much,' the woman said to Demi.

'Smile,' said Robson, taking some snaps. 'Here you go.' He offered back the phone, but the woman grabbed him in for a selfie, which made him chuckle.

'I'd better get back to cooking,' Demi told them both, then made a quick dash for the grill.

Robson went to join her as the woman went to the bar. 'Well, how famous are you?'

'I'm not famous.' Demi sorted her food, then sat down to eat. 'You can do yours as soon as I've finished.'

'No subject change.' He placed a burger on the grill, then turned to see her picking at the bun covering her chunky steak. 'Just how many followers do you have now?'

Demi didn't make eye contact. 'Far more than I thought I would.'

'You dark horse. Show me. I've not had the pleasure of seeing your content yet.'

Demi laughed as she pulled out her phone to show him her account. 'It's building fast.'

Robson smiled widely. 'Oh, wow, Dem, that's brilliant.'

'I guess.'

Robson went back to cooking his dinner, knowing she'd be finished eating soon. 'You don't use your full name much,' he muttered.

'Just been called Demi from childhood.'

He glanced over his shoulder. 'They both suit you.'

She smiled, then went back to eating.

'I can't believe I'm about to lose a celebrity chef to a B&B,' he teased, hearing her laugh. 'The way that woman draped herself over you just now, I'd say you could be your own celebrity. I'll put you on my show.'

He swirled a finger around his face as he turned to her with a cheeky grin. 'It's all about this, you know.'

'Well, you are cute. I'll give you that.'

Robson's stomach flipped, which amused him no end. He'd been complimented many times for his looks, but the words didn't normally have such an impact. He sorted his food, then joined her side, seeing as no one was queuing at the grill. 'You should tell Alice about your online gig in case you end up with fans coming in to eat because of you.' He nudged her arm and winked.

Demi shrugged. 'Stop teasing.'

'Joking aside, it could help Alice's business if people know who the chef is.'

'I'll speak to her.' Demi sighed. 'I never thought my online content would reach so many or that anyone would recognise me on the street. I only show my face for the last ten seconds to do a ta-dah moment.'

'I'd love to watch you make a video one day.'

Demi scoffed. 'No thanks. I'm embarrassed enough as it is now.'

'Don't be. You should be proud. Look at your achievements, Dem. Bloody hell, love, I wish I had half your determination.'

Her mouth twisted to one side as she met his eyes. 'I spoke about my addiction on there, and my time in prison. That woman didn't mention it, but what if others do?'

'You were obviously comfortable talking about your past, so if anyone brings it up, you'll be okay. People love a comeback story, and you rebuilding your life will probably hit a lot of your followers straight in the heart.'

She leaned her shoulder against his for a moment. 'You always say the right thing.'

Robson scoffed. 'I doubt that, but thanks.'

'I want you to know I'll never leave you stranded. No matter how famous I am.' Demi burst out laughing, but Robson could tell she meant her words.

'I might have one of those plaques made for outside my street door so everyone knows you once lived with me.'

Demi's head dipped, and he noticed her smile had faded a touch. 'If money comes with that fame, at least I'll be able to afford a sea view.'

'Or you can just take Lottie's painting.'

'Perhaps I'll rent a room at Alice's.'

'Or you could just stay right here.' He waited for her to look up, but she didn't. At least her smile was back.

What was he doing? Why was he saying such things to her?

Leah entered his thoughts. Her slim frame, soft features. What would she think about him allowing his heart to beat for someone else? Was that happening? No. He was just being daft. There was nothing but friendship with Demi.

'Shop,' yelled a customer, slapping his hand by the grill.

Robson got up to serve. 'Yes, mate. What can I get you?'

A short queue suddenly formed, so Demi jumped to his side, and they were back to working side by side as the sun began to set and the seagulls settled down for the night.

CHAPTER 17

Demi

The bereavement group spent the first half hour chatting to Marisa about the three surviving kittens who had been at the vets for the past five days. It was such a shame one hadn't made it, but at least she'd helped save the others, and Marisa was in her element knowing she could take them home soon.

'They're feeding really well, and getting stronger by the day,' she said, as proud as a parent receiving their child's positive school report.

'That's brilliant news,' said Lizzie, handing out pink wafers. 'We had a cat once, ooh, years back, but after she died, Mum said she wouldn't go down that road again.'

Marisa shook her head. 'I didn't think I would after Buttons, but how could I not fall in love with the little furballs?'

Colby brushed a wafer across his lips. 'Makes you think about love after love, doesn't it?'

'Life's for the living,' said Jed. 'But I'd never want a relationship again. I spent too much of my life with my Ursula. It wouldn't feel right now.'

Demi silently swooned at the thought of having a man love her so deeply. All Terry had done was love himself. It was time she shared her grief with the group. After all, she knew all their stories. 'I'd like to talk about my story tonight.'

Marisa stopped knitting, and Colby sat up straight. Robson gave a slight nod, and Demi wasn't sure if she should stand, as sometimes Lizzie did when talking.

Deciding to remain seated, Demi inhaled and started at the beginning, looking to Robson as though speaking only to him. 'My first partner was Ray, my daughter's dad. He was knocked off his motorbike just before Jade turned one month old. We were only nineteen. I never thought I'd fall in love again after that. We'd been together since school, so Ray was all I knew. We had it all planned. The family life, white picket fence, all the standard dreams.'

'It's like that when you're young, love,' said Lizzie, showing sympathy in her eyes.

Demi bobbed her head. 'It was such a shock, but not as much as the next death to impact my life.'

'Sounds intriguing,' said Colby, eyes wide.

Demi sighed. 'Just unexpected in a different way.'

'How so, love?' asked Lizzie.

Demi returned her gaze to Robson. 'First of all, I was in shock because Terry had been stabbed. It was a random attack that took place outside where he worked in London. He worked for a large hotel chain, and their HQ was there, so he often travelled to London and other cities. Anyway, this man started attacking people in the street, and Terry was the only one who died from his wound.'

Jed swore under his breath, but she heard him.

Marisa reached over to pat Demi's hand. 'That's too much tragedy for someone so young.'

'And that wasn't the worst part.' Demi shook her head. 'Well, it was for him, but my grief didn't stop there.'

'What happened next?' asked Colby.

She'd come this far, she might as well go all in. 'I'd just got back from his funeral, and all I wanted was to sleep forever, but this woman came to my door, and what she told me changed everything.'

'Please don't feel you need to go on if this is too hard,' said Robson, earning a glare from Colby, who clearly didn't want to be left with a cliffhanger.

'It's okay,' said Demi. 'It turned out the woman was Terry's first wife, and as they hadn't divorced, his only wife.'

Lizzie gasped. 'He had a double life?'

Demi nodded. 'Yes. She was from up north, and she knew about me. I didn't find everything out until later on down the line, mostly through solicitors, but the short version is, they were a bit back and forth in their relationship, as they had a lot of stress because they couldn't have kids. He was on a break from her when he met me, but it didn't stop him still living another life with her.'

'What a loser,' snapped Colby. 'How dare he mess with your life.'

Demi took his hand for a quick squeeze of support. 'I know.'

'It's a lot easier when you have a travelling job,' said Lizzie. 'Get away with all sorts.' She scoffed. 'Like he did.'

'In the end they did have a child. A son. He'd be six now.'

Jed shook his head. 'So even after they had a baby, he didn't change his life?'

Demi knew what they were thinking, because she had the same thoughts, but only Terry had the answers to everyone's questions, and he took those to the grave, or in his case, wherever Crystal decided to scatter his ashes. She never did find out. She had to pretend to Jade at the time that a private scattering had been done by the cremation company. At least now her daughter knew the truth about the whole ordeal.

'What a lowlife,' said Lizzie. 'I'm so sorry, love, but I'm glad you found out. A horrible way to do so, but you deserved to know you were living a lie.' She shook her head as she huffed. 'How can someone be so cruel?'

'It's called selfishness,' said Robson, and Demi noticed his fists were clenched.

'He was selfish,' she agreed. 'And I'm glad I found out, but it hit me hard. I was in such a state when his wife left, I didn't know which way was up, then the front door opened, and I got scared Jade had bumped into the woman on the pathway, so I rushed to the top of the stairs, tripped, and ended up in hospital.'

'Bloody hell,' said Colby. 'You'd think you'd cut a break after that discovery.'

Demi shook her head. 'It got worse. I had to have a knee operation, and I ended up addicted to the pain meds. Life got out of control, and I ended up serving time for theft to feed the addiction.' She quickly looked around at the circle. 'I'm two-years clean now, and I came out of prison over a year ago, so that's all in my past, but you can see why I wasn't so chatty about my grief. Honestly, I'm not sure I ever did grieve in the end. Well, perhaps for my own life.'

'Oh, love.' Lizzie got up and hugged her, which led to Colby joining in.

'Thanks,' said Demi, appreciating their kindness. 'I am okay. I go to meetings, and I've had therapy, but my therapist and mentor wanted me to do this course. Jan thinks this will help, but I don't know if I fit here. Your stories are connected to love, and although I can speak about Ray and what we had, Terry often clouds my mind, and I'm not sure I want to cry over him.'

'You don't have to cry,' said Jed. 'Jan probably wanted you to just get all the crap off your chest.'

She turned to him. 'But how will I ever find closure when I can't question him about his actions?'

Lizzie got comfy in her chair again. 'To be fair, love, liars like him wouldn't have told you the truth anyway.'

Colby nodded. 'Yeah, he would have come up with all sorts of cock and bull. Liars can't help themselves.'

Marisa agreed. 'He looked out for himself, Demi. If you had questioned him, he would have only continued to do so. Don't waste your energy on that.'

'I know it's hard,' said Jed, 'but Marisa's right. That sort of thing can drive a person mad.'

'Or make you ill with stress,' said Lizzie.

Demi nodded. 'Mostly, I'm okay, but I still have those moments where I wish I could yell at him. I lost so much because of him, and I want him to be held accountable.'

'That's understandable,' said Robson.

'Do you speak to the other wife at all?' asked Colby.

'No. I only saw her that one time. I don't want anything to do with her. She took my home, helped ruin my life, and didn't look too bothered about it either.' Demi took a deep breath.

'Wait,' said Colby. 'Rewind. What do you mean she took your home?'

'It was Terry's place, and we never bothered to add my name. Didn't think about it. We were married, raising Jade together, everything seemed normal and happy enough. I had my own inheritance after my parents passed away, and I did suggest at the time we use the money to buy a bigger property, not that we needed one, but he said he was happy where we were, and so was Jade.'

'And did the first wife get that too?' asked Colby.

Demi shook her head. 'No, because it was mine, in my bank. But as his wife, she inherited his house and any savings he had. Basically, she took the lot, and I moved in with my brother, as I was still healing.'

Silence filled the church hall for a moment, and Demi knew they were at a loss for words. It wasn't the easiest background to process.

'So, that's my story,' she added. 'I can grieve for my parents, they died of cancer, and for Ray, but with Terry, I'm just stuck.'

'Hmm,' mumbled Lizzie. 'I'm not so sure, girlie. I think you opening up about it now has shifted something. It's just a matter of time before you get the closure you need.' She waggled a finger around the circle. 'The thing with these groups is people don't often know how to express themselves, so hold it all inside. When they come to something like this, they feel they have the space to breathe because they're surrounded by others who also don't know how they're supposed to be feeling. That's why we just talk.'

'Get it out there,' said Colby.

'There are no rules,' said Jed.

Lizzie offered some more pink wafers. 'We are all just winging it, love.'

In all fairness, Demi did feel a little lighter now she'd shared her story. Normally at meetings she'd just talk about addiction-related subjects, and Terry was shoved to the back burner. Perhaps Jan had been right to push her into this group. She had no idea if talking about her so-called husband would make too much of a difference, but she'd spoken of him now, so at least the first step was completed.

Jed stood. 'I'm going to make us some tea.'

Demi watched him head off to the side room, with Lizzie following him to help. Then Marisa popped to the loo, and Colby went outside to make a quick call, leaving her alone with Robson, who offered a warm smile.

'You okay?' he asked quietly.

'I think so. It's weird saying it all out loud. I wish I could just pretend it never happened. That it was a chapter of my life I could just burn.'

'We all deal with grief in different ways.'

'It's not the grief. It's the anger. He wasted years of my life. I could have been in a relationship with someone who actually loved me, and only me. I don't want to feel that way, so it works better for me if I act like he didn't exist.'

Robson moved to the chair at her side and took her hand. 'Cutting all ties and sweeping things under the rug are two different things. One is closure, the other lies dormant, waiting to pounce when you least expect it. You need to make sure you deal with your past in a healthy way. That's how you move on. Well, it's how we try our best to cope with the trauma.'

Demi agreed. She'd heard Jan say something similar often enough. 'When I was in prison, they had this mentor group you could join. That's where I met Jan. The mentors would say all sorts of positive things to help ground the inmates, and a lot worked, but sometimes it doesn't matter what wise words a person says — it doesn't take away the pain.'

Robson gave her hand a gentle squeeze. 'Yeah, but we feel a bit better when we're not alone.'

She moved closer to him. 'You're not alone, Robson. I know our stories are so different, but it doesn't matter, we both still know pain, and I want you to know I'll always be here for you.' She had to move back, as she was sure she was about to kiss him to prove how much she cared.

His gaze fell to the floor. 'I'm here for you too,' he whispered.

CHAPTER 18

Robson

Robson sat on an ornate metal bench in the Gardens of Peace at the cemetery. Birds tweeted in nearby trees, and some perched at the edge of the small waterfall that washed down into a fish-filled pond. The heatwave had eased, but a warm breeze still blew, raking through his dark hair every so often.

He watched the golden fish, then stared over at the colourful blooms in the bedding around the winding pathways.

He'd sat in that spot many times since Leah died, and through all weathers. It never made a difference to how he felt. Calm, slightly sedated, alone.

'Hey, you,' said a voice, similar to Leah's.

Robson turned to see Leah's mum walking towards him. 'Hello, Pam.'

Pam sat by his side and kissed his cheek. 'We had a heatwave when she was born.'

Robson knew. He'd heard the story many times. He sat back and focused on the trickling water.

'Ernie's not feeling too good today, so he stayed home. He was hoping to plant another flower later for Leah.'

'Her birthday is never easy for him.'

Pam patted his hand. 'Nor the rest of us, son.'

Robson glanced her way. 'How have you been, Pam? I'm sorry I haven't been by in a while.'

'We're good, and there's no need for you to worry about us.'

He still felt bad for not popping in to see them this year. He used to visit all the time after Leah died, but then his visits became less frequent, as it was hard enough without being shown her old bedroom each time he was there. He often wondered why they had kept it untouched after she moved in with him, but he hadn't liked to say, and Leah loved taking him up to see her room whenever they visited her parents.

Just like he always said at the bereavement meetings, everyone had to deal with grief in their own way. Perhaps Pam and Ernie had grieved for their daughter in some way when she moved out.

'How are you getting on, son? Anything new happening in your life?'

He wondered if she'd heard about his lodger. But before he could reply, she took his hand.

'You're still young, Robson, and life is short, so don't think I would judge you for moving on with your life. I want you to. You deserve to be happy.'

'I haven't moved on,' he said simply, assuming her statement was to do with Demi.

Pam sat back and pulled out a small pot of bird seed from her beige handbag. She poured some into Robson's hand, then started to feed the sparrows. 'Leah was in my dream last night. Smiling.'

Robson dipped his head, shading his eyes from the sun. 'She was a big smiler.'

'You made her smile, son. She had a good life with you. Me and Ernie are always grateful for that.'

'She gave me a good life too.'

They continued to sprinkle small amounts of seeds over by the pathway closest to them.

'She saved someone recently, you know.'

Robson tilted his head. 'How so?'

'Lady at bingo said her daughter found a lump in her breast but wasn't going to get it checked out, so I told her the same thing happened to my Leah and what happened because of her not getting it sorted.' She shook her head a touch. 'Doesn't matter how old you are, you check these things out. Her girl's young too, see. They think breast cancer just affects women my age. Anyway, after hearing about Leah getting it in her twenties, they went and got her the mammogram, and she's getting treatment now. Caught it early. She should be just fine.'

Robson inhaled deeply. There were so many times when he wished Leah had told him about her lump. They could have caught it early.

A sparrow landed on the arm of the bench, close to his elbow. It was looking at him, then his hand, so he opened his palm and the little bird pecked at the seeds, then flew away as Pam turned to see.

'How long you been here?' asked Pam.

'About half an hour.'

'I won't hang around today. I don't want to leave Ernie alone too long. I'll help him in the garden when I get back. We'll have some ice-cold lemonade.'

Robson smiled. Leah's favourite drink.

'Holly's getting married this August.' She scoffed. 'Yeah, I was surprised too when I found out there was someone in this world that would take her on. I know she's my niece, but still. Horrible mare. Oh well, there's someone for everyone they say.'

He tried not to laugh. Pam was never one to mince her words.

'Might be you again one day, son.'

He mentally rolled his eyes. 'You've heard I've got a lodger, I take it?'

'Lodger, is it?'

'Uh-huh.'

'All going well?'

He threw the rest of the seeds down. 'She's just my lodger, Pam.'

Pam raised her hand. 'Not my business, son. As long as you're happy.'

He was, but it still felt awkward saying it out loud at times. How could he ever love anyone again? How would that be fair?

'Leah would want you to be happy,' she added.

'I know.'

'Tell me how the Hub is going.'

A much better subject, he thought. 'Great. It's really took off for such a small community. We didn't realise so many people would appreciate all the help on offer.'

They continued to talk about the Happy to Help Hub, Ginny's surprise baby shower later that day, and any other gossip in Port Berry until it was time for them to part ways, and no doubt not see each other again until Leah's next birthday, as Robson wasn't keen on commemorating the day she passed away.

The memory would never leave him. Lying on their bed, holding her hand, hoping she could hear the song he gently sang close to her ear. Their wedding song. Watching her fall into her forever sleep. No, that wasn't a day he would sit in stillness with. Just her birthday. Something she loved to celebrate.

* * *

As Robson and Demi arrived at Happy Farm for the barbeque Will had planned, plus Ginny's secret baby shower, he still felt peaceful, as though the world had a volume button and it was switched to low.

Demi had clearly picked up on his quiet mood, as she asked him if he was okay on their bus ride over. She looked to be still checking on him now, even though he'd said he was just a bit tired.

Robson gestured at the cake box he held. 'I really hope this is still in one piece.'

Demi laughed, then peered in the box to check on her creation. 'All good.' She knocked on the door, and Will answered.

'Ooh, what you got there?' he asked.

'Baby shower cake,' replied Robson. 'Surprise.' He laughed as he entered the hallway.

Will motioned towards the kitchen. 'That explains why Lottie brought so many flowers. I just thought they were the ones about to die at the shop, not that they look half-dead.'

Robson followed him to the kitchen. 'She didn't say?'

'No, I was waiting for everyone to arrive,' said Lottie, frowning at him.

Robson placed the box on the table, then stepped back so Demi could arrange the cake. 'Oops, sorry.'

Ginny welled up. 'Oh, bless you all. You didn't have to make all this fuss.'

Spencer put his arm around her. 'Of course we did.' He kissed her cheek, then pointed at the presents on the table. 'We wanted to buy baby gifts anyway.'

Ginny sat close by them. 'Ooh, can I open them now?'

'No,' said Lottie. 'You'll just have to wait till everyone is here.'

There was a knock at the door.

'Speaking of which,' said Will, going off to let in more guests.

Robson greeted Sophie, Matt, and Jed, along with Alice, Lizzie, and Luna.

'Benny's out with his mates,' said Alice.

Ginny smiled. 'Oh, that's okay. I can't expect a teenage lad to want to attend my baby shower.'

Sophie frowned at Lottie. 'You could have waited till we all got here before telling her.'

Lottie threw a hand out towards Robson. 'It wasn't me.'

Robson chuckled. 'I had the cake.'

Everyone praised Demi for her cake-decorating skills, loving the shape of the baby bonnet, and Ginny said they'd have it for dessert.

Sophie surrounded Ginny with presents, and Robson stood over by the back door while Ginny and Will unwrapped the gifts, which had everyone oohing and ahhing with delight.

Demi approached his side. 'Do you fancy a drink? There's some on the side there.'

'I'll have a lemonade in a minute. Just enjoying the warm evening breeze over here.'

'It is a lovely evening.'

'Do you reckon you could live on a farm?'

Demi breathed out a small laugh. 'After being in prison, I reckon I can live anywhere.'

Robson lowered his head closer to her. 'I'm glad you're not in there now.'

She met his eyes and smiled. 'Me too. And, just for the record, I prefer a sea view now I have one.'

'Right, I'm firing up the barbeque,' announced Will, heading for the back door, now that all the presents had been opened.

The gathering parted, with some going outside and others mooching in the kitchen or needing the loo.

Robson went to the fence that kept the hens secure. He leaned on the wooden top of the enclosure and stared over at the field across the way. Yep, he would definitely miss having a sea view if he moved from the harbour.

Demi joined his side, and they stood in companionable silence for a while.

It was nice at the farm, and the smell of the smoky barbeque wafting in the air made Robson smile to himself.

'It's Leah's birthday today,' he said quietly. He felt Demi's arm press against his, but he didn't look down.

'Tell me what you need.'

He tilted his head her way. 'I'm okay,' he said softly. 'But thanks.'

'Would you like to be on your own for a bit?'

'No. Your company's fine.'

Demi smiled and nudged him. 'Don't let the others hear you say that.'

He peered over at Will holding court at the barbeque. 'I'll mingle in a minute. It's just nice being over here. Feels like I'm in the middle of nowhere.'

'Sometimes, that's all you need.'

He nodded. 'That's why I go sit at the end of the pier during the night at times. It's just an empty world.' He met her eyes. 'I don't mean that in a depressing way. I just feel all worries slip away when I'm surrounded by space.'

'There's certainly a lot of space out at sea.'

Sophie came up behind them, carrying a couple of glasses of lemonade. 'Hey, you two.'

Demi said hi, then excused herself, saying she was going to help in the kitchen, but Robson wondered if she was giving him some space with his friend.

Sophie handed Robson a drink, then gave him a hug. 'Here's to Leah.' She chinked glasses with him, then raised her toast to the orange-streaked evening sky. 'To our school days and all the days.'

Spencer, Lottie, Alice, and Ginny came over, creating a semi-circle around Robson and raising their own drinks.

'We're still looking after him, chick,' said Ginny to the sky.

With everything going on, Robson wasn't sure his friends had remembered it was Leah's birthday, but as usual, they were there for him, and it warmed his heart no end.

'And you know what Leah would say right about now?' said Lottie. 'Put the music on.'

Robson laughed. It was true. Leah loved to dance.

'I'll sort it,' said Alice, skipping off to the kitchen.

Within moments, the music pumped, Sophie twirled Robson in her arms, and the quietness of the farm was over.

Everyone soon settled in for the evening, drinking, dancing, enjoying the party food and Demi's cake.

It was a couple of hours before Robson found himself alone with Demi again. She was staring down into the large metal firepit that crackled away, ready to warm anyone wanting to sit close by.

The barbeque had long died, so the fire, patio lamps, and citronella candles gave most of the light out back.

For a moment, he simply watched the golden glow on Demi's face, highlighting her raised cheekbones and full lips.

She sat on one of the padded seats, and he sat down on a chair at her side.

'Hey, how you doing?' she asked quietly.

'Almost ready for bed but tempted to sleep right here.'

She snorted a laugh. 'I know what you mean.'

Robson snuggled further into the chair. 'Let's be really quiet, then Ginny will forget we're out here.'

Demi laughed, then after a moment of silence, she said, 'I'm glad I met you, Robson. You and your friends. It's a nice circle you have.'

He closed his eyes and smiled at her warm words. She was quite the inspiration, always pushing forward, rebuilding her life. Perhaps it was time for him to let the past rest and focus on the future as well. 'I'm glad I met you, too.'

CHAPTER 19

Demi

All week, Demi had been rushed off her feet. The Jolly Pirate was down three bar staff and two in the kitchen, all with the summer flu that was doing its rounds. She hardly had time to talk to Jade, not that it mattered, as the last phone call she'd made lasted all of five minutes, as Jade was off out with her friends.

Demi and Joseph were the last to leave the kitchen, meeting the senior bartender, Geoff, by the front doors.

'You locking up tonight, Geoff?' asked Joseph.

Demi glanced around the pub as Geoff nodded his reply. 'Where's Robson?'

'He was feeling rough, so I said I'd sort things. I'll probably open up in the morning as well, judging by the state of him when he left.' Geoff's dark eyes flashed her way. 'I'll give the keys to you if you're going straight up.'

'Yes, that's fine.'

Geoff thumbed to the bar. 'I'll just set the alarm, unless Rob's taught you what to do.'

Demi shook her head. 'No. Best you do it all. You're his right-hand man. He hasn't told me the code.'

'Right you are then. You two wait outside.'

Demi smiled at Joseph as he stepped back for her to leave first.

'Let's hope no one else catches this flu. August is our busiest month,' he said as they entered the beer garden. 'We'll have to close the kitchen.' He raised his brow at her. 'Unless you think you can manage with just me.'

'I'm sure we can manage. We'll just reduce the menu until we're fully staffed again.'

'Hmm, not a bad plan.'

'Right,' said Geoff, coming over to join them. 'Send me a text in the morning if you definitely need me to set up, and if so, make sure you meet me here on time. The cleaners have to be let in before we open to the public.'

She knew the routine but simply nodded and took the keys from him.

'Night,' he said, strolling away.

Joseph gave her a slight nod, then went on his way too.

Demi hoped Robson was okay. In the short time she'd known him, it wasn't like him not to lock up himself. She did think he looked a bit peaky that morning, and he didn't go for his usual early run.

Coughing was the first thing she heard as she climbed the stairs.

Robson was lying on the sofa, one arm draped to the floor, the other flopped over his head that she could see was sweaty even from where she stood in the kitchen.

She put the keys in the drawer where he always stashed them, then went to feel his forehead.

Robson groaned.

'Jeez, you're burning up. Have you taken any paracetamol?'

'No,' he mumbled. 'I sat here, and now I can't move.'

'Hmm, well, we'll see about that. You need to be in bed.'

'My legs won't make it.'

Demi left him alone for a minute while she went to fetch some medicine and a glass of water. 'Here.' She just about managed to get some pills down his throat, as he wasn't exactly helping.

'Thanks,' he mumbled, flopping his head back down immediately after.

For the first time ever, Demi went into his bedroom. It felt weird being in his private domain, but she needed to prep his bed and sort some pyjamas, as she knew he'd be staying in there for the next few days, at the least.

A blue tee shirt and shorts were already crumpled at the bottom of the bed, so she pulled back the covers, then moved the nightwear to a nearby wicker chair.

Demi took a deep breath, gaining strength, as it was time to shift his weight from the sofa to his bed, and seeing how weak he looked, she knew she'd have her work cut out for her.

Poor Robson, he looked so pale and lifeless. She hoped the medication would lower his temperature soon. He started shivering, so she quickly moved in on him.

'Let's get you into bed. Come on.' She placed her arms around him and heaved, but it was like trying to shift a deadweight.

'I'll die here,' he muttered.

'No, you won't.' She tugged once more. 'Help me, Robson.'

He swung his legs off the sofa, and clasped his head as he leaned on her.

Demi inhaled deeply, then practically dragged him to his room, where they both slumped on the bed. Catching her breath, she wriggled free of his body squashing her, then brought over his PJs, wondering how she would play her next move.

Robson went to curl up in bed.

'Not yet.' Pulling him up a touch, she tugged off his top, then replaced it with his nightwear. At least that was the top half done. 'Erm, get those bottoms off and put on these shorts.'

He faffed about with his belt for so long, Demi got frustrated and bent to help, then stood back as he started rolling down his bottoms.

She turned, giving him some privacy and picked at a fingernail while she waited for sounds telling her the task was complete.

'Done,' he croaked, then coughed.

She tucked him in, then opened the window a touch, as fresh air was needed in the room.

He was still shivering, but hot to touch, so she whipped up his clothes for the washing machine, then brought a cool flannel for his head.

Robson sighed as she placed the damp cloth over his sweaty brow.

She checked the time, making a mental note of when he could have some more medication. She thought it best to write it down and place it by his bed with the pills and some water.

'The pub,' he mumbled on her return. He tried to get up, but she gently put him back into place.

'The pub is fine. Get some sleep.'

He seemed to settle, and his shivering wore off a little, so she went to get her own PJs on and make some tea. There was no way he was going to consume anything other than water, so she didn't bother trying. Her mum had taught her to feed a cold but starve a fever.

Demi gathered a blanket, book, and her tea, and made herself comfy in the wicker chair in his room, thinking she could just sit with him for a couple of hours before heading to bed.

The light scent of sea salt filled the air along with the cry of a seagull, stirring Demi from her sleep. It took a moment for her to realise where she was. Stretching her stiff back from snoozing in a chair all night, she peered over at the sickbed.

Robson sounded wheezy with every slow and steady breath, but at least he was sleeping.

She picked up the flannel that had fallen on the floor at some point during the night, and took it with her to the bathroom.

After a quick shower, she checked on Robson, who was still out for the count. So she refreshed his water and brought in a clean flannel, ready for when he woke, as she didn't want to disturb him.

A text message told her Joseph was closing the kitchen for a couple of days, as more people had called in sick, and he didn't feel too good himself.

Just for a moment, she pondered over the idea of running the show by herself, but it wouldn't be as easy as taking on the kitchen at the B&B. The pub restaurant held way more covers, but perhaps she could get in there and rustle up some lunchtime sandwiches to serve with crisps and salad.

She was already writing out the sign to let the customers know as she made her way to the main doors to meet Geoff, who, thankfully, was fit and well.

'Joseph messaged me,' he said, taking the keys from her. 'More kitchen staff down, but the bartenders are good, so perhaps we'll sell a few more crisps.'

'About that. I'm going to open the kitchen just for lunch, put up a sign letting the punters know the only choices we have are sandwiches, then I can easily plate up some chunky bread, crisps, and salad. All I'll need is one of your lot to serve.'

Geoff nodded. 'Yeah, that'll work. I can help with that too.'

Demi sighed with relief. 'Right, I'll just nip back upstairs to check on Robson while you sort the cleaners, then I'll be back to prep for lunch.'

It was better than nothing, and when she texted Joseph for his thoughts, he'd agreed, telling her to add a Ploughman's to her menu.

That she could handle in her sleep, she was sure.

Robson was awake, barely, so she got some more medicine in him, then placed a cool flannel on his hot head.

'I'm just going to prep some food, then I'll be right back.' She wondered if she should bring in a bucket in case he needed to pee and didn't have the strength to make it to the bathroom. He looked so poorly. She was sure any movement would be a struggle.

Placing a mop bucket by Robson's bed, just in case, she went back to the pub to see that Geoff had already put a box of ready-salted crisps in the kitchen. A batch of prawn cocktail needed to be made, and salad chopped, so she quickly checked the fridge and freezer for supplies. Luckily enough, there was plenty of cheese and ham, but not enough prawns.

'Robson gets the seafood from Sea Shanty Shack,' Geoff told her, peering over her shoulder at the lack of prawns. 'He has a tab at the shop. Just explain to Sophie what's going on here. It'll be okay.'

Demi had never been in charge of securing supplies. She headed for the fishmongers, pleased to see Sophie's shop already open.

'Hello, what can I do for you this early?' asked Sophie, all smiles.

'Robson's got the summer flu that's going around, and half the pub staff is down with it as well, including Joseph, so I'm going to put on a sandwich-only lunch menu for the next few days, but I'm out of prawns, and prawn cocktail slapped between crusty bread always goes down well with customers.

'I'll just get you some. I'll put it on Robson's tab.' She handed over a couple of large bags of peeled prawns. 'How bad is he?'

'Early days. He'll be in bed awhile. I just hope the staff come back soon. We've had some off all week, so they should start feeling better soon enough.'

Sophie gestured at the door. 'I'll pop in at lunch and help out.'

'Oh, I couldn't take you away from your shop.'

'Matt and Grandad will be here.'

Demi nodded her appreciation. 'Thank you. It would be helpful to have more hands serving.'

'Yep, I can do that.'

'Okay, I'll see you later.' Demi practically skipped out the door. How kind was that of Sophie to offer.

Little did she know that by lunchtime, Alice would be serving too, having got wind of the dilemma at the pub.

Demi's heart warmed at the love on show for Robson's business, and at least not all takings were down, thanks to the sandwiches on offer.

Robson hadn't moved much each time Demi checked on him throughout the day. He was still burning up after closing time, and he'd mentioned something about his mum a couple of times.

Demi knew his fever had him mumbling, so she ignored most of what she could make out. If his temperature didn't come down by morning, she had already decided she'd call 111 for advice.

A text message from Joseph's wife came through as Demi brought Robson some more fresh water for the night. By all accounts, Joseph was being a pain in her backside. It did make Demi laugh. She could just see Joseph refusing to stay in bed, even with flu. Somehow, through his shivering and hot flushes, he'd managed to arrange for a head-chef friend of his to take charge of the kitchen for a week and bring two members of his team with him, so that was a load off. The only problem was, they wouldn't be able to start till the day after tomorrow.

'Oh, well, that's okay.' The sandwich menu would live on.

She relayed the message to Robson, but his reply was just a coughing fit and one watery eye peeking her way for just a second.

Demi decided to make him some lemon and honey. Even a few sips should help.

All Robson wanted to do was sleep, so once more, she snuggled into the wicker chair by his bedside for the night, breathing in the cool breeze from the nearby window. At least her sinuses were clear. She just hoped they stayed that way.

CHAPTER 20

Robson

Robson sure had appreciated Demi setting up a doctor's phone call appointment for him, as he hadn't felt strong enough to get washed and dressed, let alone make the journey to the surgery, especially with his chest playing up. It was hard enough getting his legs to work to take him to the toilet all week, and there was no way he was using the bucket Demi had left out for him. He'd rather crawl — and quite often had.

The antibiotics for his chest infection were welcome, as he was certain he'd bruised a rib from coughing, and as he could finally eat again now the flu symptoms had passed, the small amounts of food Demi was supplying were slowly helping to rebuild his energy.

'Here, take these vitamins,' she said, giving him more pills to wash down.

'How's it going downstairs?'

'It's been running like clockwork all week, and Joseph reckons he'll be back in a couple of days. Not sure he was as ill as you. It didn't go to his chest.'

'He's too stubborn for germs to get one over on him.' He laughed, but it choked him, and Demi had water at his lips before he had a chance to recover.

'Most of the staff are back now. Shouldn't be too long before you can go down.'

'Perhaps tomorrow.' Neither of them looked convinced about that, but he smiled anyway.

'I'll make us a chicken stew in a bit. That'll see you right.'

'Thanks for looking after me, Dem.'

She turned and smiled. 'That's okay. You'd do the same for me.'

He nodded a little too dramatically. 'I would.'

She went to his medication notes to check the times, then placed a cool hand on his forehead.

Robson didn't mean to sigh out loud, but her light touch was so soothing, he melted slightly as he rested his head back to a plump pillow.

'It's good to see that temperature has gone. You had me worried for a while, you were that hot.'

With his eyes still closed, he smiled. 'Got to love flu.'

'Hmm.'

He peeked at her as she backed away. 'I think I'll brave the shower. I'm sure my pyjamas want to escape to the washing machine.'

'Ooh, well, if you feel strong enough for that now, I'll pop your bedding in the machine as well.' Demi looked to the wardrobe. 'Do you have any spare sheets?'

'Draw under the bed.'

'Great. You won't have to wait for it to dry.'

Robson plopped his feet on the floor. Perhaps a short lukewarm shower would be best. He was a little light-headed from going a week without food. He hated feeling so weak but understood rebuilding would take a few days.

Demi stepped to his side. 'Do you need some help?'

'What, in the shower?' He knew she didn't mean that but said it anyway to make her laugh.

'If you need your toenails scrubbing, I'm hiring a carer.'

'Good to know where you stand when it comes to the nitty-gritty.'

Demi chuckled. 'Go and freshen up. Go on.'

What a chore it was having a thorough clean while in need of a lie down, but somehow he muddled through and certainly felt better for it, especially after finally brushing his teeth.

By the time Robson plodded out of the bathroom, Demi had put some fresh bed covers on his bed, sprayed his room with some sort of disinfectant, and put a pan of chicken stew on the stove. He couldn't help but feel grateful and a little touched by how much care she offered.

'Ooh, you look better, if not a little flushed.' Demi waved him to a kitchen chair. 'Sit down a minute. I'll get you some water.'

He headed for his bedroom. 'I'll just get back in bed, if that's okay.'

'Sure, go on. I'll bring your drink in. Won't be a sec.'

Robson felt himself melt into the fresh bedding, grateful for the clean feeling and to take the weight off.

Demi came in and gave him a glass of cold water, which he quickly gulped. 'That took it out of you, didn't it?'

'Just a bit, but it's nice to feel half-human again.'

'You'll have more strength tomorrow.'

'Hope so. I miss jogging so much.'

Demi shook her head as she went to gaze out the window. 'You do like your exercise.'

'Not really.' As soon as the words left his mouth he realised how pitiful he sounded, and he was far too weary to fake a smile.

Demi turned, concern in her eyes. 'I just assumed you liked running. You always look happy when you return.'

'It lifts me, that's why, but given the choice, I'd rather not do anything.'

She pointed at his bed. 'May I sit there?'

He patted the pillow to his side. 'Come and relax your back. You've exercised enough for us both this week.'

She smiled as she climbed on the bed and sat by his side, propping the plump pillow behind her back. 'Busier than usual, but I'm okay. It was fun when I had the kitchen to myself for all of two days. I feel ready to work with Alice now.'

'Well, that's one plus, I guess.'

'It's been a hectic week, we all managed, even you with staying put.'

He raised his brows. 'I did try to pull myself together, but flu said nope, and I'm not sure what my chest had to say, but it wasn't good.'

She chuckled. 'Yes, I noticed. That was the reason I called the doctor.'

'I'll give it a couple more days, then see if I can run a little. Take Alice round the block with me, as she can normally manage that in the summer.'

'I can understand why Alice tries to exercise when she can, what with her having fibromyalgia, but why are you pushing yourself?'

He slumped into himself, not sure whether to say. There was loads of private things he knew about Demi now, seeing how she had opened up to him and their group. It seemed fair he told his own truth, and he felt safe to do so to her. If anyone would understand his troubles and woes, it would be her.

'You don't have to talk, Robson. I can see you don't want to.'

He glanced her way. 'I want to tell you.'

Her smile was soft. Friendly. 'What is it?'

'I suffer with depression, but I'm doing okay. It hasn't really bothered with me too much this year, and last year I was a lot better, but when it first struck, I was bad for quite some time.'

Demi touched his little finger, then clasped her hands on her lap. 'Grief is so hard, Robson. No wonder it did that to you.'

He shook his head. 'It wasn't Leah's death that caused my depression. It was before I got together with her.' He inhaled deeply, then carried on. 'When I was twenty-five, my uncle told me the truth about why my mum had left.'

'Hadn't you asked before?'

'Yes, when I was young. I was told she didn't want kids, as she wanted to travel the world, so she thought I'd be better off with them.'

'So what made him change the story?'

'He said he'd always planned to tell me when he thought I was old enough to handle the truth. He often worried I might find out somehow so wanted the story to come from him.' Robson pressed his head back into the pillow. 'It wasn't easy for him. He had no idea what to tell me when I first started asking. He did consider saying she was dead but couldn't bring himself to say that about his sister.'

'Sounds like he was left with a heavy weight.'

Robson nodded. It took a few days to process at the time, but in the end, he knew his uncle only did what he thought best.

'He could have raised you to believe he was your father and your aunt your mum.'

'They knew the locals would know the truth. My mum had been seen pregnant. They did consider moving, but this was their home, so they just got on with it, and their friends never raised the subject.'

'It seems to me your uncle could have carried on that way forever, but something about it niggled away at him.' Demi sighed. 'I guess nothing about Terry's situation weighed on him.'

'Some people don't carry guilt. My uncle just thought I had a right to know everything about my own life.'

Demi nodded. 'One of the things that angers me most about Terry, is that he hid part of my life from me, like he had that right, and no one has that right. I can totally see where your uncle was coming from.'

Robson could too, especially when he had heard the truth. What a terrible secret for his uncle to carry. The man never said, but it must have been such a relief to unload the burden, no matter how hard.

'Are you sure you want to share this with me, Robson?'

He slowly bobbed his head. 'The real reason my mother had nothing to do with me was because she couldn't bear to look at my face.'

Demi glanced at him.

He looked back. 'She was attacked one night, walking home. I'm the product of that night.' He heard Demi's voice hitch. 'She thought she could handle having me, but within weeks, she couldn't, so she left, telling my uncle she never wanted to see me or Port Berry again.'

'I'm so sorry, Robson.'

'She contacted him a couple of times over the years, just to let him know she was safe and well, but it took her a long time to rebuild her life. She never asked about me, and he wasn't allowed to show her any photos, even though he assured her I looked like their side of the family.'

'Did they catch the attacker?'

'No. She didn't report it. Said she had no clue who he was anyway, as he wore a balaclava, so all she could see were dark eyes.'

'Jeez, that poor woman.'

Robson nodded. 'My uncle said it affected her badly. She was nervous around people and only went out if he was with her. There was talk of termination, then adoption, but in the end it was me who stayed and she left the family instead.'

'Have you ever thought about contacting her?'

'She's dead now. Died a few years back, brain tumour.'

Demi took his hand. 'Oh, Robson. I'm so sorry.'

'So that's when the depression started. I felt sick to my core that I came from such evil. I went through a stage where I worried I would turn out like him, then I kept thinking he could be someone who came in the pub every day, and little by little, my self-worth crumbled, my confidence disappeared, and I spent a couple of years just feeling numb.'

'Did your uncle and aunt get you some therapy?'

He gave her hand a light squeeze. 'Yep. Been there, done that. I wouldn't take any medication, and that's when my uncle came up with the suggestion of exercise to see if it would help, as he'd read it would, so I took up running.'

'And you've been doing it ever since.'

'It works. So does therapy.' He met her eyes. 'I still have some from time to time, but in all honesty, getting together with Leah helped. The love I felt for her showed me I did have love inside me, because I had convinced myself I wasn't made of any, so how could I possess any?'

'Oh, I see lots of love in you, if my view counts for anything.'

He smiled softly. 'Thanks. It's okay, I know I'm not a monster like him. That was sorted with therapy. But it was a long hard road.'

'You have to remember that none of us are our parents. We're all just us. Whoever that piece of shit was, that's certainly not who you are. Not one ounce of him is in you. You are kind and generous, thoughtful and friendly. Robson, you're the best friend I've ever had.'

Her words smacked him straight in the heart, bringing a lump to his throat and a tear to his eye. He blinked hard, hoping he could disguise his emotions and put it down to tiredness from the dregs of influenza.

He slid down further beneath the covers, taking her hand with him, holding it close to his chest. 'Thanks,' he mumbled, finding words hard.

Demi shifted to his side, simply staring into his eyes. 'Get some sleep,' she whispered. 'Dinner will be ready when you wake.'

He didn't want to close his eyes, even though he was tired. Witnessing the kindness on her face was soothing enough. 'Not many know my story,' he said quietly.

'I won't tell.' Her voice was just as soft.

'Sometimes I still don't know how I should feel.'

'Just remember who you are.' Her eyes held a warm smile.

'Thanks for listening.'

'I'll listen anytime, and when the depression hits, you tell me what to do. If you just need me to sit with you and say nothing, I will. Whatever you want. Just know I'm here. I'll always be right here.'

He closed his eyes, repeating her words in his head, focusing on the gentle tones, the meaning behind her eyes. They knew each other's truths now. All the grit and grime. And somehow, through it all, they'd both survived.

CHAPTER 21

Demi

Demi huffed as she read the text message from Alana telling her not to bother coming around, as Jade was in bed with flu. Fat lot of good that was to Demi, who was already on the bus, halfway there.

Typical of Alana to leave it to the last minute, and she probably wouldn't have said anything if Demi wasn't due for a visit.

Sometimes Demi felt she was back in prison, what with all the rules and visiting times. Alana and Colin had instructions and lists, and God forbid Demi went off-road.

She turned to the window and sighed onto the glass. It was only the rolling hills and wild meadows maintaining her peace. At least Robson had been back on his feet the last few days. It was good to see him looking healthy again. She hoped Jade wasn't in bed too long with the illness.

She understood Jade had little trust in her, but she hoped with time that would change. They had made some progress, it was just slow. Still, it was better than nothing, as she hadn't seen her daughter at all when she was in prison, not wanting Jade in such a place, and Colin had agreed.

Demi's mind drifted to those days. Locked up, feeling beat up, and ever so alone. Often baffled as to how her life had ended up that way. Worried she'd never recover all she'd lost, which was mostly herself.

If it wasn't for the help she'd received, the likes of Jan and The Butterfly Company, she dreaded to think where she might be.

She put her phone away, ready to get off at the next stop to head home, but then she remembered wanting to visit the Sunshine Centre to discuss hosting the odd cooking class as a form of therapy, perhaps.

Demi shuffled back into the seat, deciding today was the day she tried to be a helper.

It wasn't long before she'd arrived at the centre. The big colourful flowers painted on its white-washed walls brought a smile to her face immediately, and the wide lilac door looked even more welcoming. The front garden held an array of raised flowerbeds and large metal ornaments in the shape of ladybirds, hedgehogs, and hummingbirds. It really was a splendid sight, and she could see just from the driveway how appealing everything was.

Demi stepped inside, inhaling the scent of freshly baked bread. The kitchen was in good use already, and she wanted to follow the smell and join in with the cooks, but she figured her best bet would be to knock on the office door, rather than wander around without a pass or something.

Before she had a chance to approach, the door swung open, and out walked a middle-aged woman. 'Hi, I'm Debra. How may I help?'

It was then that Demi noticed the camera over the back of the reception area spying on her.

'Hi, I'm Demi Carter. I was wondering if you had a minute for a chat.'

Debra flashed a wide smile. 'You're Robson's friend, right? Chef at the Jolly Pirate?'

Demi nodded. 'That's right. He told you about me?'

'No. Word gets around. So, what can I do for you, Demi?'

'I was wondering if I could volunteer my services as a chef. I was thinking perhaps I could host a cooking class once a month, as it's something that helps my mental health.'

'Oh, wow, yes, that sounds like something I could look into.'

'I need to let you know straight away that I do have a criminal record for theft. That's all in my past, but you have to know, as I heard children also come here, and DBS checks are needed, not that I'm asking to work with them. I had my mind set on adults. If I'm allowed, I propose simple, quick meals.' She tapped her handbag. 'I can show you some examples on my phone.'

'Come into my office so we can talk in more detail.' Debra waved her forward. 'I'll have to do an assessment, and because we have vulnerable adults here, yes, you will still need to go through a DBS check, but mostly these things depend on the seriousness of the crime.'

Demi took the seat offered, got comfortable, and explained her past. 'So, you see, I really want to give something back. I never thought much about what was happening outside my own life before it got turned upside down, and now I can see there are so many people out there willing to help others when the going gets tough. I want to be like them. I want to try to make a difference, plus it helps me too.'

Debra thoroughly understood and was happy to delve deeper into the proposition.

Before long, Demi was back in the fresh air, pleased with how her unplanned interview went. Heading for the bus stop she took in the now overcast sky. She hadn't brought a brolly and hoped it didn't rain, although she couldn't see the plants being in agreement. The heatwave had left the ground parched.

'Hello, love,' said Luna, plonking herself down on the seat in the bus stop's shelter. 'We've got to stop meeting like this.'

Demi snorted a laugh. 'You're my bus buddy.'

'Seems that way.' Luna offered a mint, which Demi took.

The bus pulled up, so they got on, grabbing a seat next to each other.

'You going straight home?' asked Luna.

'Yes. I was supposed to see my daughter today, but she's got that summer flu that's doing the rounds.'

Luna sucked on her mint, making a slurping noise. 'So, you've been out for a wander instead?'

'I popped in to the Sunshine Centre to see if I could become a volunteer.'

'They do great work with people there. When do you start?'

Demi folded her hands on her lap as she sighed. 'I have to wait till I get the all-clear from one of those police checks.' She shook her head a touch. 'Sometimes I feel like I'll be haunted forever by my past.'

'It'll fade, love. The past has a habit of doing that.'

Demi faced her. 'Not sure about that. Not a day has gone by yet where my ex hasn't popped into my head. Not in any good way. Just . . . I don't know.'

'That's because you haven't let go yet. I know your story. I know what you're doing wrong.'

Demi bit back a laugh. 'Well, I'm all ears.'

'You just need to put it to bed, love.'

'If you're talking about closure, I'll never have that. Terry's dead. It's not as though I can call him to have it out with him.' She looked up, then down, wondering where he might have ended up.

'Do you want me to try to communicate with him for you?'

Demi widened her eyes, not wanting to reveal amusement. But what if the old lady really could talk to the dead? Should she just have a row with him through her? Even though she'd had conversations with Terry over and over in her head, what would she really say to him if she had the chance? She glanced at Luna, sitting quietly.

The bus stopped to let two teenage girls on, and all eyes focused on them until they sat.

'I think talking to him would be pointless,' Demi whispered. She was sure Luna's mouth quirked for a second.

'Oh, and why's that?'

Demi shrugged. 'He was a liar. There's no point asking a liar a question.'

'But you have questions?'

'Loads.'

'You also have the answers.'

Demi shook her head. 'Not sure about that.'

'You want to know why he did that to you. What's the answer?'

'When I spoke about it at the bereavement meeting, the answer for everyone was, because he's selfish.'

Luna linked her fingers. 'That explains everything.'

It certainly did, and Demi had to admit that. She breathed out a small laugh. 'Is that my closure?'

'If you like. Unless you want me to intervene.'

And just like that, for the first time ever, Demi didn't want to talk to Terry.

'No, thanks. I actually think I'm done with him.'

'Makes sense. Liars aren't worth time nor effort.'

Demi mentally nodded. Luna was right. Terry didn't deserve any more of her energy. She had to laugh. Who knew it would take a bus ride with a psychic to finally figure that out?

The bus pulled up along Harbour End Road, and Demi and Luna parted ways, with Demi going down to the sea to sit with the boats for a while. She'd had an unexpected morning and just wanted to be alone for a bit before heading to the pub.

The waves were a tad rough, curling and slapping against the shore, and some seagulls perched along a wall, huddled into themselves as the breeze ruffled their feathers.

Demi enjoyed the light spits of seawater spraying up and hitting her face every so often. The salt in the air was familiar now. Home.

Was it all so simple? Just breathe. Forget. It seemed that way, because Demi hadn't felt so relaxed in such a long time. The harbour had her wrapped in the cosiest security blanket, inviting her to stay.

'Hiya,' said Matt, approaching the bench. 'You okay?'

Demi nodded and patted the seat. 'Yeah, I'm good. Come and join me. I'm just enjoying the view.'

Matt sat by her side. 'Bit gloomy out today, looks like rain is on the way, but I still love the view.'

'It's therapeutic, isn't it?'

'Yep. This whole place is. Brought me back to life.' He glanced her way as he bobbed his head. 'From the moment I stepped into the Happy to Help Hub, it was like an angel touched my shoulder and gave me a blessing.'

'You make it sound so magical.'

He smiled. 'Sophie and Jed are the magic to me. They gave me back my life.'

'Don't take away your own credit, Matt. Every day you fight to live. I know. I'm the same.'

'Yeah, I know, but it's so much easier when you're surrounded by love and support.' He sighed, resting back against the hard wood, hooking one foot over the other. 'My childhood wasn't all that, and being an adult didn't make anything better. I'd never had peace in my life, not real peace.' He thumbed behind them. 'But here, I'm just so settled, it amazes me half the time.'

Demi blew out a quiet laugh. 'Maybe Port Berry does hold magic.'

'You doing okay here?'

'Mostly. I have some family problems, that's all.'

Matt nodded. 'I cut all ties with mine. We never had much in the way of connection anyway, and a few months back I decided to contact my mum to let her know I was safe and happy, and getting hitched, but she just said "good luck to you", then hung up on me. So, that's me done.'

'Didn't that hurt you?'

'Nope. Used to it. Not sure why I even bothered, if I'm honest. I knew what was coming, but hey ho.'

Demi stared at the rolling waves, gaining height as they crashed against the end of the jetty. 'I feel like I'm the distant aunt in my family who only pops up at Christmas.'

Matt sat straighter and turned to her. 'You struggling, Demi?'

'I was, but I think I had some sort of epiphany today. When I first came out of prison, I thought things would go back to normal. Well, you know, as normal as normal can be. But I was wrong. My daughter had a new life. One that didn't include me, and she was happy. I've been trying to force my way in, but my family don't trust me.'

'Give it time. They'll see.'

'That's what I thought, but now I've decided to be the distant aunt they've made me. I'll show my daughter I'll be there if she needs me, but I'm not going to try to squeeze in the door anymore. It's too much, you know?'

Matt nodded. 'It's not just addiction we have to recover from. We can have family trauma too. That's why my life is so good with Sophie. She's my safe place.'

Robson sprung to mind. He gave her safety and peace. He carried the weight of his own demon, and yet, there he was, caring so much about others.

Matt cleared his throat as he pulled out his phone. 'Can I give you my number? I want you to know you can call me if you're ever struggling.'

Demi smiled. 'That's kind of you.'

'Do you have a sponsor?'

'Yeah. You?'

'Yep, but it doesn't hurt to have another friend close by who understands.'

She got her phone out and swapped numbers. 'And the recovery meetings at the church.'

'They're a godsend, eh?'

'I used to rely on them to get me through the week, but now I just like having somewhere to go where I'm not judged.'

'Hmm,' said Matt. 'You feel that from your family?'

'A bit.'

'And at work?'

Demi shook her head. 'No. Nowhere else. Work is just the same as before my life changed, but my circle since coming here has improved. I love Port Berry, and the people around here are the best.'

Matt chuckled. 'They certainly are.' He gave her elbow a gentle nudge. 'Hey, I'm glad you're doing okay.'

His soft words, filled with meaning, warmed her heart.

'I'm glad you're doing okay too.'

They shared a knowing smile, then Matt stood. 'Right, best get back to the shop.' He pointed up. 'Don't stick around too long. It's going to bucket down soon.'

She gave a small wave. 'I'll just have two more minutes.'

He said goodbye, and she watched him jog across the road before she turned back to the huddled seagulls.

Even though rain was on its way, she was relaxed on the bench, feeling at one with the scenery. Perhaps she could join in with the art classes at the Sunshine Centre, as it would be nice to paint something as beautiful as what she could see before her. So wild. So alive.

Demi inhaled the scent of the sea as she stood to move closer to the wall to take one last look at the fierce waves. The boats continued to bob, and the sky grew the darkest shade of grey, threatening to disturb her peacefulness any moment now.

A muffled sound mingled in with a whistle of the wind, gaining her attention.

She straightened, frowning, as she was sure she'd just heard a whimper. Turning to face the large birds on a break from scavenging, she heard the noise again, and it definitely wasn't them.

A car passed by behind, followed by a motorbike, then some people rushing to escape the impending downpour.

The whimper came again, and Demi followed the cry, leading her along the wall.

Peering over at the shingles, she gasped at the sorrowful sight before her.

Lying on its side was a scrawny light-grey-and-white dog, covered in old scars and dried blood. Its bones were visible through its thin, dishevelled coat, and its dark eyes were full of fear. The poor thing was shivering and whining.

Demi jumped the wall and slowly crouched close to the dog's narrow pointy nose. 'Hey, there. It's okay.' Her soothing words did nothing to calm the distressed animal.

She noticed it was a boy, and he looked far too sickly to have the strength to bite her, so she took a chance and reached out to the side of his neck, allowing him to see her hand approaching.

The dog's breathing was shallow at first, but it quickened as she touched him. He tried to lift his head, perhaps to get away, maybe to ask for help.

'It's okay,' she said gently. 'You're safe now.'

Whether or not he could sense she was kind, he didn't react, looking far too weak to do much at all.

Demi checked his limbs for breaks, and when she was sure she could move him, she whipped off her coat and placed it over his body. Taking a deep breath, she scooped her hands beneath him and managed to lift him into her arms.

Had he been well kept, he would've surely weighed too much for her to carry, but he was nothing but skin and bones, so she clambered back over the wall with ease.

It wasn't long before she had the quaking creature resting on Robson's sofa, hoping the comfort and warmth would soothe the poor thing a touch.

It didn't.

She quickly sent Robson a text, asking him to come upstairs as soon as possible, then she brought a small bowl of water to the dog, but he wouldn't drink.

'Chicken,' she said, mainly to herself, before picking some sliced pieces from the plate in the fridge.

The dog whimpered, not taking the food.

Demi dipped her finger in the water bowl, then traced the tip against his mouth to see if she could hydrate him somehow.

Heavy footsteps ran up the stairs, and Robson appeared in the kitchen.

'Demi, you okay?'

She waved him over. 'I'm okay. But look what I just found down by the sea.'

He rushed to her side, resting on his knees as he peered at the dog. 'Jeez, look at the state of it. Did it get run over?'

'I don't know. Looks more like neglect.' She pointed out a worn scar on his leg. 'I'm trying to get some water in him, but I think he's just too scared.'

'I just saw Neville downstairs with his cab. I'll run down and get him to take us to the vets.'

Demi blinked back tears. This was not the time to fall apart. This dog needed her to step up, so she sprinted upstairs to the cupboard along the landing and pulled out a large towel, thinking that would work better as a cover for the dog.

Robson was back in no time. 'I'll carry him. You lock up.'

Demi set the alarm at the flat, then hurried to the cab.

The ride to Lane's Vets didn't take too long, even with the rain pelting down.

Michael was just saying goodbye to a woman with a hamster, when they rushed in with the dog. He quickly gave the animal the once over, then took him out the back to be sedated for an X-ray and a scan. Demi had told him she'd pay for any care needed.

Demi and Robson sat in the waiting area, reading over leaflets, posters, and checking out the supplies on sale. Anything to fill the time.

'I don't understand how people can treat animals so badly. First the dumped kittens, and now that poor thing.' She stabbed a finger in the direction of the surgery's door.

'Happens more than you'd think,' said Michael, coming out of another doorway.

Demi jumped up. 'How's he doing?'

'Nothing broken. No internal bleeding. More malnutrition. Looks like he's been on the street awhile.'

'He has so many scars,' said Robson, joining Demi's side.

Michael nodded. 'Yeah, he's definitely been abused, then either tossed out or he ran away. I checked to see if he's been chipped, but nothing.'

'We'll look after him,' said Robson, and Demi quickly nodded. 'When can we take him home?'

'Normally, I'd prefer to keep him overnight, but we have staff shortages, thanks to flu doing its rounds. So if you just give me some time to rehydrate him, you can take him home soon. He'll sleep off the meds, then it'll just be a case of you building him up slowly. He's hardly eaten anything in a long time, so I'll give you some food to start with that's high in fat and protein.' Michael went off to sort everything, leaving Demi wondering if they could get the dog to eat at all.

Robson was over by the animal supplies. 'I'll buy some bits here now, then we can order some more online.'

Demi pointed out a comfy bed. 'He'll need that.' She opened her bag to pull out her purse, but Robson placed his hand over hers.

'I'll pay for his bits and pieces, and I'll help with the bill too.'

She shook her head. 'It's okay. I have my savings.'

'That's for your new home, and you wait till you see that bill. It won't be pretty. Let me go halves with you. We can get into it all later.'

'Small meals, little and often,' said Michael, returning with some puppy food. 'He's fully grown, but this is best for him for now. You should see some weight gain in a couple of weeks.'

One of the assistants or nurses, Demi couldn't be sure, went to the reception desk to type up some details and hand over an invoice, letting them know some of the bill would be paid by the charity that helped with injured animals off the street, so that was a weight off. Robson had warned Demi of the cost, but she didn't think it would be so much. She sure appreciated his help as well.

'I'll call a cab when it's time to leave,' said Robson, taking back his credit card from the young woman. 'For now, let's sit down and check out some dog bits and pieces online while we wait.'

It seemed to take forever for the dog to be ready to leave, but at least when he was returned his shaking and whimpering seemed to have stopped.

'Oh, you poor thing,' whispered Robson, taking the dog in his arms.

Demi leaned over to stroke the sleepy animal's ear.

'I've got some cream for his sores and ointment for the infection in his ears,' said Michael, handing Demi the instructions. 'Don't bath him. Just keep his wounds clean, then apply some cream. They're only minor, so everything will clear up soon, especially now he's got the treatment he needs. Oh, and if you're going to keep him, I recommend pet insurance.'

Demi thought that a good idea too, after seeing the bill.

The assistant brought a large box from out the back and filled it with the goods purchased while Robson took the dog to the cab he had booked.

'Don't forget this,' said Michael, placing a medical cone on top of the box. 'He must wear this to stop him from licking and scratching.'

Demi eyed the plastic collar, sure the dog wouldn't be comfortable wearing it all day.

Robson was on the back seat with the dog on his lap by the time she got to the cab. The driver placed the box in the boot, then she clambered in the front, looking forward to going home. It had been a long day, and it wasn't just their new pet that needed feeding.

As soon as Robson got the animal settled on the new comfy brown dog bed, Demi washed her hands and got a cottage pie out of the fridge to place in the oven.

'He's a real fighter, I can tell,' said Robson, stroking the top of the dog's leg.

Demi nodded, peering over his shoulder. 'A proper champ.'

'Hey, that's what we could call him. Champ.'

She smiled, agreeing. 'Let's just hope he eats something when he wakes.'

'He will. He'll soon see he's safe.'

Demi nodded as she sat by his side on the floor. 'He won't ever be abandoned again. Not on my watch. You hear that, Champ. You've got a family now.' She breathed out a small laugh, not finding much funny. 'He might be all I have.'

Robson curled her hand in his. 'You've got me too, Dem.'

She smiled down at their connected fingers. 'You know we've just become dog parents.'

Robson quietly laughed. 'Does that mean we've got to have a shotgun wedding?'

Demi leaned into his arm, muffling her laugh so as not to disturb Champ. She closed her eyes for a moment, absorbing Robson's warmth. He felt so good, and she realised she didn't want to move.

CHAPTER 22

Robson

The weather had turned hot again but it wasn't about to stop Robson from his morning run. He had hoped to take Champ along, but the dog had only just started to regain weight, and so short walks were all he could manage for now.

Robson bent to rub behind Champ's ear, receiving a lick on the cheek in return. It was early, and the dog showed no signs of leaving his snuggly bed anytime soon. 'You be good and don't wake your mum yet.'

Champ wagged his thin tail, then shoved his face into a cuddly teddy bear.

Robson stood to warm up. He was meeting Alice outside the pub soon, as she was going to jog around the block with him this week, which meant he wouldn't run at his usual pace, as Alice's jog was more of a power walk. He didn't mind though, as he liked being her running buddy whenever she felt fit enough to exercise.

Champ was watching him, Demi was upstairs, still sleeping, and life at home was better than ever. Just adding a dog into the mix seemed to fill in gaps he didn't know were there.

His flat looked lived in. And as unconventional as their setup was, it somehow worked.

Robson stared at the dog, who thumped his tail. It was good to see Champ so relaxed and happy. It didn't take long at all for him to settle with his new owners and see they were kind people.

Demi fussed the dog no end, and she fussed Robson on occasion, which always made him smile internally.

He made sure there was a pee pad by the balcony door, just in case Champ decided to get up after all. Then Robson said goodbye to his furry friend and headed downstairs to find Alice by the entrance to the beer garden.

'Morning,' she sang.

'Have you warmed up?'

She tipped her head to one side as she huffed. 'Yes, boss. I know the drill.'

'Come on then.'

They set off, with Alice talking all the way, as usual. Robson was used to listening to music when on a run, but with her, he just followed her lead.

'It's going to be sweltering later on. What you got planned?' she asked, puffing already.

'Just work. But I'll open the grill for dinner. Oh, wait, we've got vets at lunch. Champ is getting a check-up, and we're having him chipped.'

'How is he? I thought he might join us today.'

'He's doing great, but he's not strong enough for anything other than short walks at the mo. Besides, he gets scared. He's still afraid of people, and especially other dogs.'

'He loves seeing Benny.'

'Yeah, he's been good coming up to visit. I think Champ knows Benny's not an adult.'

Alice laughed. 'Try telling that to Benny. Ever since he turned fifteen this year, he's suddenly a man.'

Robson remembered being that age and feeling so grown up. 'You've got yourself a good kid there, Al.'

She smiled, slowing her jog. 'I know.'

They continued at a slower pace along a row of terraced houses, then picked things up going down a hill as they came back to the harbour. Robson could tell Alice wouldn't be going for round two today, but at least he could head off to the park afterwards.

'I was thinking, Al. How about that little party to celebrate you being the new owner of Seaview B&B now? Mabel is off next week, so we could combine the two. Wish her well and that.'

They came to a stop outside the B&B, and Alice leaned against the chalky wall at the front of the pathway.

'That would be lovely.' She pointed at the door. 'I'll see what Mabel thinks. I'll just pop in before I head home.' She turned on the path. 'And don't forget, you're part of the moving-in crew once she's left. Benny's already packed all his stuff.'

Robson chuckled. 'Yes, I remember. See you later. Pop by the grill for dinner.'

'Will do.'

He waited till she went inside, then turned to look over at the lighthouse in the distance. The rising sun was sparkling against its tip as the cry of seagulls woke the sky.

'Morning, son,' said Jed, passing. 'You're late on your run today.'

'Oh, I've already been round once with Alice. I'm about to—'

A scream came from the B&B, startling both men. Robson and Jed immediately ran into the building.

'Alice?' called Robson, heading straight across the hallway to the reception desk.

Alice came from out the back. Her face was pale, cheeks damp from tears. 'It's Mabel.' Her voice hitched. 'She's dead.'

Jed sprinted behind her, leaving Robson to wrap Alice in his arms.

'It's okay, Al. Try to take a deep breath.'

'I just found her on the floor.' Alice sobbed.

Robson rubbed his hand in circles on her back, trying to soothe her. At least calm her a touch. Mabel meant the world to Alice. She was like another grandmother.

'She died alone, Robson.'

He didn't know what to say.

'I called an ambulance, but it's not like they can do anything,' called out Jed. 'She's gone.'

Alice peeled herself off Robson's shoulder to go back to Mabel, and he thought it best to call her mum.

Lizzie was shocked to hear the news and came round straight away, leaving Luna in charge of the newsagent's.

A lot of commotion took place over the next hour, with medical people coming and going, Alice having to contact Mabel's girlfriend to break the sad news, and neighbours poking their heads in the door to see what had happened.

Lots of tears were shed, and Robson made tea for anyone in need.

Sophie, Lottie, and Spencer sat in the dining room with Alice, and Lizzie stood out front with Jed and Will.

Flowers had already been placed at the entrance by the time all the shops in the area started to open for the day, and the heat was irritating everyone.

Robson went over to the front of the pub and looked up at Demi's bedroom window. No doubt she was awake by now but might not have noticed what was going on outside, so he called her phone.

Demi gasped at the news, then opened the window, looking over at the B&B. 'I'll get dressed and come down.'

He shook his head. 'No need. They're about to take Mabel away now, and I'm sure the guests aren't bothered about having breakfast there today.'

'I'll come and see to them. Sort something quick and easy.'

He got off the phone, wondering if any of the guests would complain that breakfast wasn't waiting. They had paid for it, after all. He headed back to see everyone gathered outside as Mabel was taken away.

Alice burst into tears again, held up by Sophie and Lizzie.

Benny came hurtling around the corner of the street, running straight to his family. His dark hair was all that could be seen as he buried his face into the huddle of women.

Robson went straight to the kitchen, with Will hot on his heels.

'Tell me what to do, mate.'

Robson shook his head. 'Demi's on her way to feed the guests, so perhaps try to clear everyone who doesn't need to be here out the door.'

Will nodded. 'Yeah, I can do that.' He went back to the hallway, and Robson could hear his muffled voice moving people outside.

A lady entered the dining room, and Robson spotted her through the serving hatch. He quickly went to greet her.

'I heard the previous owner passed away this morning. Is that right?' she asked softly.

'Yes, I'm afraid so.'

'Oh, that's so sad.' She grabbed Robson and hugged him, taking him completely by surprise.

Demi walked in and met his eyes.

Robson wriggled free of the tight hold. 'Erm, this is Demi. She'll make breakfast today.'

Demi gave a brief smile, then headed for the kitchen, with Robson close behind. 'Who is she?' she whispered.

He shrugged. 'A guest. She just hugged me when I confirmed Mabel had died.'

Demi washed her hands, then made a beeline for the bread. 'It's an emotional time.'

He watched her place down the small monitor device they had bought online so they could watch Champ when he was left home alone.

'He's had his food and used a pee pad on the balcony to do his business, but I'll walk him after this,' she said, popping slices of bread in the toaster.

He peered over her shoulder to see Champ curling up in his bed. A smile hit his heart as Demi leaned back into his chest a touch.

'It's sad, isn't it?' she added quietly.

Resting his head next to hers, he agreed. 'She'd been around forever.'

'She was always nice to me.'

'Mabel was a real gem.'

Demi's hand came around to clasp his, and Robson curled his arm around her waist and kissed her temple.

They stayed still for a moment, then Demi told him to go see if any more of the guests had arrived yet and if they wanted tea or coffee.

Luckily enough, the B&B wasn't full that week, so they only had four tables to cover, and that didn't take long, as most of the guests said they were going out for the day and seemed keen to leave as soon as possible.

Alice was sitting out the back, where Mabel used to live, so Robson went to sit with her for a while.

'Hey, how's it going?'

'Mum's in the bedroom talking to Betty on the phone. It's going a lot worse for her. Poor Betty was all ready to move to Jersey with Mabel next week. She's devastated. Mum's been on the phone for an hour. Shame Betty lives so far away, else she'd be here, not that there's anything she can do. She'll want to come by soon, though, to sort Mabel's things.'

'Any news of Mabel's grandkids?'

Alice shook her head. 'I called the prison to let them know. I'm not sure how they'll go about telling Jamie.' She sighed deeply. 'As for Shannon, well, I couldn't find a number for her, but there was an address, so I'll have to write. Does it take long for mail to reach Australia?'

'No. Not long.'

'She never had anything to do with Mabel, so I don't even know how recent that address is, but it's all I've got to work with.'

Robson tapped her hand. 'Don't stress it, Al. Let's get everything sorted for Betty.'

'Yeah, knowing how organised those two were, I'm guessing Betty will know Mabel's funeral plan.' Alice slapped a hand to her eyes and sobbed. 'I can't believe she's gone.'

Robson leaned over to hug her close just as Lizzie came back into the living room.

'Betty will be here tomorrow.'

'I don't mind driving to Devon to pick her up,' said Robson, releasing Alice into Lizzie's arms. 'I could borrow Spencer's van.'

Lizzie waggled her finger his way. 'She's sorted for tomorrow, love. It's all good.'

He left them to it, heading back outside to see who was around.

Sophie came down the stairs, carrying a duster. 'I've cleaned the rooms, so that's out the way until the morning.'

'Kitchen's back to normal,' said Demi, entering the hallway.

'Neighbours have all gone about their business now,' said Will, coming in from the front door. He held a warm smile as he gazed at a vase of flowers on the side. 'This is where I stayed when I first came to Port Berry. Mabel was a good friend to me. I'm really going to miss her.'

Sophie sniffed, walking towards him. 'Come on, let's get back to work — I can hear Mabel telling us off for loitering.'

They shared a small smile as they waved goodbye.

Robson turned to Demi. 'Might be best you start work here tomorrow for the breakfast shift. What do you think?'

She nodded. 'I was going to suggest the same. Joseph's already told me I've only got one more week left at yours. I guess it won't be too much for him if I leave now.'

'No, it won't. Leave it to me. I'll sort it.'

Demi glanced around. 'Where's Alice?'

'Out back with her mum.'

Demi's head dipped as she inched closer to him, and he pulled her into his arms.

'You okay, Dem?'

'Yeah. It's just sad.'

'It was supposed to be a different kind of farewell for Mabel.'

'You just don't know what's around the next corner.' She gazed up at him, and Robson felt his heart skip a beat.

He leaned a touch closer, about to rest his head on hers when Alice called out to see if he was still out there.

'Yes,' he called back. 'One sec.' He turned to Demi. 'I'll help Alice here today. I'll be back home in a minute to get changed, then I'll open up and leave the staff to it.'

'Okay. I'll pop in and out between shifts. And don't worry about the appointment at the vets. I'll sort that. I've got the cab office's number.'

'I really need to get a car. We'd both get use out of it.'

She smiled softly, leaned up to kiss his cheek, then told him she'd see him later.

Robson followed her to the door and watched as she walked to the pub. It was quiet outside again, and he took a moment to inhale the warm salty air before going back inside to see Alice.

CHAPTER 23

Demi

Demi had just finished a shift at the Hub, and it hadn't been quiet. She'd stocked shelves, handed out baby clothes — which she had to run upstairs to the office to collect — and helped a young man fill out an online job application form, and that was all within the first hour. Then she encouraged a new mum to join the parent and baby group that took place in the church hall, and steered a middle-aged man towards the homeless hostel, having called them first to make the arrangements.

All in all, she'd had a productive morning while Mabel's funeral took place, then Matt came in to take over.

Her phone rang, and she assumed it was Robson, back at the pub for the wake, but to her surprise, it was Jade. She could count on one hand the number of times her daughter made contact, so immediately her heart flipped, thinking something was wrong.

'Hello, Jade?'

'Hi, Mum.'

'Is everything okay?' Demi looked both ways before crossing the road to sit on a bench overlooking the boats.

'Yes, I wanted to tell you how the results day party went.'

Demi frowned as Jade chatted away about some venue, the dress she had worn, and the speeches made by her group of friends. Half of what she said floated in one ear and out the other. She didn't even know Jade had got her results.

'We're going to visit the uni again this Sunday. Alana said we could make a week of it up there. See the sights. Give me a good idea of the area. Oh, Mum, I'm so excited. Wait, I'll send you a picture of me with my exam results. We had the best party. Colin danced the night away, showing everyone his funky moves. You know what he's like.'

Demi glanced at her phone, then tapped on the messages to see Jade looking so happy, even more so in the second picture of her with Alana and Colin. A slight smile twitched, but her heart was so broken it was a struggle to know how to feel. 'You look beautiful,' was all she managed, swallowing down the pain of not being there to witness her baby in such an important moment of her life.

'I can't wait to start uni. I wish I was there now.' Jade sounded so happy.

Demi stared out at the glistening sun twinkling on the tips of the water. Even though she'd made the decision to take a step back in Jade's life, where she'd been placed anyway, she didn't for one moment think she would be excluded from the big things. No one had bothered to call to let her know what results Jade had got, let alone mention a party. Perhaps it was her own fault for forgetting to keep up with it all, what with so much going on. She should have called Jade. She shouldn't have backed off so much.

Jade's voice faded in. 'I'm going shopping to buy some things for uni. I know it's not till September, but it's best to get sorted now. I won't have much time once we get back from Spain. We'll be . . .' Her voice faded out.

So they were off to Spain before uni started. Good to know. Demi gave up the ghost.

'Sorry, Jade, I have to go. Work.' And with that she hung up.

A woman walked past with a teenage girl, and Demi's heart thumped.

A memory hit of Jade taking her first steps. The cheers, claps, the magnitude of the moment.

Slowly, Demi made her way home. Not much seemed to matter anymore. All she wanted was to feel the comfort of somewhere she belonged.

Champ scooted to her side as soon as she entered the kitchen, bouncing around her feet and licking her ankles while wagging his tail.

Demi headed straight to the sofa and curled into a ball, and Champ snuggled his nose into her cheek before flopping to the floor by her side. She dropped one arm to rest her hand on him, then closed her eyes, blocking out the world. Her life.

'Hey, Dem. You okay?' Robson's soft voice floated through the air.

Had she drifted off? A tad dazed, she opened her eyes to see him standing over her. 'Robson?'

He smiled. 'Yeah, it's me.' He blew out a laugh. 'Guess you needed to catch up on your sleep.'

She yawned as she sat up. 'I only closed my eyes for a moment. What time is it?'

'Gone lunch. I thought you were coming in for the wake. Thought I'd better check everything was okay.'

She went to tell him it was, but then remembered she wasn't okay at all. Without warning, she burst out crying, slapping a hand to cover her face.

'Hey, hey.' Robson was at her side within seconds, holding her close.

'I'm sorry,' she muttered, sniffing. 'I'm so sorry.'

'There's nothing to be sorry about. Hey, come on, Dem. What's this all about?' He raised her chin slightly, and she met the concern in his eyes.

'I'm just feeling sorry for myself.' She dipped her head, ashamed she had crumbled.

'We're only human, you know. We're allowed to have the occasional pity party.'

Demi leaned into him, resting her head on his shoulder, inhaling the woody scent of his cologne. 'Jade passed her exams, got into the university she wanted, and they all had a party. I wasn't invited. I was just shown photos.' She felt his chest steadily rise and fall.

'I won't lie. That's pretty shitty of them.'

Those weren't the words she was expecting. She sat up and sighed. 'Yeah, you're right. It bloody well was, and I'm not crying over this crap anymore. Sod the lot of them.'

Champ whacked his tail on her leg as he shuffled onto his back. His way of asking for a tummy rub.

Robson had one hand on Demi's back and the other stroking the dog.

She slid to the floor, giving Champ more attention. At least she meant something to him. 'This is my life now, and I'm not going to let my family mess with my head any longer. I don't even know if they know they're doing it, but it stops now.'

'What are you going to do?'

She stood, causing the dog to jump to his paws. 'I'm going to let them know. Make it clear.' She slammed her hands on her hips for a moment, then dropped her stiff stance. 'What do you think?'

Robson shrugged. 'You know them, not me. Would your words make a difference?'

Demi shook her head. 'I honestly don't think they would. They've made up their minds about me, moved forward as though I don't exist, and snubbed me whenever I try to involve myself.' She raised a finger. 'Actually, I'm going to write it all down and send them the letter.'

'They do say that gets it off your chest, and at least they can't interrupt you. But think about it first, Dem. Don't write things in the heat of the moment. You could end up with regrets.'

Demi scoffed. 'Regrets? Oh, I'm so over regrets.' She touched the top of her head. 'I've had it up to here with regrets.'

'Maybe you could arrange a visit with them instead.'

She whipped out her phone, waggling it in the air as her cheeks flushed. 'Or I can yell at them for how horrible they make me feel at times.'

Robson stepped forward, but she waved him away, determined to use her words while she had some.

A message popped up, letting her know the dog food she had ordered online would be arriving tomorrow, and that simple text had her sitting down, taking a breath.

Robson joined her side. 'If you need to get it off your chest, go for it,' he said softly. 'But if you think your words will fall on deaf ears, then perhaps it's best to use your energy on yourself.'

He was right. She knew that, and it was the Terry situation all over again. As Luna had pointed out, there would have been no point talking to Terry, as he would have avoided the truth. There was no point telling her family she thought they were thoughtless, because all they were doing was living their life the way they knew how, plus Jade was happy.

'Why is it always me that has to let things go?' she asked herself more so than Robson.

'We do that to help ourselves.'

She smiled at him. 'You sound like Jan.'

'She taught me a lot.'

Demi pressed against his arm. 'Oh, Robson, I understand why my family are the way they are with me, but it can be so annoying at times.' She shook her head at herself. 'You know what, I can't be angry about this. We all suffered, and my daughter ended up in therapy. Healing takes time, and I've no right to expect anyone else to move at the same pace as me.' Sighing deeply, she smiled softly at him. 'Sometimes I just need to blow off steam, or take a break from it all would be good.'

'Sounds like you need a holiday.'

'I'm helping Alice with the B&B, that's about as close as I'll get to a change of scenery.'

His smile was soft, filled with warmth. 'You're missed in our kitchen.'

She laughed. 'I don't believe for a second Joseph said that.'

He playfully nudged her elbow. 'I'm saying it.'

'You hardly came into the kitchen.'

He showed his palms. 'I'm just saying. And speaking of kitchens, how about you have something to eat, seeing how you slept through lunch.'

Demi looked over at the fridge. 'I'll make a sandwich.'

'There's plenty of food downstairs.'

'Nah, I'll have something here, check my emails, then pop down for the wake.'

Robson gently patted her knee. 'You stay there. I'll make you something. Chicken okay?'

Champ jumped up and let out a muffled bark, which he only did when excited.

Demi placed a finger to her lips. 'Shh, you said the magic word.'

He laughed as he set about making her food. 'Come on, Champ. You can have a snack too.'

Demi watched him place some chicken in the dog's bowl, then checked her emails and social network account. She had thousands more followers now, she couldn't believe how quickly her content had been noticed. It was just mind-blowing on every level. Perhaps after the wake she could make some more content. She was certainly inspired to do so. She went to tell Robson of her plans, when a message made her gasp.

Robson swirled around. 'What is it?'

'Oh my goodness!'

He rushed over, leaving Champ to mooch in the kitchen, looking for more chicken.

'Look at this,' she added, tugging him down to the sofa.

'Is it your family?'

Demi showed him the screen. 'No. It's a company asking me if I'd consider advertising their product on my page. They'll pay me. Look who it is. Blimming heck, they're a huge name.'

He pulled her in for a hug, cheering close to her ear. 'How brilliant is that, Dem?' He shuffled back, grinning while gesturing at the kitchen. 'I've got their frying pan.'

'They're asking if I have an agent or should they deal with me direct. How am I supposed to know if it's a good deal or not? I don't have an agent.'

'First thing's first, do the video chat they're proposing, then see how the land lies. If you're mates with any of the other influencers online, ask them for advice. You never know, one might be helpful.'

Demi widened her eyes. 'Influencer?'

Robson nodded. 'That's what this is, Dem. When you have so many followers, these companies start knocking on your door, and your bio does state you're up for collaborations.'

'Yeah, but I didn't think anyone would take any notice.'

'You're in a good position to advertise anything to do with cooking now. Why not get paid for it?' He gave a small fist bump to the air as he beamed her way. 'I'm so excited for you.'

Demi smiled back. 'I'd love my own products to sell. You know, cooking equipment, kitchenware. Cups and plates with my own designs.'

'What designs would you have?'

She shrugged, as she hadn't got that far in her dreams. 'How about the seaside?'

'Sounds good. I'll be your first customer.' He took her hand, lifting her from the sofa to spin into a dance, making her giggle.

'I'm going to do it,' she told herself more than him as she stepped back from his arms. 'I'll set up a chat with them, then do what you said about asking some of the others. There's one woman who messages me sometimes with praise. She has a similar page, but hers is more about sweet treats, and she advertises all the time.'

'Great. Can I do anything to help?'

Demi gestured at the kitchen. 'You can make my sandwich.'

Robson laughed. 'I can do that. Got to keep the superstar's strength up.'

Demi snorted a laugh. 'You know, if I can make some more money this way, I won't need to save for rented accommodation. I could save to buy my own property.'

'Good idea.' His back was turned so she couldn't see his expression, but his tone was on the quiet side.

'Do you really think so, Robson? Or are you thinking the same as Colin?'

He turned. 'What do you mean by that?'

'That if I'm an owner, I can sell and have more money to keep up my habit or turn the place into a drug den. And to be honest, perhaps Colin's right.' She flopped back into the comfy sofa and sighed.

'Don't let him plant seeds in your head that scare you. You're stronger than he knows, and you've got goals that remove you so far from that world.'

Demi shrugged one shoulder. 'Sometimes it's scary. Living like this is simple. I don't feel I'm taking on too much, but if I buy a place, then what? Will I fold under the pressure of mortgage repayments? And why is that any different to rent?'

'You're overthinking this, Dem.'

'I know, right! But this is what Colin does to me. His voice just appears in my head whenever I think of moving.'

'Didn't stop you moving in here.'

She sat up straight. 'No, he didn't.' Stabbing a finger in the air, she added, 'I'm going to see what these advertising offers are, and if I can get some more, and look into creating my own brand, and if I can afford to buy a house by the sea, then I'm going for it. I haven't come this far to stop now.'

'Good for you.' He brought her sandwich over. 'So, by the sea, eh?'

She smiled at him, loving the twinkle in his piercing eyes. 'I don't want to live anywhere else. I love this place.'

'Well, there's no rush for you to move. Stay here as long as you like. You'll figure it out soon.'

'But this is supposed to be a temporary arrangement. You're supposed to be getting used to having a lodger not a full-time flatmate.'

Robson went back to the kitchen. 'You're not my lodger or flatmate. This is your home, and you choose when you're ready to move on.'

Champ curled up on her feet as she bit into her sandwich. She didn't know how to respond to Robson's soft words.

'Right, I'd better get back to the bar. See you downstairs in a bit.' Robson darted off before she could reply.

She gazed down at the happy dog snoozing on her feet and smiled.

CHAPTER 24

Robson

It was early, and Robson should have been out on a run, but instead he was standing outside the gate to Colin's house, wondering what in the hell he was doing interfering in Demi's life. She was so up and down the day before, thanks to basically being told she had been left out of Jade's celebrations. He had no idea what she would say, but he had a fair idea what Colin was about to.

Warm air left his mouth in a sigh as he pressed the button on the intercom at the gate. He shouldn't be there. He should turn and walk away, but he couldn't. Someone had to have Demi's back.

'Hello,' croaked a female voice.

'Hello. I'm Robson McCoy. I live with Demi.' He wasn't sure if he should use her full name, but it didn't matter, the gate unlocked.

He walked the driveway, glancing left and right at the colourful bedding and neat shrubs.

It was Alana who opened the door, looking as though her morning yoga session had just been interrupted.

Colin rushed down the stairs, wearing a dark robe that covered matching PJs. 'What's wrong? What's my sister done?'

Robson silently fumed at Colin's first thought. 'Nothing, but I do want to talk to you about her. Is Jade awake?'

Colin and Alana exchanged glances before looking back at him.

'Why are you here?' asked Colin.

'I told you. I want to talk to Demi's family.'

Alana scoffed. 'Did she send you?'

Robson cocked his head, eyeing their shiny hallway furniture. 'No.'

Colin huffed. 'It's early. Get to the point. Has she started taking pills again?'

Jade came down the stairs, concern in her eyes as she stared at Robson. 'Has something happened to my mum?' she asked him.

'No. She's fine, but I'd like her to stay that way — that's why I'm here.'

Colin frowned. 'Excuse me? What's that supposed to mean?'

'It means she's healing, and it's not easy.' Robson kept his gaze on Colin. 'She needs love and support. Kindness and understanding, and so far, all I've seen from you lot is disrespect and selfishness.'

Alana's mouth gaped as Colin stepped forward.

'I don't know who you think you are coming round here, telling us—'

'You're messing with her head,' said Robson, just wanting to get his point across.

'Is my mum struggling?' Jade twiddled with the belt on her pink dressing gown. Her gaze on her slippers.

'Only when she's left out of important family occasions. You know, like her daughter visiting universities, having parties, going on holiday.' He tried to remain composed while his heart fluttered away, pounding at his chest. 'It really hurts her and brings her down when she's doing so well. I wish you could spend more time with her so you can see what I see every day.'

'Oh, what would you know about anything?' yelled Alana, making Colin jump. 'You have no idea what trouble Demi can cause.'

Robson was facing what Demi often saw. Her past. 'She hasn't been that person for a long time. She's moved on. Rebuilt her life. She doesn't need you constantly dragging her back to that nightmare. Give her a break.' He didn't mean to say the last bit, but emotions were running high, and he hated seeing Demi hurting.

'I have done nothing but help my sister, before, during, and after.' Colin looked to his wife, who nodded. 'But we don't want her at our celebrations, around parties and alcohol. We worry she might turn that way to get a high if she needs one and can't get her hands on any drugs. Why do you think I'm so against her living above a pub. Working in one?'

'She doesn't work there anymore, but the booze wasn't her addiction. It didn't push her off the edge, and it doesn't tempt her. She doesn't drink at all. She's been working in restaurants since she came out of prison. She goes in supermarkets every week, passes off-licences. There is access to alcohol everywhere, and drugs aren't that hard to come by either. And yet, here she is, two-years clean, still pushing towards her goals each day, just wanting peace and normality for her life.'

Colin's face was turning purple. 'My sister is none of your business.'

'Yes, she is, because I care about her.'

'I love my mum,' said Jade, sounding upset.

'And she loves you so much, and I know she's sorry for what you went through. I can't even begin to imagine how hard this has been for you.' Robson took a breath. 'I'm sorry.'

Alana pushed Colin out the way as he went to take another step closer to Robson. 'You listen to me. We were the ones who saw Demi full of drugs and all that entailed, not you. We were the ones who tried to get her the help needed, not you. We were the ones bringing stability into her daughter's life, not you.' She stabbed a finger towards his chest. 'Don't act like you know the story when all you see is the Demi now.'

'But that's my point,' said Robson. 'She's a different person now. All you have to do is accept her for who she is today. Tell her you're proud. Let her know she's welcome at your table. After all she's been through, the strength and courage it's taken to turn her life around after Terry's death, his wife turning up, losing her home, having an accident, the addiction. Bloody hell, I'm surprised she's still standing, but she is, and she's amazing. Take a look at her rise instead of just her fall.'

Colin pointed at the threshold where Robson perched, his bottom lip trembling slightly. 'Go away.'

'Wait!' cried Jade. 'Where is my mum?'

Robson checked the time on his phone. 'Feeding the dog. Getting ready for work.'

Colin frowned. 'But you said she doesn't work at the pub anymore.'

'What dog?' asked Jade.

'Perhaps if you showed an interest in Demi's life, you'd know these things.'

'Tell us now,' demanded Alana.

Robson stepped back, shaking his head. 'Invite her for dinner. Ask her about her life. Show her you're interested in what she's become. Do something or very soon you might just find you've lost her forever, and it won't be to the drugs. It'll be because she's had enough of you lot not accepting her.'

'You've got a bloody cheek, do you know that?' spat Colin, following him onto the driveway.

'No,' said Robson calmly. 'I've got a heart.'

'I have a heart. We all do, we're just taking things slowly with my sister because we're wary. If you knew the impact her addiction had on our family, you would be more understanding.'

'I do know. Demi told me, and I can see your point of view, honestly I can. I just want you to know Demi is doing so well, and she's determined to stay that way. I just want you to be completely on her side, to cheer her on, not worry and bring those worries to her.'

Colin said something else, but Robson blocked him out as he made it back to the road, feeling he'd said too much.

The noise of the main gate opening behind him caused Robson to turn, ready for more words with Colin or Alana, but it was Jade who came speeding out in a car, and he had an idea where she was heading.

He swore at himself under his breath. What on earth was he thinking getting involved? Had he gone too far? It wasn't as though he was going to hide his visit from Demi, but now it would come across far worse.

CHAPTER 25

Demi

Champ's croaky bark startled Demi. Someone was banging down the door. She was used to delivery drivers wanting to drop off and run as quickly as possible but that kind of thumping was going too far.

Frowning, she sprinted down the stairs to swing the door open, surprised to see a tearful Jade standing there.

'Mum!' Jade cried.

Demi pulled her into her arms. 'Jade, what's happened?' There were palpitations but she couldn't tell if they were coming from her or her daughter.

'Can I come up?'

'Of course.' Demi closed the door as Jade climbed the stairs. She noticed her daughter was wearing nightclothes, and her mind went into overdrive as she rushed to the kitchen.

Champ darted to his bed, eyeing the newbie in his home with suspicion.

Demi turned Jade to face her — she was staring over at the dog. 'Is it Colin? Is he hurt?'

'No, Mum. It's you. It's me. All of us.' She burst into tears, and Demi had no idea what was going on. All she could do was hold her child until she regained her breath.

Champ made a whining noise.

'Is the dog okay?' asked Jade, sniffing while pulling back.

'Yes. He just gets a little nervous around strangers.'

'Should I go say hi?'

Demi tipped her head at Champ still staring at Jade. 'Don't you think you should talk to me?'

Jade nodded but approached the sofa anyway to sit close to Champ. 'What's your name, eh?'

'Champ,' said Demi, sitting on the floor next to him in his bed.

Champ crawled over onto Demi's lap. 'I found him down by the harbour. He was in such a state, bless him. All he needed was some love, right, Champ?' She snuggled her face to his, and he licked her cheek.

'Like you, Mum.'

Demi glanced up. 'What do you mean by that?'

'Robson was right. We haven't been as supportive since your release, but I do love you. So much.'

Demi's heart flipped as adrenaline pumped. 'What's that about Robson?'

'He was just at our house. Told us off for not seeing you for who you are today.' Jade dipped her head to the dog. 'For not inviting you places with us as a family.'

'He did *what*?'

'He cares about you, Mum.'

That wasn't the point. What a cheek he had going to her daughter's home, spouting his opinion!

Champ stretched his head towards Jade's knee for a sniff but ducked away when she tried to stroke him.

'Jade, tell me what happened this morning for you to run out in your nightwear.'

'I just wanted to see you. Let you know I care. I'm sorry we never invite you anywhere, but we just worry about putting you in any kind of hyper zone.'

A laugh escaped Demi before she had a chance to hold it back. 'Sorry, I don't mean to laugh, but honestly, what do you lot think I'll do?'

'We didn't want anything to tempt you.'

'I live with temptation every day, love. I don't have to be at a party or on holiday. You don't need to worry about me. I'm doing just fine.'

Jade sniffed again. 'Robson said you have a different job.'

Demi sighed. 'Seems like Robson had a lot to say.'

Champ smooshed his nose into Jade's leg, making her giggle.

'I'm still a chef,' added Demi, pleased to see her dog trying to bond with Jade. 'I'm now at Seaview B&B, just along the road. The new owner wants me to create a lunch menu, so I'll be doing that and breakfast duties.'

'Sounds like fun for you. You've always been so good at cooking.'

Demi nodded, patting the floor for Jade to join them. 'I've got something else going on that you might find fun.'

Champ slid a paw onto Jade's lap and finally let her stroke him.

'What's that?'

'I'm an influencer now.'

Jade laughed. 'Mum, do you know what that is?'

'Erm, excuse me.' Demi giggled. 'Of course I know. I have my own social networking page and loads of followers.'

Jade's eyes nearly popped out her head. 'What? Shut up! Since when? And more to the point, doing what?'

'I used to get bored in the evenings on my own in the bedsit, so I started making meals for one and creating videos of the process. Quick, affordable, that sort of thing. I decided to share my tips with the world, and, well, it took off.' She showed her phone so Jade could see the cooking page.

'Whoa!'

Demi smiled. 'Yes, I was a little surprised too, and now I'm about to start advertising products on my page.'

'Well done.' Jade ruffled behind Champ's ear. 'I didn't know this about you.'

Demi held in her sigh. 'I planned to tell you next time we met up for a coffee.'

Watery, pale eyes looked up. 'You really have changed your life, haven't you, Mum?' Demi could see some pride sitting there.

'Just pushing forward. We all are.'

'Do you think I've held you back at all?'

Demi shook her head. 'No, love. You've had to deal with so much because of me, and I don't blame you for not wanting me around all the time. I brought pain and misery into your life, destroyed your safe place. I know it couldn't have been easy having an addict as a mother. But I'm not that person anymore. I just want my family to give me the same chance I'm giving myself.'

'It was Terry who stole so much from us, Mum. He started all this with his lies. I hate him so much. I hate how it all fell apart.'

Demi pulled her into her arms, kissing the top of her head. 'I know he hurt you too, and I'm so proud for how you've handled everything, including things with me.'

Jade hugged her mum tightly. 'I'm proud of you, Mum, honestly I am. I've just been so scared most of the time.'

Demi raised Jade's face so she could look into her eyes. 'There's nothing for you to fear anymore, my beautiful baby girl.' She rolled back tears as she smiled. 'We survived, didn't we?'

'Yep.' Jade's tears fell freely. 'I love you so much, Mum.'

Demi hugged her again, her heart settling along with her daughter's breathing. *All will be well, just breathe.*

'I'm going to make sure I call you every day when I'm at uni.'

Shaking her head, Demi pulled back. 'No, love. You just focus on your schoolwork and new chapter.'

'But I don't want you to think you're alone.'

A few choice words rolled around Demi's brain as she thought of Robson.

'I know I'm not, Jade.'

'It's just been hard, Mum.'

'I know, love. But it's important we focus on the future now, not past.' Demi wiped Jade's damp cheeks with her fingertips, then pushed back her hair and smiled softly.

'That's pretty much what Robson said.'

'Where is he now?'

Jade shrugged. 'He didn't come here with me. I just jumped in my car, thinking of you.' She huffed down at her clothing. 'I haven't even brushed my teeth yet.'

Demi chuckled. 'Then I suggest you go home, clean up, and we'll see each other later.'

'Come for dinner.'

Demi settled Champ back in his bed as Jade stood, knowing it wasn't as simple as that. 'I'll have to speak to your aunt and uncle.'

'No need. We always have room for you at our table.'

'See what Colin says first. Text me later. Let me know.'

Jade nodded as she made for the stairs, Demi following. 'Are we all right, Mum?'

'Always, love.' Demi kissed her head, then walked her to the door, wishing she didn't have to say goodbye, but it was for the best for Jade to get washed and dressed and settled. That's all Demi ever wanted for her child, to be happy and settled. 'Drive safely.'

Jade gave her another tight hug, then a small wave. 'See you later.'

Taking a steady breath, Demi went back upstairs and called Robson, who answered straight away.

'I can explain,' were his first words.

Part of her wanted to tear into him for his interference, but another part was so touched by how much he cared.

'You had no right,' she said, sitting at the table in the kitchen.

'I know. I'm so sorry, but I was worried they were making life harder for you. I just want you to have peace.'

She wanted that too, but still. 'It's not your place.'

'It won't happen again, Demi. I promise.'

She hung up, but only because she didn't know what to add.

It wasn't long before Robson was home, apologising before he'd even put his door keys on the table.

Demi chewed her gum, contemplating her next move. She watched him fuss Champ, then sit opposite her at the kitchen table. His head was dipped as much as his shoulders.

'I'm sorry, Dem,' he whispered.

'I've been invited to dinner tonight. First by Jade, then by Colin, who just texted.'

He looked up, holding the smallest of smiles.

'You shouldn't have gone round there, Robson. I don't care if you were sticking up for me or worried. My family. My business.'

'Got it.'

'I'm happy right now, and I don't need trouble.'

His head bobbed. 'I'd never intentionally bring trouble your way.'

Demi inhaled slowly, believing him. 'I know. But I don't want anyone else controlling my life, and that includes you trying to make things better for me and my family. I do things my way, and in my own time.'

'Yeah, now I've had time to think things through properly, which was only on my way back here, I can see that.'

'I need the people in my circle to trust in me, not be my voice.'

Robson reached for her hand on the table and she let him, enjoying his gentle touch. 'I'm a right idiot.'

'Yep.'

'What can I do to make amends?'

'Just let me live my life my way.'

He nodded.

'And be on poop-a-scoop duties for the next two weeks,' she added, quirking one side of her mouth.

He kissed her knuckles and smiled. 'Deal.'

'Oh, and one last thing.'

He met her eyes.

'You're coming to dinner at Colin's with me tonight.' She saw him gulp.

'I am?'

'Yes. I want them to meet you properly.'

'Okay, but why?'

Because you mean so much to me.

'Because it's time they started getting to know my circle, and they can start with you — seeing how you've already introduced yourself.'

'I best pop to Berry Blooms for an apology bouquet.'

'Thank you. I like pink flowers.'

He went to speak but closed his mouth and grinned. 'On it.'

She smiled to herself as he headed out the door, then glanced at Champ. 'Your dad is an idiot.'

Champ thumped his tail.

'Perhaps a lovable one,' she added quietly to herself.

CHAPTER 26

Robson

Agreeing to go back to the house where he had ripped into Demi's family wasn't something Robson thought he'd be doing, but after his outburst, it was the least he could do. Plus, Demi seemed keen for him to meet them under better circumstances.

Colin's home appeared friendlier as dinner was served in a large dining room that looked fit for a showroom.

Robson was scared to touch anything in case he left a smudge or knocked something over. The house definitely didn't have the relaxed vibe his home had. He couldn't imagine Champ sneaking onto the sofa here, which is what he'd started to do at home when he wanted more comfort than his bed.

Alana was being the perfect host, and seemed genuine when she thanked him for the flowers he'd brought.

'Look, I have to say something about the way I acted before,' he blurted, after a gulp of lemonade.

'There's no need,' said Jade.

Alana quirked a perfectly groomed eyebrow. 'Let's hear what he has to say.'

Robson could tell she wanted him to squirm. Swallowing his pride, he apologised once more for interfering in their family. 'I just want what's best for Demi and Jade.'

Demi twisted her lips to one side as her head bobbed a touch.

'It's what we all want,' said Colin, cutting into prime steak. He turned to Demi. 'And I want you to know we are proud of you. Robson reminded us of how much you have had to overcome, and I know I've been a little hard on you at times, but it was just my way of trying to fix your problems.'

Robson observed everyone around the table. All eyes were on Demi, with both Jade and her cousin, Damien, showing a kind smile. The only thing keeping Robson breathing properly was the fact Demi looked relaxed.

I'm so proud of you, Dem. You hold that chin up high, love.

As though reading his mind, Demi lifted her head a touch. 'I understand, Colin, and I've always been grateful for the help you've given. It wasn't easy.'

Colin offered a small nod. 'And now it's time we moved forward with you. You're doing so well, and we need to focus on that.'

Robson wasn't sure who smiled the widest, him or Jade.

The rest of dinner went well, with polite conversation and a lot of attention on Demi's future.

Robson stayed quiet, only joining in when spoken to. He was glad to see Demi happily talking about her plans. Her eyes held a sparkle, and there was a warm glow to her cheeks. Right or wrong, he'd made some sort of difference to the dynamics in her family. All he wanted was for them to see what he could in her. So much determination. So much talent. He could see everything and more. So much beauty.

Demi flashed him the occasional smile as she spoke, bringing more than joy to his heart, and he felt the evening was a success.

Jade and Damien went to the living room to set up a computer game they wanted Demi to play, and Robson couldn't help think he should leave them to their night as he stood in the kitchen with Alana, handing her items for the dishwasher.

'I'm glad Demi has someone nice around her. You seem . . . nice enough.' Alana's expression was neutral, so he couldn't be sure if she meant her words.

'We all need a happy circle,' was all he could think to say.

'And you don't think she has that with us.'

He shook his head. 'No, that's not what I was saying.'

'But you do think we're too strict with her. That we hold all the cards. Tell her what to do with her life. Control her.'

'Hey, those are your words. Is that what you think of yourself?'

Alana scoffed. 'We support Demi.'

A noise at the kitchen doorway had them both turn to see Demi and Colin.

'Speaking of support, I want to talk to you both about my money,' said Demi, entering. 'I know you have your own thoughts on it, but I have some too.' She gestured at the table, and they all sat. Robson too, as he wasn't sure of his place in the conversation.

'You want some to help build a business, perhaps?' asked Colin, looking to his wife.

Demi shook her head. 'Actually, I've decided I don't want any of the money. I'm making my own now, so, I've decided to give Mum and Dad's money to Jade. It can pay her uni bills so she doesn't leave with a debt, and when she's ready to move into her own home, she can use the rest for that.'

Robson looked at each person in turn, wondering what was going through their heads.

'If that's what you want,' said Colin.

Demi nodded. 'It will be helpful for Jade's future.'

'I guess,' said Colin, sounding at a loss for words.

Robson remained silent.

Alana offered a small smile. 'I see a bright future for us all.'

Demi smiled back as she stood. 'Thank you, Alana.'

Alana went over to the fridge. 'How about some dessert now? I'll bring it through to the living room.'

Demi waggled her fingers at Robson. 'Come on, let's play a video game. I bet I can beat you in the car race.'

It was obvious the money issue was over now, and he was pleased to see relaxation wash across her face. 'Ooh, I don't know about that. I'm a bit of a champion in that area.'

'Is that right?'

They nudged each other as they departed for the living room, where Jade and Damien screeched with laughter in front of the telly while competing for first place.

Robson relaxed fully for the first time since entering the house. Whether or not Demi's brother and sister-in-law were going to start trusting her again, he couldn't be entirely sure, but one thing he *was* certain of was the joy on Demi's face when Jade snuggled to her side to play the game.

CHAPTER 27

Demi

It was Demi's first cooking class at the Sunshine Centre, now that the DBS and assessment checks had been cleared, and she felt a little sick with nerves, way more than she had felt having dinner at Colin's two nights ago. At least it had gone well, and she could move forward once more.

Looking around the kitchen, there were only four attendees, including Debra, who she was sure was there just to keep an eye on things.

The other three women were quiet, looking just as awkward, so Demi got her act together quickly. It was one thing for her to crumble, but she was damned if anyone else would on her watch.

She gave a quick introduction, pointing out the ingredients each person had at their station, and assured them making a cottage pie would be quick and easy and that she'd help at all stages.

The women seemed happy enough to make a start, so Demi explained the first step before approaching each lady in turn to give assistance.

'Hi, I'm Keely,' said a young woman with blonde braids. 'Is it really true that cooking can de-stress you?'

Demi thought about all the times it had done exactly that, even in the prison kitchen, where she had worked daily. 'I find it a good escape because you're concentrating on something else for a while and you get a sense of achievement at the end.'

Another woman at the back agreed. 'And I think it's healthy to cook from scratch, rather than those microwave meals, which, I won't lie, I find myself living off of most days. That's why I'm doing this. I heard being healthy in the body helps keep your mind healthy too.' She shrugged as Demi looked her way. 'I want to feel all-round good about myself, and I haven't for so long. I was so pleased to hear about this class. Thanks, Demi.'

Demi smiled, feeling a touch emotional. 'Thank you, Coral. It's good to get some feedback on my first day.'

The youngest woman in the group raised her hand. 'I've always wanted to be a chef, but my anxiety is too high to do a cookery course at a college, so when Debra mentioned this class, I knew it might be the only chance I have at something similar. I sometimes make cakes here with the baking group, but I don't really want to be a baker. Not that it matters. I only do things here that I can't outside.'

Demi approached her, seeing a mixture of sadness and longing in the woman's dark eyes. 'You never know, Serena. Perhaps this will be your first step towards your chef dream.'

Serena smiled shyly. 'Wouldn't that be nice.'

Demi remembered her first day in culinary school. She was uncertain of herself. It wasn't the same though, she knew. Serena had severe anxiety, and if the centre was the place she relaxed, then Demi was determined to make the cooking classes the best they could be.

Debra offered an encouraging nod to Demi before going back to her own cooking, showing clear signs she needed little in the way of help.

It wasn't long before the women were chatting happily away to each other and laughing over any mess they made.

Demi was so pleased she'd created a kitchen so unlike the busy ones she had worked in. The atmosphere was chilled, filled with friendly vibes, and positivity, all of which she wanted for her group.

Coral pointed at the small radio on the side. 'Hey, how about a wooden spoon dance while our dinner cooks?'

Keely frowned. 'What's that when it's at home?'

Coral raised her spoon in the air and wiggled her bum. 'We move like this.'

The women laughed, and Debra switched on some pop music, keeping the volume on low. The door to the kitchen was closed, and the sensory rooms at the centre were sound-proofed, but still, it wasn't the place for a party.

Demi grabbed her wooden spoon, holding it aloft, and joined in with Coral's dance routine that had everyone giggling until they were out of breath.

'Now, this is my kind of group therapy,' said Keely.

Demi smiled on the inside. The women had become members for different reasons, but the one thing they had in common was needing respite from their lives — and Demi knew exactly how that felt.

Debra switched off the radio and waved them back to their stations. 'We'll have to join one of those dance keep-fit clubs.'

'Only if it's here,' said Serena.

Coral waggled her spoon. 'You'll be all right with us, love. I'll help you. We can do the salsa.'

Serena blushed as she lowered her head, focusing on cleaning her table. 'Thanks, Coral,' she mumbled.

Demi had tossed and turned all night worrying her class might go belly-up in a thousand different ways. She couldn't wait to tell Robson how well it went.

She walked around to the ovens to check on the pies as thoughts of Robson warmed her more than the heat in the kitchen.

Just the thought of being able to go home and share her day with someone — with Robson — brought joy to her heart.

* * *

As soon as she was home, Demi made a start on creating more cooking content, the skip in her step from the Sunshine Centre helping push her along. It really had been the best day, and all she wanted was to keep cooking.

Robson entered with Champ, and the dog headed straight for his water bowl for a drink. 'I need some water myself.' He paused as he noticed the phone set up on the kitchen table with some ingredients laid out in bowls. 'Oh, have I just walked into your video?'

Demi laughed, waving him towards the sink so he could have a glass of water. 'No, I'm just getting ready to start. Good walk?'

'Yep. Champ was happy. How was the cooking lesson?'

'Brilliant. I can't stop smiling.'

Robson gulped his drink as he nodded. 'I can see.'

'Have you ever just wanted to actually jump for joy?' She clasped her hands together and beamed, making him laugh.

'You jump as high as you want, Dem. And why not? I'll jump with you.' And with that, Robson leapt into the air. 'Woo hoo!'

Demi burst out laughing at his star jump, then joined him, grabbing each other as they tumbled.

Champ barked, his two front paws pouncing to the table, knocking the bowl of flour to the floor. He jumped back and barked at the metal bowl as it crashed near him, then he darted through the flour, spreading it everywhere.

'Oh no, Champ, stop.' Demi was laughing too much to chase him, but Robson sprinted around the table, skidding in the mess, which only made Demi laugh harder.

Champ bounced out of Robson's arms and wagged his tail, his tongue lolling, looking as though he, too, found the incident amusing.

The flour was spread all over the kitchen floor, and now on one of Robson's knees as he stood, and Demi couldn't help herself as she scooped up the rest in the bowl and tossed it on his other knee.

'Now they match.'

Robson quirked an eyebrow. 'Oh, like that, is it?' He wiped himself down, then came at her with white dusty hands, and Demi squealed as he smeared some on her cheeks, quickly burying her head into his chest to stop him spreading any more on her.

'I surrender,' she said, giggling into his top, knowing full well the flour had transferred from her face to his clothing. She pulled back and pointed, and Robson tugged her back into him.

'Take it back.'

Demi chuckled. 'To share is to care.'

'I'm the only one covered in flour.'

'I'm a professional chef. I know how to stay clean in the kitchen.'

They shared a laugh until Champ padded over to the sofa to plonk himself down, powdery pawprints lining the cushions.

Demi shifted out of the warmth of Robson's arms, her smile still firmly in place as he smiled directly into her eyes. 'I guess we should clear up,' she whispered, as her voice had cracked.

Robson gave a slight nod. 'I guess we should.' But neither of them moved for a long moment.

Champ let out a small whine as he sniffed his paw, and the attention turned his way.

'I'll clean him. You clean yourself, then I'll sort the floor.' Demi handed Robson a tea towel, and the thought of helping him remove his top sprung to mind, making her laugh to herself.

It really had been a fun day, and the happy atmosphere at home certainly was the icing on the cake.

CHAPTER 28

Robson

September had arrived, and Robson and Demi were visiting Ginny at Happy Farm to discuss the farmers' market. They went straight to the outbuilding, as Ginny didn't answer the door to the farmhouse.

'Ooh, you scared me half to death,' Ginny said, rubbing her back.

Robson glanced around, pleased with how ready the place appeared to be. 'What you up to in here? You're supposed to be taking it easy.'

Ginny huffed. 'I'm pregnant, chick. I think I can manage a walk to the barn.' She pointed at some hay bales. 'It's not as if I'm lifting anything, but they could do with moving over here.'

Robson laughed and got to work.

Demi laughed at the scarecrow wedged into some hay. 'I love him. Where did you get this?'

'Will made it, and very proud he is too.'

Robson glanced over his shoulder. 'Looks like him.'

'I'll tell him you said that.' Ginny huffed, flopping to a hay bale by a wooden cart.

Demi approached her. 'You okay? You look a bit pale?'

'Rough night, back ache. It all adds up. I thought pregnancy was supposed to make you bloom, but nope. I feel like I've been through the wringer.'

Demi chuckled. 'I remember that feeling.'

'You didn't bloom either, chick?'

'I threw up a lot.'

Ginny rubbed over her large baby bump. 'I'm fit to burst.'

Robson dropped a bale along the back wall. 'Is this where you want them?'

Ginny turned her head. 'Yep, that'll do.'

'So, any news on if we can open this market?' asked Robson, reaching for another bale.

'With all the red tape to get through, Will reckons we should focus on opening next spring, but I think autumn would be nice, and people still food shop during the winter.'

Demi sat on a bale next to Ginny. 'Aw, he's probably thinking it's a bit much with the baby due any day now.'

Ginny wrinkled her nose. 'He's probably right.'

'It's my fault, pushing you into these things while you're having a baby. I think springtime would be best too,' said Demi, shifting so Robson could move some of the bales behind them.

'I agree,' he said, smiling. 'It'll give us more time to sort the pathway, tidy up the front, and section off some of the drive.' Robson sat on the ground and dusted his hands down his top.

Ginny nodded, then gestured to the doorway. 'It's a bit hot. Excuse me, I'll just go get some water. Won't be a sec.'

Robson turned to Demi as she sat to his side. 'It's not that hot today.'

'Yeah, well, you're not carrying a baby.'

'True.' He glanced around. 'So, what do you really think of the spruce-up in here?'

'It's great. I think people will love it. I'm definitely shopping here.'

'If you have time. You're as busy as me.'

Demi laughed. 'Alice has assured me she won't serve the lunch menu on Sundays. She wants to steer everyone towards the pub.'

'She doesn't need to do that. Sunday dinner always packs out my place.'

'I think she wants the break herself.'

'How's she getting on over there?'

'Not too bad. Slowly moving in. Making it her own. We'll get the lunch menu out there soon. I'm just waiting on her say-so.'

Robson bobbed his head. 'And I see things have improved with Jade.'

Demi smiled. 'Things are much better.'

'That's good.'

'My family like you a little bit more since you came to dinner.'

Robson blew out a laugh. 'Yeah, that started off awkwardly.'

'But ended well.'

'If you ever want to invite them to dinner at ours, feel free.'

'Small steps.'

He grinned. 'Okay.'

'I'm glad they've met you properly now though.'

'Me too.'

They shared a smile, and Demi moved closer to him, about to speak, but a muffled scream wafted in with the light breeze, causing them both to still for a moment before running to the house.

Ginny stood at the back door, staring blankly at the ground. 'My waters broke.'

Robson reached for her arm. 'What do we do?'

Demi guided her into the kitchen. 'Are you in any pain?'

Ginny placed one hand on the wall as she yelled through gritted teeth.

'Pant, Ginny. Pant,' said Demi.

Robson took his phone from his pocket. 'I'm calling an ambulance, then Will.'

'We can drive her to the hospital. She won't give birth straight away,' said Demi.

Ginny shook her head, catching her breath. 'I might.'

'Are the contractions close?' asked Demi. 'Have they just started?'

'No. I've been in pain since last night, and I knew it was a different pain to any I've had before, but I thought it was those Braxton Hicks thingies so ignored it. It's mostly in my back, so I didn't take it too seriously.'

Robson held the phone to his ear as he looked at Demi. 'Is that good, bad?'

'It's on its way.'

'I wish this bloody ambulance was. Oh, hello, I need an ambulance.' He waited a second to be connected to the right department, then a woman asked what the problem was. 'My friend's about to give birth.' He turned to Ginny. 'I think.'

Ginny slid to the floor. 'I can feel it. I need to push.'

'Don't push,' said Robson. 'The lady on the phone said try not to push.'

Ginny cried out again, then started to sob. 'Call my midwife. Her number is on the fridge. And call Will.'

Without thinking about the operator giving advice, Robson hung up to phone the midwife.

'I'll just fetch some towels and water,' said Demi. 'Just in case the baby comes before anyone else.'

'Upstairs landing,' said Ginny, gritting her teeth. 'And my hospital bag is made up in the nursery. Grab that. There are baby bits inside. Blankets, clothes. Just bring everything.'

Robson ended his call. 'Midwife is on her way.'

Ginny reached for him as Demi sprinted off. 'Sit with me, Robson. My back hurts. Jeez, everything hurts.'

He curled around her back, propping her up against his chest, trying to keep his breathing under control while hers was all over the place.

'I'm scared, Rob.'

He brushed back her damp hair. 'Hey, it's going to be fine. You've got this.'

'I shouldn't have ignored the pains. I should have told Will. Oh, God, Will. He doesn't know.'

Robson noticed he'd left his phone on the worktop. 'I'll get Demi to call him as soon as she gets back. Oh, shit, I should have left one of the experts on the phone.'

Ginny gripped his hand as pain ripped through her. 'Robson, if anything happens to me, look after Will. Help him with the baby.'

'Don't talk like that.'

'Promise me.'

He kissed her head. 'I promise, but you're going to be fine. I'll never let anything happen to you, Gin. You're one of my best mates, and I'm here for you.'

Ginny started to cry. 'What if I can't do it? What if I'm a crappy mum like my own? She was horrible. What if I'm like her?'

'Whoa, whoa, whoa. You stop that.' He took her hands back in his. 'You're one of the kindest people I know, Ginny Dean, and you're going to be the best mum ever.'

'But she was so cruel.'

'You are not her. None of us are our parents.' His own came to mind as the words left his mouth. He knew the fear. His father was a monster, an evil man.

'Yes, you're right. We're not them. I wouldn't do what she did to me. I don't know why that hit me like that.'

'It's just the trauma talking.' He hugged her. 'You're a good person. Keep remembering that.'

She clenched her jaw as a contraction took over, and Robson started doing some breathing exercises with her.

'You're doing great, Gin.'

She settled a touch in his arms. 'This baby will be so loved.'

'Definitely.'

'A good mum, a brilliant dad, and the best godfather in you, Rob.'

He grinned, reaching for the tea towel hanging on a cupboard door handle by his side. Patting her brow with the cloth, his heart warmed at the honour. 'You want me to be godfather to your child?'

'Yes. Will and I discussed it. We were going to ask you once the baby was born, but now is as good a time as any.' She yelled out once more, digging her fingertips into his hands.

Robson gritted his teeth.

Demi sprinted into the kitchen, arms full with bags, towels, and a large plastic bowl. 'Right, I think I've got what we need, and I finally got through to Will. He's on his way.' She started placing towels by Ginny's bottom and one over her own lap. 'I need to look, Gin.'

Ginny nodded, and Robson peered down at Demi playing midwife.

'You're crowning,' said Demi.

'What's that mean?' asked Robson. 'Is that bad?'

Demi looked up. 'It means I can see the baby's head.'

'Bloody hell, Dem. Make sure it doesn't come out,' he told her.

Demi blew out a laugh as she rolled her sleeves up. 'Doesn't work that way. They come when they're ready, and this little one is so ready.'

Ginny groaned. 'I want to push.'

Robson shook his head at Demi, but she had her head down and hands ready.

Sirens filled the air, much to everyone's instant relief.

'Yes!' cheered Robson. 'Hear that, Gin. Paramedics.'

Demi's brow was crinkled as she glanced his way. 'I can't leave her now.'

'Run?' he suggested. 'Open the door for them, then get back.'

She didn't look too sure, but darted to the door and was back in seconds. 'They're just getting out.'

'Argh!' Ginny pushed back on Robson, and he mopped her head, not sure what else he could do.

'It's coming,' said Demi, her hands beneath Ginny's dress.

Two female paramedics rushed in just as the baby came into the world in Demi's hands. One of them quickly took over as Demi flopped to the floor and Ginny slumped into Robson.

He kissed her head. 'You did it, Gin.' Swallowing hard, he laughed. 'You bloody did it. And look — it's a baby.' He couldn't believe his eyes. There, being checked over by the paramedic, was an actual baby. Tears pricked his eyes as Ginny gasped, giving his hand a light squeeze.

The paramedic smiled, wrapped the baby in a blanket, and handed the little bundle to Ginny to hold. 'You have a beautiful boy. Congratulations.'

Robson cried. 'It's a boy.'

Ginny cooed over her son, and Demi got up to wash her hands.

Robson was happy to stay squashed between the cupboard and Ginny all day long. What a wonderful sight before him. There was nowhere he'd rather be.

'Let's get you cleaned up and on the sofa,' said the paramedic.

Robson couldn't take his eyes off the baby as everyone set to work, and as soon as Ginny was transferred to the living room, Will came rushing in.

Demi stood in the doorway, watching the happy parents, and Robson joined her side.

'How lovely is that?' she whispered.

Every inch of him warmed from the perfect sight. He placed an arm around Demi, and warmed even more when she hugged him back.

'That's what you call magical,' he whispered back.

'Let's go home and leave them to enjoy this moment together,' she said quietly, turning in his arms to face him.

Robson looked deeply into her eyes. 'Yeah, let's go home.'

'Hey, you two, get over here,' said Ginny, looking up from her son who now appeared to be asleep in her arms.

'I want to thank you both,' said Will.

Robson smiled down at the snuggled baby. 'No worries.'

'He's so perfect,' said Demi quietly.

'Can you call the others?' said Ginny. 'Let everyone know the news.'

Robson nodded. 'Will do. I'll call a cab first, as we're going to leave you to it, then I'll let everyone know.'

'You don't have to leave,' said Ginny.

'You'll be swamped enough with people wanting to meet junior here soon enough,' said Demi. 'Have some quiet time alone.' She blew a kiss to them, then headed for the door.

'We'll see you soon.' Robson smiled once more at Ginny.

She smiled back. 'See you soon, chick.'

He went out to the hallway to see Demi on her phone, arranging their taxi, so he wandered to the driveway, inhaling the fresh scent of wild flowers in a warm breeze.

Thank you for taking care of Ginny and her baby.

He had no idea who he was talking to in the sky, but felt the need to say something.

'Cab will be here soon,' said Demi, joining his side.

He put his arm around her as if it was the most natural thing to do in the world. 'Dem, I think we need to talk.'

Her head rolled up his shoulder. 'About?'

He met her eyes. 'Us.'

She smiled softly. 'Do you mean how close we've become?'

He gave a slight nod, not losing eye contact. 'You feel it too?'

'Yes.'

Slowly, he slipped his hand into her locks and dipped his head until the tips of their noses brushed against each other.

Demi pushed her lips to his, then stayed still, as though waiting for his permission. She didn't have to ask.

Robson pulled her closer, losing himself in her completely, and it took a while before they came up for air.

'I thought you wanted to talk,' she mumbled, placing a finger to his mouth, a slight quirk to her lips.

'I think that spoke volumes.'

'What should we do now?'

The cab pulled up at the end of the driveway and the driver beeped the horn.

'Go home,' said Robson, not taking his eyes off her.

Demi smiled, taking his hand, as they walked to the car, and Robson felt his heart grow just that little bit more.

CHAPTER 29

Demi

'How you feeling?' Demi asked Robson as they entered their home.

'I won't lie. A bit weird.'

Champ bounced around their legs, earning himself a ruffle on the neck.

'After Ginny giving birth today, perhaps it isn't the best time for us to get into a deep and meaningful.' She put the kettle on, then sat at the table.

Robson gave the dog a treat, then sat opposite her. 'It was seeing Ginny and Will so happy that overwhelmed me, I guess.' He shrugged, bending to untie his trainers.

'There was a lot of emotion in the air. I think we got carried away.'

He peered up at her. 'You think that?'

Demi wasn't sure what to think. Was it wise getting into something deeper with someone who had become such a good friend to her? Maybe it was being on Happy Farm, surrounded by so much love, that gave her ideas above her station. All she knew was, seeing Ginny and Will with their baby melted her heart, and she wished she had such love in her life.

'We have a lot going on, Robson.'

He stared at her for a moment, then got up to put his shoes by the stairs. His silence wasn't helping matters, not that she was sure what matters they had. Was she adding complications where there weren't any?

'Robson, I—'

His phone rang, cutting her off.

She watched his blank expression turn stern as he listened to the caller.

'Bloody hell. I'll be right over.' He hung up and went straight to his trainers. 'That was Alice. There's been a fire in the hallway.'

Demi jumped up. 'What?'

'Yeah, I don't know any more than that. I'm going there now.'

'Wait, I'll come with you.' She quickly flicked the kettle off, then snuggled Champ in his bed.

'It's just one thing after another this year.' The huff in Robson's voice made Demi think he might be talking about her.

Shrugging it off as they headed to the B&B, Demi turned her attention to a flustered Alice on the pathway.

'I put it out,' she told Robson as he approached the doorway.

'What happened?' asked Demi, cradling Alice's arm in hers.

'I don't know. I was out the back, and I smelled burning. I came out here and saw a piece of the carpet on fire by the door.'

Demi glanced at the large burnt hole. 'Flipping heck. Lucky you got to it quickly.'

Robson was searching the area, for what, Demi wasn't sure. She turned back to a shaky Alice.

'Did you call the police?'

Alice frowned. 'No. Why would I call them?'

'In case someone did this deliberately.'

Robson scoffed from over by the reception desk. 'Jamie isn't out yet, is he?'

Demi saw Alice's expression switch to anger for a split second before turning neutral.

'No. He is still in prison, and even if he wasn't, he wouldn't come in here and set fire to the carpet.'

'Wouldn't put it past him, after all the carnage he used to cause around here with his thug mates,' said Robson.

Alice let go of Demi's arm to march over to him. 'He's not the same person he was.'

Robson looked up from behind the desk. 'How would you know?'

'Because hardly anyone's the same person as they were eight years ago.' Alice turned to Demi. 'He's talking about Mabel's grandson, Jamie. He's my age now, thirty-one, and I'm pretty sure he's grown up.'

'He's been inside eight years?' asked Demi.

Alice nodded. 'He was in with a bad crowd round here. Obviously, it didn't end well.' She spun back to Robson. 'What are you looking for?'

'Security cameras.'

'Oh, Mabel was a bit old school. She didn't go in for any of that.'

Robson shook his head as he straightened. 'I know a bloke who has a security business. Did mine at the pub. I can give him a call for a quote.' He headed to the door. 'You up for this, Al?'

She gave him the thumbs-up, then looked at Demi as he went out the front. 'Hey, in other news, Will called to tell me the news, congrats on delivering Ginny's baby! I bet that was fun.'

Demi laughed. 'More like mind-blowing. I swear, I didn't have time to think, let alone feel, until it was over. I was glad the paramedics turned up when they did. The midwife arrived just as we got in the cab to leave.'

'Aww, I can't wait to see him. We're popping over tomorrow.' She scowled at the damaged carpet. 'Well, we were, but now I'm going to have to call someone about flooring.'

'Perhaps wooden flooring would be better out here?'

Alice nodded. 'Yeah, I was thinking that.'

'So, how do you think this happened?'

'It wasn't anything to do with Jamie. Probably kids, or an accident. I can't see any of the guests coming clean about it, as they won't want that on their bill.'

Demi glanced at the ceiling. 'Didn't the smoke alarm go off?'

'Nope. I'll check the batteries.' Alice went off to get a step ladder, and Demi followed.

'You know, my family thought I'd be the same when I came out of prison, but lots of people change.'

Alice tugged the metal ladder out of a tall cupboard. 'Oh, I know. It's just Jamie caused a lot of trouble for Mabel and mud sticks and all that. Robson just worries about me. He over-cares when it comes to the people he loves.'

Demi had that much figured out already. 'Do you feel unsafe at all now?'

Alice gave a slight shrug. 'I won't lie. It gave me a bit of a wobble when I first saw it sparkling away. But I don't think I have anything to worry about.'

'Report it to the police anyway. It could have been some lad who has a grudge against your Benny. Something like that happened to me once when Jade was young. She fell out with some girl, and the girl keyed my car. Luckily a neighbour caught her, so her mum paid for the paint job. Had to. I told the police.'

'Well, now you've said that — I will ask Benny.'

'It's worth exploring. Did you see any cigarette butts or anything suss?'

Alice shook her head. 'Nope. There wasn't any chemical smell either.'

Demi took the ladder from her and set it up beneath the smoke detector in the hallway. 'I'll do it, Al.'

'Thanks. My knee's playing up a bit today.'

Demi pressed the button on the alarm, but nothing happened, so she unscrewed it to take the batteries out. 'Have you got any more?'

'Yep. Won't be a sec.'

Demi sat at the top of the ladder, staring over at the stained-glass picture of a boat in the top of the main door.

Robson came back in and looked up at her. 'This place needs an update on the smoke alarms as well.'

Demi motioned towards the burnt hole. 'Apart from thinking inmates committed the crime, what's your take on it?'

Robson quirked an eyebrow at her sarcasm. 'I only mentioned Jamie because it's a bit fishy Mabel's not long died, then this happens. The last time the B&B had trouble at its door was when he was here.' He shrugged. 'Who knows if he got one of his mates to come around.'

'But why would he do that?'

'I don't know. He was the first person that came to mind.'

Demi frowned. 'It's not nice being judged on your past.'

His shoulders dropped. 'Yes, I know. I'm sorry.'

Alice came back with new batteries. 'I'm going to sort all updates this place needs as soon as possible.'

'Al, I'm sorry for accusing Jamie,' said Robson quickly. 'It was a stupid thing to say. Demi's right, people change.'

'Forget it,' she replied, handing the batteries up to Demi.

Demi put them in place, then screwed the lid back on. 'Right, cover your ears.' She pressed the button, and a screech rang out for a few seconds.

Alice lightly clapped. 'Yay. I'd better test all of them now.'

'I've got someone coming day after tomorrow about the camera,' Robson told her.

Alice frowned. 'Oh, couldn't they come today?'

Robson shook his head. 'That was all he had available, but, hey, I was thinking, if it's all right with you, I can sleep here until the security is up and running.'

Demi saw Alice's eyes light up. It was obvious she was worried someone had burned the carpet on purpose.

'Oh, you don't have to do that,' Alice replied coyly.

Robson placed his arm around her. 'I'll be your doorman.'

Alice laughed. 'Okay then. There's a fold away bed you can use. I'll make that up for you in my living room, as the guest rooms are all booked. Is that okay?'

Robson nodded. 'I'll nip home now and sort an overnight bag.' He turned to Demi as she climbed down the ladder. 'Will you be all right in the flat on your own for a couple of nights?'

'Of course. Don't worry about me. I'll be fine. Plus, I have Champ.' She only meant half of what she said, because she already knew she would miss his company.

He headed off, and Demi followed Alice around the building to check all the alarms.

'You two are like a couple,' remarked Alice, pointing up at another alarm.

Demi didn't want to lie. 'I know.'

'Do you like him?'

She glanced at Alice to see a hint of mischief in her eyes. 'You trying to matchmake?'

'Nope. Just asking. Friend to friend.'

Demi twisted her mouth to one side, then set off the alarm, proving that one worked. 'I like him very much,' she admitted with a smile.

Alice let out a quiet squeal. 'I didn't want Robson to spend the rest of his life alone.'

'I never said we're together.'

'I know, but he deserves another shot at love.'

Demi sighed. 'It's hard when you're still healing.'

Alice's face held a sympathetic look, as though she understood. 'I think everyone out there is walking around with a healing heart. Pain is part of life, isn't it?'

'And not much we can do about death.'

Alice shook her head. 'Today is supposed to be a joyous day, what with Ginny giving birth — but now it's turned to doom and gloom.'

Demi knew what she meant. She was feeling it too. 'Let's perk up. We'll put the ladder away, then knock on doors and ask the guests if they saw anything.'

'They're not all in this time of day.'
'Well, we'll ask when we see them.'
Alice nodded. 'Might as well.'

Only one person was in their room when they got around to knocking on doors, and the elderly man hadn't seen or heard anything. Demi stepped out to the pavement to stare at the sea for a bit while Alice called Benny.

There weren't many people about and just a few boats sailing the calm sea. A lone man smoked a cigarette over by the pier, and Demi wondered if he could be the fire starter. She laughed to herself at her lack of sleuth skills. The only crimes she knew about were the ones that had landed her in prison.

She turned to face the pub. A few days not wrapped around Robson would probably do them both a bit of good. At least then she'd have the space to consider if being together could help them heal. The last thing she wanted was to make waves with what they had. It was so special, she needed to protect it at all costs.

CHAPTER 30

Robson

Grabbing a sports bag, Robson shoved some overnight bits and bobs inside, knowing he could just nip home for anything else. He wanted Alice to feel comfortable in her new home and was sure once the security cameras were up and running, and the fires and safety measures set up, she would feel a lot safer.

'I'll still be back and forth to see you,' he told Champ, snuggled with his teddy on the floor. 'You keep your mum company at night, which means no sneaking in my room to sleep on my bed.'

Champ buried his head into the bottom of the sofa.

'Right, I'll see you later, Champ.'

Champ thumped his tail, and Robson headed off to the B&B.

He figured he'd get his things sorted there, then go to work if Alice didn't need him hanging around during the day. Whatever, he needed a good distraction from his kiss with Demi.

All he could think about was her blowing him off as soon as they got home. It was his own stupid fault for moving the goal posts.

He stopped in his tracks at the front of the pub, as over by the pier stood Demi, talking to a man Robson knew used to be a drug dealer. His heart dropped immediately. Had he done that to her? Put so much pressure into their relationship? Built an awkward atmosphere that raised her anxiety levels?

They were smiling and chatting away, but Robson only saw red flags.

Sprinting across to the pier, he called out her name.

Demi turned, still smiling, but Robson's attention was on the man smoking a cigarette.

'You stay the hell away from her, you hear me?'

The man in his thirties grinned. 'Good to see you too, Rob. Been a while.'

'Get lost. No one wants your sort round here.'

The man dropped his cigarette and stomped on the butt. 'Yeah, whatever, mate.' He walked off, not looking back.

Demi tugged Robson's arm. 'What on earth was that about?'

He narrowed his eyes as he glanced at her clenched fists. 'What's in your hand?'

Demi frowned as she uncurled her fingers. 'Nothing, why?'

'Did you just buy drugs from him?'

Demi scoffed, eyes wide with a mixture of amusement and anger.

'It doesn't matter if you did,' he added quickly. 'We can get rid of them. Go to a meeting or something. Anything. Just don't take any. Please?'

She dipped back to one heel and raised a palm. 'Okay, take a breath. You've got this all wrong.'

Robson thumbed down the road. 'I know who he is. He's a dealer. Well, he used to be the last time I saw him about five years ago.'

'I didn't know that. He didn't talk about his line of work.'

'Why were you talking to him?'

Demi pointed at the sea. 'I was going to sit on the pier for a while, and when I passed him by, he said hello, so I said it back, then we started chatting about the weather. I was about to say goodbye when you came over.'

Robson watched a seagull soar the pale-blue sky as he inhaled deeply, settling his racing heart. 'I just saw him, and I thought—'

'Yeah, I know what you thought.'

He lowered his gaze. 'I'm sorry. After everything I said to your family, then I go and do that.'

'There's no need for that. You saw what you saw, and I would have thought the same if the shoe was on the other foot.'

He quirked an eyebrow. 'You would?'

Demi gave a small shrug. 'Of course. I'm a recovering addict. He is, or was, a drug dealer. It's not rocket science.' Her sigh was deep. 'I understand, Robson. I've been dealing with lack of trust for quite some time, and I guess now you know how my family feel. And I appreciate you looking out for me, I really do, but what I need is you being my friend and supporting me, not rushing in thinking you can fix things.'

'I was so scared. I thought you had slipped because of me. That I'd made you struggle and—'

'Whoa, whoa, slow down.' Her hand curled around his. 'Why would you think that?'

'Because of earlier. The kiss. How you were in the flat.' His heart was thumping so badly, he was sure she'd be able to notice.

Demi headed to the end of the pier, taking him with her, which he didn't mind, as her touch was instantly soothing. They sat, dangling their legs over the side, and stayed silent for a moment.

'It's hard, Dem,' he said quietly, watching a yacht in the near distance, wishing he were on board, enjoying the open water.

She met his waiting eyes. 'Do you mean us?' Her soft words melted into his heart.

'After our kiss, I thought it was possible for me to be with someone else. Falling for you made me feel like I was cheating on Leah, so I tried to hold back. Not fall for you. Keep you as my friend. So, when I did cross the line, it wasn't an easy step for me — then you took a step back as soon as we were home. I thought I'd messed us up. Brought challenges to your door you didn't need.'

Demi gave his hand a gentle squeeze. 'You didn't do anything wrong. I'm scared too, Robson. I'm in a good place right now. Something I built by myself, and it's been so, so hard.'

He nodded.

'I live in a house of cards,' she added. 'I know how easy it is for my life to come tumbling down. Every day till the end I'll have to fight to stay in control. Unless someone invents a cure for addiction.' Her smile was small. 'I fought long and hard to regain my peace, and I'm very protective of it now. I have to be.'

'I understand. I want peace and calm in my life too.'

Demi gestured to the road. 'Each time I get the itch to use again, I call my sponsor or Jan or go to a meeting. I even have Matt's number now, so I can call him too. Whatever it takes, I'll try, because I know what it felt like back then. How much I hated myself, and I never want that life again.'

'I'd help too. You only have to let me know what to do. And if it means not taking our friendship any further, I'll do that.' He shifted to face her full on. 'Dem, I want peace for you, too. I need you to know I'd never want you to feel uncomfortable.'

'I was trying to figure things out. Take a moment. You don't make me feel anything bad, and I would have spoken to you about all of this earlier, but we got the call from Alice.'

He sighed and looked back out at the gentle rolling waves heading his way. 'I like that we have peace in our home.'

'We all need it, even Champ, bless him.'

They shared a warm smile.

'Let's take a few days to decide what's the best move for us,' said Robson. 'There's no rush. We were feeling emotional after Ginny gave birth. We'll know soon enough if we mean more to each other than friends.'

Demi took his hand to her lap. 'I think we know that much already.'

He bobbed his head. 'Okay, but me sleeping over at Alice's will give us the room we need, and it doesn't matter if you decide you want to stay mates. Whatever's best.'

She agreed.

He looked heavenward, wondering if Leah could see him. What would she say? She'd told him on her deathbed he must live. Was another relationship what she'd meant? Would she really approve?

Emptiness swirled for a second, swiftly followed by the lack of ability to think or feel anything at all.

'I'll just get my things over to the B&B,' he said quietly, slipping his hand from hers as he stood.

Demi jumped up. 'Robson.' Her voice was strained, her stare filled with concern.

He turned at the same time her arms came swinging around his body. Heat from her closeness brought a twinge of life back into his soul.

'You okay?' she whispered.

'I will be.' Because just like her, he too fought each day for his peace.

She cupped his cheeks, forcing his eyes to hers. 'I want you to be okay right now.'

A fizz of something delightful hit his stomach as he witnessed the love in her gaze, and he decided right there on the pier that even if they lived a life of just being together without intimacy, they would be happy, and they would have peace.

'Come on,' she said softly. 'Let's drop your bag off at Alice's, then take Champ for a walk.'

Walking the dog with Demi was one of his favourite things to do, so he nodded his agreement and took the hand she offered.

CHAPTER 31

Demi

It had been quiet while Robson was away. Demi kept herself busy making a cooking video and advertising products as best she could without feeling too awkward. Other influencers made it look so easy, and Jade had given her some content ideas to play with.

Champ had been the best company, even sleeping in her room, which was mainly down to her taking his bed upstairs.

It was different when she was in the bedsit, getting used to the loneliness, but now she was used to Robson being around every night.

'Daddy should be home tomorrow,' she told Champ, getting ready to take him for his night-time walk.

Champ brought his teddy over.

'No, we're not taking that with us. If you lose it, you'll cry all night. Remember when teddy was under the sofa and we couldn't find him, eh? He can stay home.'

The phone bleeped, and Demi assumed it was Robson, as he'd been sending more messages than usual since sleeping at the B&B.

'Oh, it's your sister,' Demi told the dog. She frowned at the clock, thinking Jade must have just got back from her holiday in Spain.

Champ dropped his toy and slumped to the floor as if knowing his walk would have to wait.

Demi saw that Jade was asking if she was still up, so Demi rang her phone. 'Hey, it's not that late.'

'Best to check,' said Jade.

'You just got back?'

'Not long. I'm putting my pyjamas on as we speak.'

'Thanks for sending me pictures. It looked lovely.'

'You and me should book somewhere when you have time.'

Every part of Demi beamed. 'I'd like that. You'll have to let me know when your uni breaks are.'

'Speaking of uni, that's why I wanted to talk to you. We're moving me into my accommodation next weekend, and I wondered if you wanted to come with us?'

That was a yes in all areas. 'Will there be room in the car?'

'Should be. We're using both Colin and Alana's cars because Damien wants to come, and we've got lots of stuff to take.'

'Won't you take your own car up there?'

'No. Colin reckons I'll be better off on foot if I'm out and about with uni mates — getting drunk, as Damien added.'

Demi frowned. 'I want you to be sensible around alcohol, Jade. I—'

'Don't sweat it, Mum. If anyone knows what people are like when they're wasted, it's me. Ooh, I'm *sorry!* I didn't mean anything spiteful by that. I just meant I'm not the type to want to get off my head.'

'It's okay. I understand.' Demi hadn't realised her addiction had affected Jade in that way. She assumed her daughter would go out drinking — and likely drinking too much — with friends.

'Hey, Mum, how about we book a spa break for this Christmas? A little treat just for you and me. I'll be home then, and we can talk all things festive.'

Demi smiled. 'That would be great. Meanwhile, we can get together so I can teach you some quick and easy dishes to make when you're at uni. We can go shopping and buy a few bits for your kitchen.'

'I'd like that. I still have a couple of things to get. I could do with a saucepan.'

She heard Jade yawn. 'Oh dear, someone sounds ready for bed.'

'Getting there. Are you about to snuggle down for the night?'

'No, I'm just off out for a walk with Champ.'

'Okay, have fun, and stay safe. Have you got one of those hi-vis tops for him?'

Demi laughed. 'No, but he does have something similar on his night collar, not that he walks off on his own. He hates any traffic, so I keep him close, which he prefers anyway, even when we get to the grass.'

'Aww, bless him. Give him a kiss from me, and tell him I'll see him soon.' Jade yawned again.

'Will do. Night, love.'

'Night, Mum.'

Demi set about getting Champ ready for his walk, giving him a smooch from Jade. 'Now, wasn't that a nice phone call?'

It was quiet along Harbour End Road, with only a couple of customers sitting in the beer garden out front of the pub. The patio lights were on, as the sun had gone to bed for the night, but it was quite warm for September.

Demi stopped to gaze at the outdoor grill area. The memory of working side by side with Robson filled her vision. They always had so much fun. It had been a great summer. She was so pleased she had moved to the harbour.

Champ tugged on the lead, eager to get to the grass at the end of the road.

She passed the B&B, staring up at the balconies, then carried on until Champ could relieve himself.

'Hey, Demi.'

She turned towards Robson's voice.

'Thought I saw you two passing a moment ago.' He reached to give the dog a scratch behind the ear.

'You enjoying the mild air as well?'

'I'm just waiting to lock up for the night.'

Demi laughed. 'I'll come sit in the beer garden for a bit, if you like. We'll keep you company while you shoo the stragglers out the door, won't we, Champ?'

Champ went back to sniffing long dried grass around the base of a tree.

'Thanks, that'll be nice.' He smiled her way and just for a moment she couldn't remove her gaze from his.

'Erm, so, you're back home tomorrow,' she muttered, swallowing hard.

'Yeah, the cameras are finally getting fitted first thing. I say finally, but really he's squeezed the job in because I told him how worried Alice has been since the fire.'

'Aw, that was kind of him. Any news finding out how it started yet?'

Robson shook his head. 'No, but an old fella said he was smoking by the door and hoped it wasn't his fault. Guess we'll never know for sure.'

'Alice said wooden flooring is going down soon.'

'And your lunch menu starts next week. You ready for action?'

Demi beamed as she nodded. 'Can't wait.'

Champ mooched to her side, letting her know he didn't need to do another piddle, so they started to walk towards the pub.

'He's missed you of a night,' she said quietly, glancing his way to gauge his reaction.

A slight twitch hit the corner of his mouth as he glanced back. 'Has he?'

She nodded, pressing into his arm for a moment.

'I've missed my bed.' Robson blew out a laugh as he rubbed his back.

'You're a good man, Robson McCoy.'

'Hmm.'

'Ooh, I have some news.' She almost bounced on the spot, she was that happy.

'Tell all.'

'Jade has invited me to help with her move into uni accommodation. They're going up to York next weekend. They're taking two cars, so it shouldn't be a squeeze. Depends how much stuff she's taking. And we're going shopping together to buy a few bits to add to her kitchenware.'

He stopped walking and took her hand. 'I'm so pleased for you, Dem. That's great news.'

'And Jade wants to book us a spa weekend at Christmas when she's home.'

'Brilliant.'

She pressed up on her toes and kissed his cheek. 'Thanks for making a breakthrough with them. Things only changed after your speech.'

He grinned. 'Not sure *speech* is the right word.'

They carried on walking.

'Whatever you want to call it, it gave them another point of view,' she told him, clinging on to his arm.

'So, what you got planned for the rest of the week?'

'I've got a couple of shifts at the Hub, and a work meeting with Alice to finalise things, giving Jade some cooking lessons, and, ooh, Ginny's baby get-together is tomorrow night.'

'Yep. We're going to find out little man's name.'

Demi giggled on his arm. 'It's exciting, isn't it?'

'What, finding out what they called their son?'

'No. Having so much to look forward to. Being happy in the now. Just feeling alive.'

They entered the beer garden, and Demi took Champ over to the far corner to sit out of the way of customers that would be leaving soon.

Robson sat by her side. 'We have to appreciate the good days.'

Demi smiled. 'Work through the bad.'

He nodded. 'We've got that covered.'

'Yeah, we're doing all right.'

Robson gestured at the doorway. 'Do you fancy a hot chocolate?'

'Ooh, yes, please.' She watched him walk into the pub. Her night had just got a whole heap better. Then Terry sprung to mind.

There were so many times she thought she had a happy life with him. The odds of being with someone else living a double life were slim to none, but it didn't stop the wariness lurking.

Life in Port Berry was a different chapter in her story, and she simply needed to remind herself of that fact. Terry was long gone, and so was the life she'd lived with him. Robson rarely went far from home and was struggling with his own insecurities. He was nothing like Terry.

Demi glanced over the road, loving the sea view, even if it was turning as black as soot out there. Just knowing the sea was steadily breathing close by made her insides glow. How had her life changed so much? So dramatically? It was all so surreal at times, as though it hadn't happened to her at all, just someone else's story she'd read in a book.

Robson came back with a tray carrying two tall glasses of hot chocolate and a bowl of water.

Demi gave Champ his drink, which he slurped once before settling back across her feet, then Robson's slow sigh and wide smile had her attention. 'What are you grinning about?'

'It's a nice night.' He chuckled, and she watched his arm come around the back of her chair.

He was right. It was nice, and tomorrow when he was back home, it would be even better.

CHAPTER 32

Robson

Robson felt like Father Christmas as he opened his street door to call upstairs to Demi.

Her head poked around the top of the stairs. 'What's up? I'm in the middle of wrapping a baby gift for Ginny and Will.'

'Come look.'

Demi jogged down the stairs, closing the door behind her. 'What's with the soppy grin?'

'I have a surprise.' He waved her towards the road. 'Ta-dah!'

Demi looked left and right. 'What am I looking at?'

Robson dropped his shoulders, then took her hand, leading her towards a blue hatchback. 'I bought a car.'

Demi smiled. 'This is yours?'

'Well, I thought we could both get use out of it, if you'd like me to put you down as a named driver?' He watched her eyes widen with delight, and it went straight to his heart.

'Really?'

'Makes sense. Vet trips, famers' market, when it opens, back and forth to the Sunshine Centre. And Champ can be chauffeured to the park. He'll love not walking along the road.'

Demi chuckled. 'Sounds like you thought of everything.'

'We can give it a run in a bit up to Happy Farm.'

'You drive there and I'll drive back?'

'So you're happy to share the car?'

She shrugged. 'We share everything else.'

He went to speak, but Sophie came whizzing along on her bicycle, stopping when she saw them.

'Hello, you two. I'll see you soon at the farm. I'm just heading home now to get changed. Any guesses on the baby's name?'

Demi shook her head. 'Nope.'

'Ginny will just call him chick, anyway,' said Robson, grinning. He gestured at the car. 'What do you think, Soph? I just bought it.'

'Ooh, lovely. It'll make life a bit easier.' She waved as she set off.

He turned to see Demi peering in through the side window. 'I've been fine without a vehicle for ages.'

'Yeah, but Sophie's right. They do come in handy.'

He opened the door for her, and she quickly clambered inside. 'Second-hand, but it looks quite new, doesn't it?'

'Smells it too.'

He climbed into the driver's seat and smiled. 'This will do us.'

Demi smiled. 'Right, I best get back to wrapping that present, then we can get ready to head off.'

He was proud of himself and his new car and so pleased Demi wanted to be part of it with him.

Geoff had everything covered at the pub for the evening, so Robson headed upstairs for a quick shower.

It wasn't long before Champ had been fed and settled, and Robson and Demi were off out for the night.

Even though they hadn't spoken about their relationship yet, it wasn't lost on him how much they acted like a couple.

Perhaps it was for the best if they weaned themselves onto each other for a bit longer. Whatever they were doing, it worked. It was just hard not to kiss her at times.

'I love Happy Farm,' said Demi as they entered the driveway.

'But our sea view more?'

She grinned. 'Yep. Although I think Champ would prefer it here. It's a lovely place to raise kids.'

'Yeah, I guess. But so is anywhere in Port Berry. I was raised above the pub, and I was all right with that.'

She glanced his way. 'You never went far, did you?'

Robson laughed. 'Don't need to. I love my home. But we can take a holiday if you like?'

'Ooh, where you got in mind?'

'I haven't. Just thought of it, but seeing how you love this place so much, how about we rent something similar for a week, next spring perhaps?'

She nodded as she climbed out of the car. 'Okay, as long as the place accepts dogs.'

'And that when we have to leave, you want to go home.' He chuckled, thinking she'd be sold on farm life.

Demi looked serious as she replied, 'I always want to go home. Now I live with you.'

He blinked hard as his heart skipped a beat.

The door to the farmhouse flew open, and out came Will, waving them forward. 'Come on in. Hope you're hungry. Ginny's laid out enough food to feed an army.'

Robson grabbed the baby gift from the back seat and followed Demi inside.

Jed and Luna were the first to greet him in the hallway, then Lizzie, who took his present to place with the others on a side table.

'We're in the kitchen and out back,' said Jed.

'Baby's asleep in the living room,' said Luna.

Lizzie held a baby monitor aloft. 'I'm guardian at the moment.' She beamed at the screen as she walked away.

Robson entered the kitchen to see Lottie and Samuel plating up some food. Will wasn't exaggerating about the amount on offer.

'Tuck in before it all goes,' said Lottie, grinning while adding prawn sandwiches to her plate.

Sophie came up behind him and kissed his cheek, swiftly followed by Spencer who did the same, making Robson laugh.

'Beth's outside with Archie. He loves that donkey,' said Spencer, snaffling a sausage roll.

'Matt's out there as well,' said Sophie, pouring out some orange juice. 'Although he's more a fan of the chickens. Smaller and less likely to nip him.'

'Oi,' said Ginny, walking in from out back. 'My Ralph doesn't bite.'

A black cat brushed up against Robson's leg. 'I think Lucky can smell the prawns.'

Ginny picked her up and placed her by the back door. 'No you don't. Go on, out you get.'

Robson went outside to say hello to the others. He spotted Jan straight away and automatically gravitated towards her.

'Hey, how you been?' she asked, giving him a hug.

'Good.'

'Your health?' she asked.

Robson bobbed his head, knowing she was referring to his situation depression. 'A lot better. The dark moments are becoming less and less.'

Jan peered around his arm at Demi, talking to Matt over by the hen house. 'And you and Demi?'

He was sure he blushed but blew it off. 'Very good.'

'I'm so happy for you.'

When Jan walked away to talk to Beth, Robson made his way over to the barn to take another look at what might well be a farmers' market next year.

Sophie waved as she approached. 'Looks good, doesn't it?'

'I really believe it'll go down well with the locals.'

'Yeah, and we'll all help.'

He nodded. 'That's what I was thinking. Set up a timetable or something.'

Sophie flopped to a hay bale and smiled out at the field. 'Been so many changes for us lot these last couple of years.'

He smiled as he joined her, sitting at her side. 'Bet you never thought you'd meet your soulmate.'

'I wasn't expecting love in my life, but it just happens when it happens, doesn't it? Makes you wonder if we even get a choice.'

Robson looked over at the farmhouse. 'Ginny was on her own for a long time, and now look. Will and a baby.'

'You never know what's around the next corner.' She turned to face him. 'And life's short, right, Robson? So we need to grab those good moments when we can.'

'Are you going to go on about Demi now?'

She bit her bottom lip while grinning. 'I've just seen the way you look at her, that's all.'

'She brought my heart back to life.'

'So what are you going to do about it?'

He shrugged, knocking her arm. 'We're taking it slowly. Trying to see what works best for us.'

'That's the trauma talking. If neither of you had that, you'd be a couple already.'

It was true, but what could he do about it? It was what it was. Demi was wary of so much, and he had Leah in the back of his mind.

Sophie leaned into him. 'What do you truly want for your life, Robson?'

'What I have now. I'm happy enough, Soph. Demi has just been a bonus. She moved in and made my place feel like a home again.'

'Sounds like you've got a second chance at love, and as long as she's kind to you, she's all right by me.'

He smiled warmly. 'She is very kind.'

Sophie tapped his thigh. 'Right, let's get back over there then, and you can tell her how much you love her.'

He breathed out a laugh as he stood. 'Why is declaring your true feelings always so complicated?'

'We're programmed to protect ourselves. Not sure how, when, or why, but it's how we are. I guess it's a human thing.'

He watched her skip off into the arms of Matt, who kissed the side of her head as they hugged.

Beth was leaning on the paddock fence, talking to Demi while Jan took Archie for a stroll in his pram.

Robson admired the view for a moment, pleased to see Demi laughing so much she doubled over. He was about to laugh too, but then he noticed something didn't look right. Beth leaned over Demi's back, and her hand came down in one big bang right in the middle of Demi's spine.

'Help,' yelled Beth, and Robson darted towards them.

Demi's face had turned a shade of purple, and her eyes held fear and water as she gasped for air.

Beth banged on Demi's back again. 'She's choking on a sandwich.'

Lizzie came running over with a bottle of water as Demi continued to wheeze.

Robson was having his own struggle with air, as watching Demi gasping while reaching out for his hand had his heart jammed solid in his throat. 'It's okay. It's okay.'

Lizzie shoved the water in Demi's face. 'Try, love. Drink.'

Demi swallowed but coughed, tears streaming down her face.

'I might need to do the Heimlich manoeuvre in a minute,' said Beth, banging Demi's back some more.

Lizzie leaned down and stuck her fingers in Demi's mouth, rummaging around for obstructions as everyone ran over to see what was going on.

Demi gagged, causing Lizzie to move back, and as she did, Beth thumped once more on Demi's back.

Something shot out of Demi's mouth, and she spluttered as a gasp left her lungs. She dropped to her knees as Robson slid beneath her to catch her fall.

'Bloody hell!' mumbled Lizzie, glancing up at Alice while resting one hand on Demi.

'You okay, Demi?' asked Sophie, leaning over.

'Well done, Beth,' said Samuel.

Beth was taking her own deep breaths.

Robson swept back Demi's damp hair, gauging her flushed face. She fell forward into him, and he wrapped his arms around her back.

'Mum,' said Lizzie. 'Make Demi a warm tea. Her throat will need soothing.'

Luna gave a sharp nod. 'Will do.'

Lizzie gently stroked Demi's shoulder. 'Come on, love. Let's get you inside. You've had a nasty shock.'

'Just a minute,' Demi croaked into Robson's chest.

'Okay,' said Lizzie, straightening. 'You come and get your tea when you're ready.' She waved a finger around at the onlookers. 'A bit of space, please,' she added softly.

Robson waited till everyone left, then slowly lifted Demi's chin. 'Hey, you all right?'

Her eyelashes were still damp, but her breathing had settled.

'It's okay,' whispered Robson, running his finger beneath her eye to catch a falling tear. 'You're okay now.'

Demi exhaled, sounding a tad shaky. 'Scared me.'

He rested his head against hers for a second before pulling back. 'Scared me too.'

'I was laughing while chewing, and . . .'

'It's over now.'

'I didn't think I could shift it.'

'Beth had other tricks up her sleeves to try, thankfully, because I was about as much use as a bike with no wheels.'

Her mouth quirked slightly. 'Good thing someone's trained in first aid.'

'I am. I just froze when I saw you couldn't breathe. Jeez, Dem, I thought . . .' He pulled her into him, holding her as close as he could. 'I love you so much. Don't ever do that to me again.' He felt a small laugh rumble on his chest.

'I'll try my very best.' Demi sat up, meeting his weary eyes, and Robson kissed the tip of her nose. 'Do you really love me so much?'

His smile was small but held meaning as he nodded. 'Just seeing you like that, thinking you could die, and me feeling helpless like I felt when I watched Leah die, it just jolted something in me. And I don't want to take time to think things through or go slowly now. I want us to be a couple, Dem. To love. To share a life. I don't want to waste time, not when I know how I feel about you. We have no idea how much time we have, and you just . . . If we . . . Bloody hell, Dem—'

Demi pulled him to her mouth, taking away the rest of the words attempting to form in his frazzled mind. 'I love you too, Robson,' she mumbled on his lips.

'Then be with me properly, Demi. Be my partner. Let's do this.'

'Yes,' she whispered, then cupped his face. 'I know we're both healing, but we can walk that path together. We'll be there for each other.'

'I'm not going anywhere. I'll be with you always.'

They shared a warm smile, then a light kiss.

'Let's get you some tea for your throat.' Robson stood, taking her hand.

'I feel okay now, but I'll still have that drink.'

He tugged her back into his arms for one more hug, not wanting to ever let go.

'I'm okay, Robson.'

He made himself step back. *I thought I was going to lose you!*

Demi smiled softly. 'I got a bit worried for a moment, but I'm fine, and we're okay. And we're not going to fight our emotions any longer.'

There's no chance of that. He had no hope of managing it.

'All okay?' asked Ginny, leaning around the back door.

They both nodded at her as Robson squeezed Demi's hand.

'My girlfriend and I are just fine,' Robson said sounding confident and knowing every word was true. He matched Demi's smile.

Ginny waved them inside. 'Great. In that case, I think it's time I announced the baby's name.'

Luna gave Demi a cup of sweet, warm tea as soon as they entered the kitchen, and Will led everyone to the living room, where Alice was holding the newborn, snuggled in a cream knitted blanket.

Ginny took the baby as everyone gathered around, finding places to sit or stand. 'Will and I talked this over, and seeing how Robson and Demi were there to help bring this little one into the world, we've decided to take that into consideration. So, on that note, please allow me to introduce the newest member of our family . . . Robert Demetri Pendleton.'

Lots of oohs and ahhs went around the room while Robson and Demi beamed at each other.

'I feel honoured,' said Robson, determined not to shed a tear.

Ginny brought the baby to him. 'Here, you have a cuddle.'

Little Robert looked up at the man holding him, and Robson smiled.

Demi placed her arm around him as she peered at the baby. 'If you ever want your own, let me know,' she whispered, taking him by surprise.

'You want that?' he asked quietly as the people in the room started chatting to each other.

'I want everything with you.'

He smiled and kissed her head, a rush of love filling him. 'I want everything with you too, so it looks like we've got more plans for the future than farm holidays.'

'Looks like we have.'

They rested against each other, safe in the knowledge that so much of them had healed.

THE END

ACKNOWLEDGEMENTS

This story is dedicated to everyone on a healing journey. You are powerful, resilient, problem-solving masters who know how to survive the deepest, darkest pits of hell. Remember that, next time you doubt your strength.

Huge thanks goes out to the Choc Lit/Joffe Books team for their help, support, and encouragement for the Port Berry series. Much appreciated.

Also sending a cheer to my readers who are a constant support to my author journey. I want you all to know that I'm so completely and utterly grateful to each and every one of you.

As always, sending lots of love and light your way. Keep reading. It's good for the soul.

ABOUT THE AUTHOR

Hello, I'm K.T. Dady. I write uplifting love stories filled with friendship, family, and community set here, there, and everywhere, as love happens anywhere and under all sorts of circumstances. But whatever challenges my characters face along the way, there is always a happily ever after.

Feel free to join my newsletter over at my website, where you can download a free Pepper Bay short story that you won't find anywhere else. Newsletters go out once a month and often contain free gifts, previews, and writing tips amongst the news. Head over to my website at ktdady.com

If you enjoyed reading my book, please leave a rating or review on Amazon or Goodreads. It really helps to bring the story to more readers. Thank you so much.

You'll also find me on my social media accounts.
Instagram: @kt_dady
Facebook: @ktdady

THE CHOC LIT STORY

Established in 2009, Choc Lit is an independent, award-winning publisher dedicated to creating a delicious selection of quality women's fiction.

We have won 18 awards, including Publisher of the Year and the Romantic Novel of the Year, and have been shortlisted for countless others. In 2023, we were shortlisted for Publisher of the Year by the Romantic Novelists' Association.

All our novels are selected by genuine readers. We are proud to publish talented first-time authors, as well as established writers whose books we love introducing to a new generation of readers.

In 2023, we became a Joffe Books company. Best known for publishing a wide range of commercial fiction, Joffe Books has its roots in women's fiction. Today it is one of the largest independent publishers in the UK.

We love to hear from you, so please email us about absolutely anything bookish at choc-lit@joffebooks.com.

If you want to receive free books every Friday and hear about all our new releases, join our mailing list here: www.joffebooks.com/freebooks.